Until We Meet Again

Until We Meet Again

A Woman With a Gun story

A Novel by K D Ryder

UNTIL WE MEET AGAIN

Copyright © 2014 by Rancho Lazarus Publications

ISBN 978-0692342213

First publication November 2014

Published in the United States of America

Dedication

This book is dedicated to my father, who taught this woman with a gun
how to shoot one

.

Until We Meet Again

Prologue

I SUPPOSE EVERYONE HAS ONE day in their life they would give anything to be able to delete from their past. Mine was a perfect sunny day in October. That was the day my bubble burst. Or maybe I should say – it blew up in my face.

It was the Chief himself who called me in to deliver the news. I never liked him anyway. He always thought I was too enthusiastic about my work and took every opportunity to remind me of that fact. I couldn't help it. I loved being a cop. It really stung to have him be the one to tell me it was over. He seemed just a bit too happy about it.

Nevertheless, at the insistence of everyone from the commissioner to the mayor to the district attorney to forty-seven irate citizens, I, Angela Virago, was fired at the age of twenty-eight from the one job I had dreamed about since I was a little girl. I would be a police officer no longer. It was over.

My tenure as a cop with the Myersburg police department had been brief. I spent the first four years after high school working as a civilian in the department while taking college classes in Criminal Justice. After my divorce at the age of twenty-two, I went through the police academy and graduated – by the skin of my teeth, to be sure, but I graduated. My granny always said I had turnips for brains and I damn near proved she was right, but somehow I made it through.

I was the only female police officer in the department. I heard once that the only reason they hired me was because of some Equal Opportunity thing. I was their token female. I heard they got some kind of grant because of it. There had been no other female applicants, so I was put on the streets despite the conclusion reached by the county shrink that I would probably better protect and serve the citizens of Myersburg, Utah, by moving to another town.

Somehow, the shrink who had done my psychological profile had gotten the notion that I would be a bit trigger-happy. I heard through the grapevine that "Loose cannon?" had been penciled in the margin of his report. I had passed the psychological evaluation, but it seems he was concerned that a bad hair day might put me over the edge.

But my partner and mentor, Tim Reed, had managed to keep me in check and we were a great team for almost six years, even pulling off the bust of a minor mobster – although that was more a matter of dumb luck than any skill or expertise on my part.

Tim also enjoyed being a cop and shared my enthusiasm for the job, but in his years on the force before I came along, he had learned to control his impulses and was able to help me control my own. Even the Chief had once grudgingly admitted to me that I wasn't a half-bad cop when I was working with Tim. We both got promoted to detective in my fifth year on the force, much to the surprise of the Chief. But by then I was used to following Tim's lead and he kept me out of trouble. We actually got a commendation on the bust of the mobster and I felt I'd finally proven myself.

Then just a month after the verdict came down, sending the mobster away for eight to twelve years, Tim's wife went into labor with their first child and I was left on my own that day and managed to let a drug suspect engage me in a pursuit, and the rest – including my career as a police officer – was history.

It wasn't my fault. I didn't tell him to drive into the reservoir. And how could I know that several packages of heroin would break open on impact and contaminate the water supply? Could have happened to anyone.

But there was an immediate uproar in the media about it, and three days later, after what must have been the fastest Internal Affairs investigation in history, I was ordered to hand in my badge and clean out my locker. At least I still had the gun I'd bought as a graduation present to myself – the thirty-eight special I affectionately called Charley. At least he couldn't take that from me.

Tim came to help me pack and to say goodbye. "I'm really sorry, Angel," he said. "If I'd been there, this wouldn't have happened." He gave me a hug.

"It's not your fault, Tim," I murmured into his Kevlar vest. "I should have known better than to let that guy bait me like that." I turned away from him and closed the locker door. "Not like you haven't told me a thousand times to think twice before chasing."

"What are you going to do now?" he asked.

"I've got some money my grandmother left me that I'll get in a couple of years," I replied. "And I have her house, but it's in Clarkdale,

Colorado. I guess I'll go there and try to get a job until I get my inheritance."

"You know you'll never get work as a cop again."

"I know." I sighed. "Maybe I can be a PI. I really screwed up my life, didn't I?"

He patted my shoulder. "You'll land on your feet. Maybe you'll meet Mr. Right and not have to worry about a job. You can stay home and cook and clean and take care of two-point-five children and a Cocker Spaniel."

I socked him lightly on the arm. "Chauvinist," I said. He grinned. I grinned back. I knew he was kidding. Then I sighed. "I'll never get married," I said, a bit wistfully. "Nobody will ever want me."

"Someone will," he assured me. He picked up the box with my possessions in it and we walked toward the door. "Marcus was a shallow jerk. He was lucky to have you and too stupid to know it. You're smart and tough but soft inside. You just need the right man to find you."

Marcus was my first husband, who had left me when I was twenty-two for a stripper he found somewhere with more boobs than brains. I laughed. "Yeah, sure, I'm like a stale marshmallow. With turnips for brains," I added. "Some combination." We reached my car and I opened the trunk. Tim set the box inside it and I closed the lid. I turned and looked up at him. "I'm going to miss you something awful," I said, blinking back tears that sprang into my eyes.

He took me in his arms and gave me another hug. "I'll always be here if you ever need me," he said.

I pulled away and unlocked my car door. "I'll be okay," I said and slid behind the steering wheel. I looked up at Tim. "Don't let them win, okay?"

He smiled at me sadly. "They already did, Angel. They got you out of here."

I nodded and started the car. I looked at him one more time through the open window, choked out, "Give my love to Jenny and the baby," and drove away, tears running down my face as I left the parking lot for the last time. I did not look back again.

Chapter 1

Three years later

HE SWEPT INTO MY OFFICE like a hormonal hurricane – six feet of lean, sinewy testosterone – and I couldn't take my eyes off him.

From the windblown dark brown hair to the unclipped mustache to the long, tanned arms to the mouth that looked like it was perpetually amused about something, this man shouted one thing from every fiber of his body to every fiber of mine: "Your place or mine, honey?"

Well, it was a nice fantasy, but it would have to wait. I didn't even know why he was there. My secretary, Felix, had told me only that, "The sexiest man in the world is here to see you. I've already gotten his phone number. If you don't use it, can I?" Now the man who had turned Felix's head stood before my desk and every hormone in my body was on point.

"How may I help you, Mister ... ?" I inquired. It didn't occur to me to be embarrassed that I'd already forgotten the man's name. It was written on a piece of paper in front of me but I didn't want to take my eyes off him long enough to read it.

Mr. Testosterone merely replied, "Andrew Field, Ms Virago." He shook my hand firmly but with all gentlemanly propriety and I dismissed a fleeting fantasy that he might throw me to the desk and make passionate love to me on the spot. Oh, well. Maybe Felix *was* his type.

I slapped my hormones into submission. "So very pleased to meet you, Mr. Field," I said with all the formality I could muster. "Please call me Angela."

"Only if you will call me Andrew." He seated himself in the chair I indicated and I sat back behind my desk, crossing my legs carefully in what I hoped was a non-seductive and ladylike fashion.

"How can I help you, Andrew?" I inquired demurely.

Most of my clients were women, and it was probably for the best. I've always had a habit of falling, hard, for the wrong men. When I first opened my own investigative agency, I did it with the knowledge that my clients would be mostly women. After all, what red-blooded American male is going to come to a woman and ask that his wife be put under surveillance? I knew going in that most private detective work in a small town consisted of just that – divorce-related work, with a few pre-employment checks and the occasional insurance fraud investigation thrown in to break up the day. I had spent two years doing just that kind of grunt work for another PI before my trust fund came in and I hung out my own shingle a little over a year ago.

So far I'd managed to avoid any emotional entanglements with clients – but suspected that was about to change.

I studied Andrew Field. The laughing brown eyes crinkled at the edges, and the upper lip twitched slightly as if amused. Was he laughing at me?

"Angela, I've come to you because I think my problem needs a woman's touch."

"What problem is that?"

"I'm being followed," Andrew Field answered.

"Followed? By someone dangerous?" My hand unconsciously reached out to touch the handle of my right-hand desk drawer, where I kept the thirty-eight special I called Charley. The mere suggestion of danger made me itch to grab my gun and get after the bad guys.

"I don't know. I don't know who's following me. I don't know why. But I think you're the one who can help me, at least that's what I've heard."

I was silent for a minute, studying my newest potential client. I could easily understand why any member of the female sex and ten percent of the males would follow this man anywhere. Entering the office, Andrew Field had moved with the lithe grace of a cat, his chest and back muscles rippling smoothly beneath the stretch knit shirt he wore. His tight, white jeans emphasized his masculinity in a most appealing way.

I studied the chest hair that was visible over the open neck of the light blue shirt. My eyes drifted upward to his face, where I again found amusement in his eyes. I pulled my gaze away from him and turned to some papers on my desk. "Let me get some information from you first, Andrew."

I began asking him the basic questions for my case file – name, address, phone, age, occupation, *marital status.*

"Single," he replied without hesitation. I had already flicked a glance at his left hand and found only what looked like some kind of class ring. "Never married," he added.

Oh, what the hell, I thought, get the question settled and be done with it. "Are you gay?"

"No."

Sorry, Felix.

"Good. I mean, that's all the preliminary questions. Now tell me why you think someone's following you." I clicked on my recorder. I rarely take notes since I can seldom read my own handwriting. Later, I would have Felix type a transcript of the conversation.

He proceeded to tell me that he had been noticing a certain car in his vicinity lately wherever he went. A yellow Toyota Celica. No, he hadn't been able to get the license number. No, he couldn't see the driver. The car never got close enough, and every time he tried to get where he could see it better, it turned off onto another road.

"Why do you think I'm the best one to handle this case?" I asked. He probably heard that my fees are lower because I'm trying to build a clientele, I thought.

"I think it's probably a woman."

"So?" Send a bimbo to catch a bimbo, was that it?

"I think you'd have a better chance of catching her than a man would. If a man started tailing her, she'd might worry about being stalked by a rapist, but with a woman on her tail, maybe she'll be less on her guard."

Well, I suppose there was some logic in that, I had to admit grudgingly, but only to myself. "Why do you think it's a woman?"

For the first time, Andrew Field looked nervous, evasive. "I think it's my –" He broke off at the sound of a commotion in the outer office.

I heard Felix's voice. "No, you cannot go in there! She's with a client and can't be disturbed!"

There was a scuffling sound, a muffled "Ooof!" followed by the sound of someone thudding heavily to the floor, a "God damn it, I'm her fucking husband!" and I jumped up and bolted to the door.

"Excuse me," I said over my shoulder to my startled client. "Reginald!" I shouted at the man on the floor. "What the hell are you doing here? And you are *not* my husband, goddamn it!" At five-foot six and about one hundred and twenty pounds soaking wet, the skinny little wimp should have known better than to cross anyone over the age of seven, but he always had been long on ego and short on brains. The problem was, while he had either the balls or sheer stupidity to antagonize someone bigger than he was, he didn't have the brawn to back it up.

Reginald raised himself from the floor, keeping a watchful eye on Felix, who was poised to kick the crap out of that worthless piece of garbage with whom I had once had the misfortune of cohabitating for two months.

Felix didn't look it, but he was black belt Karate. He wasn't physically large, only about five-foot eight or so, but had a deceptively solid build. He had appointed himself my protector, a role he took seriously, and twice had turned away business when his instincts told him the potential client was dangerous. Now he had just decked my least favorite ex-lover and I bit back an approving smile as Reginald slowly climbed to his feet.

"Call off your dog, will you?" Reginald said warily, rubbing his ass.

Felix almost imperceptibly shifted his weight to his right foot, preparing to lash out with his left at the slightest excuse. "It's okay, Felix," I said. "He's harmless enough. Even I can whip him."

"And I do miss that, sweetheart," Reginald said.

"What do you want?" I demanded tersely, mindful of the fact that I had a *real man* waiting in my office with a problem for me to solve.

"I just wanted to see you again." He seemed unsteady on his feet and I bent closer to him and sniffed.

"You're drunk! Get the hell out of here! I told you I never wanted to see you again, you weasel! Get out of here before I have you arrested!"

Reginald never was one to stand his ground against me, and as he shuffled out with his tail between his legs, I almost felt sorry for him for a moment – but just for a moment. "Thanks, Felix," I said. "If he comes back, call the police."

I returned to my office and found Andrew Field on his feet, studying a picture on my wall – a picture of me in my Myersburg police uniform, taken the day I graduated from the academy so many years ago. A glance at my desk told me he had thoughtfully turned off the recorder after I bolted from the room.

"Sorry about that," I muttered, blushing slightly, embarrassed by my unprofessional response to the disturbance. I should have let Felix handle it instead of running out on a client like that.

"Ex-husband?" he inquired politely.

"Not exactly. I had the bad judgment to shack up with the jerk for a couple of months. I kicked him out when I caught him in bed with the cleaning lady."

"Oh," he said.

"She was fifty-three." At thirty-one, it had been a bit of a blow to my ego to learn that Reginald found it possible to bed all two hundred and forty pounds of that ugly cleaning woman *the day after* the son of a bitch had told me how much he loved me and how he was so lucky I was exactly his type. His type! Anything with an orifice was "his type."

Well, actually, she probably only weighed about a hundred and fifty, and I suppose *some* people might find her attractive. Apparently Reginald did, anyway.

She was lousy at her job, too, leaving streaks on the bathroom mirror every week and refusing to do windows. I had wondered why Reginald hired her in the first place. She'd been working for us for only three weeks when I figured it out.

"It was a long time ago," I finished lamely. Well, three months ago was a long time for me. "Anyway, we were talking about your problem," I added, suddenly realizing I shouldn't have just spilled my guts to a complete stranger.

"My problem." Again he looked uncomfortable. I looked at him closely, my hormones having been driven far, far underground by Reginald's scene, and I realized he was not the carefree bachelor of my fantasy, but someone who was truly troubled.

Curiously, I leaned forward, encouragingly. "You were about to tell me who you thought was following you," I reminded him gently, switching the recorder back on and pushing the microphone in his direction.

"There's a good chance it's my ex-boss," he finally admitted.

"Your ex-boss? A woman?" Why did I sound so surprised, anyway? Wasn't I a woman boss myself?

"Yes. A woman. That's why I had to come to you," he said quickly. "I mean, this whole situation is so crazy, no man would believe it, but I think a woman could relate to it. That's why I came to you."

"Tell me about it," I said, leaning back in my chair.

"I told you I worked at Computech. Her name is Cassandra Bellamy. She was my boss, the manager of my section. She promoted me to be her assistant about a month after she was made manager. I wondered at the time why I got the job. There were other people with more seniority, you see, but I was told I was better qualified. I'm trained in computer design and Cassandra's section was about to begin a new project for some high-tech firm. She told me she wanted only the best in her section and that's why she chose me."

"Are you the best?" I asked.

He shrugged. "Maybe. The thing is, she had no way of knowing that. I'd only been with this particular firm for a couple of months when she chose me. She hadn't had a chance to see what I could do."

"So she chose you as her assistant. Then what?"

"At first, everything seemed all right. We got the specs for the job and started work. I was responsible for the overall planning, but there were three designers under me who did most of the actual graphics. Cassandra and I spent a lot of time together, going over the project, meeting with the client. I suppose when it comes right down to it, she really wasn't doing much of the actual work, but I'll get into that later."

"Okay." So far this didn't sound like much of a case. I suppressed a yawn.

"Then she began to do things like rubbing her leg against mine when we were sitting next to each other looking at charts. She'd find excuses to pat me on the back, and her hand would stay there. I mean, it's not like I really minded – she's a great-looking lady – but I was starting to wonder what she was trying to pull."

"Was she married?"

"Yes. With children."

"Were you involved with anyone at the time?" Or now, for that matter, I wanted to add.

"I was engaged."

Damn. "Okay, so you thought maybe she was coming on to you. Did you confront her about it, ask her to stop?"

"Well, one night we were working late, just the two of us. I made a suggestion she liked and she threw her arms around me and said she was so glad she'd hired me for that job, that I'd probably saved hours and hours of work with that suggestion. Then she kissed me."

"She kissed you," I repeated. Not a bad impulse, actually. "On the mouth?"

"Yes. Then she asked if I'd like to go out for a drink."

"What did you say?"

"I pulled her arms away from my neck and said I was engaged, that I didn't want to get involved with anyone else, particularly not my married boss, and I thought maybe we shouldn't keep working late at night."

I leaned across the desk. "Let me get this straight. You're working alone at night with a woman you admit is attractive, she practically throws herself at you … "

"No practically about it," he interrupted. "She did throw herself at me."

"… and you tell her, basically, sorry, but I'm not that kind of guy?"

"My work is very important to me, and I think in that moment I realized that the only reason she requested me as her assistant was because she had the hots for me."

"And this is a bad thing."

Andrew Field stood up. "I thought a woman would understand about sexual harassment. Maybe I made a mistake coming to you. Maybe I just have to deal with this myself."

"Please don't leave, Mr. Field," I said. "I'm sorry, but you must admit this is not how sexual harassment usually works. And apparently there must be much more to the story than this."

To my relief, he sat back down. "I can't blame you for wondering why I didn't just jump at the opportunity, but at the time there was my fiancée to think of."

"At the time? Not anymore?"

"A week after this incident, my fiancée was killed in a freak accident. Her car went over an embankment."

The back of my neck prickled like it always does when I scent danger. "And you think your boss did her in?"

"No, in fact I was her alibi. The accident happened while Cassandra and I were together making a presentation to a client. Just a freak accident."

I suppose I didn't quite succeed in keeping the disappointment out of my voice when I said simply, "Oh."

"About a week after the funeral, Cassandra called me into her office at five o'clock one evening and said she was truly sorry about Gail's death, and she understood how difficult it must be for a virile young man such as myself to find myself suddenly alone. She said if there was anything she could do to help, anything at all, to let her know. I didn't have to be a rocket scientist to know what she meant by *anything*."

"So she still had the hots for you," I prompted. This babe has my sympathy so far, I thought.

"It got worse. She started with the late nights again, pawing me at every opportunity. By that point she was pissing me off. I mean, Gail was hardly buried and she expected me to take up with her, just like that? I kept telling her I wasn't interested. Then she started with the threats."

"What threats?"

"She finally told me point blank that she'd always been attracted to me and if I didn't go to bed with her, she'd kick me out of her department, perhaps have me fired."

"So what did you do?"

"I had suspected this was coming up. It would have been easy for me to play along with her, but I worked too hard to get where I did in my career. I wasn't about to be anybody's boy toy. I had a recorder on in my pocket, and the whole conversation was recorded."

"You blackmailed her."

"No! I knew if I let her know I had the recording that she would lay off, but that would have been a form of blackmail, and I've always believed that blackmailers are just asking to be shot. No, I didn't want to put myself in that position, and there were other issues involved anyway. I went to the head of our personnel office and played the recording. I told him I was afraid my job was in jeopardy but I didn't think it was appropriate for me to sleep with my boss especially since she was married."

"And after he stopped laughing, what did he do for you?"

Somehow Andrew Field no longer looked like he was about to laugh about something.

"He fired her. And they gave me her position. I finished the project myself and they gave me a big bonus."

I considered what that would have done to Cassandra's ego – first, to be rejected by the man she wanted so badly, then to lose her job over having made the pass in the first place. And the second place, and the third place, I reminded myself. "She was pissed at you."

"She had to be. She was earning over a hundred grand a year in that position. But worse still, word got out of why she was fired and her husband kicked her out, kept the kids, the house, and the dog, and sent her away with a ten year old Plymouth and an empty checking account. Or so I heard through the grapevine at work. That was four months ago. I heard the divorce was final two weeks ago. That's when all this started."

"And you think she's following you? In a yellow Celica?"

"She swore when she was packing up her desk that day that she'd get even with me."

"You think she'd try to kill you? Did she threaten your life?" My hand slid unconsciously toward my right drawer again and I pulled it back.

"No, she won't kill me. She swore that she'd make me wish I were dead. That she was going to ruin me and see me homeless and drunk on the streets before she was through with me."

The intercom buzzed. "Ms Virago," Felix said, "your next appointment is here." I had instructed him to buzz me anytime I was with a client more than thirty minutes, whether anyone was waiting or not. Gave the clients the impression I was busier and more important than I really was. Made them more willing to pay their bills. At least, that was the theory. I was never sure it worked.

"Thank you, Felix," I replied.

"Is my time up already?" Andrew asked, looking at his watch. "I'm really not through with the story yet."

"Go on. I'm still not sure what you want me to do for you."

"She's been sending me hate mail, believe it or not. Never signed, but I know it's from her." He pulled several papers out of his hip pocket and handed them to me. I glanced through them, then set them aside.

"Looks pretty tame to me," I said lightly. Actually, they looked very amateurish. Real threats are usually more specific, but these just said things like, "You're going to regret this for the rest of your life." It would have piqued my interest more if they'd said something like, "I'm going to blow your fucking head off, you cocksucking swine." It's much more fun to deal with something tangible. These letters were a big yawn.

"Well, I really wasn't too worried until I got the phone call yesterday."

"Phone call. Did you check with the phone company to see if they could trace it?"

"Caller ID was blocked and they just said it was a local call and there was no record of where it came from. But I know who it was. I recognized the voice."

"What did she say?"

"She said she was going to ruin me. That somewhere, there was a skeleton in my closet and she was going to find it and ruin me for what I did to her."

"And is there a skeleton in your closet for her to find?"

He looked right at me then, his dark brown eyes under those heavy dark eyebrows under that shaggy dark hair boring right into mine. I saw the corner of his mouth twitch, ever so slightly. My heart beat faster. Shit, who could blame her? He smiled, dazzling me with perfect white teeth, and said simply, "That's what I want you to find out."

I stared at him, puzzled, without speaking. He needed me to find out if he had a skeleton in his closet? Didn't he know? Then his smile faded and he added soberly, "You see, Angela, if she finds out enough about my past, we're both going to end up dead. I know that – but she doesn't. I've got to know what she knows. My life depends on it. And on you."

Chapter 2

AFTER ANDREW LEFT, I SPENT OVER AN HOUR discussing with Felix what we needed to do. My first task was to confirm if it really was Cassandra Bellamy following Andrew Field, and to discover what her situation was now that she was jobless, homeless, and husband-less. Had she found a sugar daddy already? Somehow she didn't sound the type, but from what Andrew had said, it didn't sound like she had the wherewithal to trade the Plymouth for a thirty-plus thousand dollar sports car.

While I pursued the all-too-understandable Cassandra Bellamy, Felix would begin a preliminary investigation into the life of Andrew Field. Andrew had refused to tell me anything else about himself, other than his date of birth, social security number, where he was born, and his mother's maiden name. He wanted me to investigate him cold, since Cassandra Bellamy didn't know much else about him either. He wanted to know what about him it was possible to learn without his cooperation.

It sounded like he did have a skeleton in his closet, but was hoping it could stay there. Public records are funny. Sometimes the most innocuous facts show up, and the most heinous go unreported.

He refused to explain why he felt he would be in mortal danger if she found that skeleton in his closet, or from whom the danger would come.

Felix would check the usual sources, and, depending on what he learned, I would do any necessary interviewing of witnesses or family members. I told Felix to check court records, DMV, the U.S. military, the newspaper morgue and anything else he could think of.

Although I'd been open for over a year, I didn't have much business yet and this case would be a real boost in the checking account. I had opened the agency with some of the inheritance I had received from my maternal grandmother. She had died when I was twenty-five, but her will had stipulated that I not receive the money until I proved I had "the sense God gave a common turnip, or at age thirty, whichever came first." Apparently my misspent youth had caused her to think I would do likewise with any windfall received sooner than that.

I had committed some of that money to hiring Felix two months ago, hoping an investment in a more professional image would yield more business and reduce the rate at which I was using up my granny's bequest. There had been several responses to my want ad but I didn't want to have some empty-headed blonde bimbo sitting in my front office attracting all the wrong kind of clientele. Felix was perfect. His sexual orientation would keep anything from developing between us, and his male presence would act as a deterrent to the occasional scumbag who might try to take advantage of a woman working in an office with only an empty-headed blonde bimbo for protection.

Felix had quickly demonstrated a knack for figuring things out that went way beyond his job description and I was constantly grateful for whatever twists of fate had brought him to my door. I didn't know much about his background, other than that he had been born in Los Angeles to Latin American parents twenty-five years before and had a last name I gave up trying to pronounce in our first and only interview. We had hit it off instantly and I had hired him on the spot. Now he was my first line of attack on any database in existence.

He was dark and handsome and had an infectious wide grin. In the outer office, he had a no-nonsense professional demeanor that tended to command respect – from everyone but idiots like Reginald, anyway. Privately, he enjoyed the freedom I gave him to be himself in my presence and I found him to be intelligent, witty, and charming.

He was more than a secretary to me; he was already a good friend.

With the preliminary investigation into Andrew Field's past left in Felix's capable hands, I took on the case of the oversexed lady boss. My God, what if I turned out to be just like her?

I started out by casing Andrew Field's neighborhood at five o'clock the next morning. My first priority was to be sure there wasn't some other person involved here. I mean, there wasn't a whole lot of point in investigating Cassandra Bellamy if she had innocently moved to Oregon after being fired and some person Andrew didn't even suspect was really behind the letters, phone calls, and the wheel of that yellow Celica.

But it wasn't very likely, I knew. Andrew's ex-boss had a ton of motive to do him damage, physically or psychologically. I picked out a spot at the end of Andrew's street and waited to see what I could see.

He lived in an upper-middle-class neighborhood. The cars I saw emerging from oversized garages were mostly high-end sedans, several full-sized SUV's along with a scattering of newer-looking sports cars.

Folks here were not exactly filthy rich, but definitely well-off. I figured the average incomes to be in the high five figures to low six figures.

Andrew Field owned a gray Chevy Suburban and a black Harley-Davidson cruiser. It was the motorcycle he rolled out of his garage that morning at about six-fifteen. I watched him buckle on his helmet, adjust his left-hand rearview mirror, and ride up the street in a black leather jacket that only served to further excite hormones that had perked up at his first appearance in the door to his garage.

I pulled my eyes away from his retreating back and began studying the area. He had barely reached the corner two blocks away when a yellow Celica passed my parked car and followed him out of the neighborhood.

Apparently the driver hadn't been following yesterday when Andrew came to my office or if he had, he didn't notice my Firebird, for the car drove right by without the driver showing the slightest interest in me. I pulled away from the curb and followed. I tried to get a look at the driver, but the glance was too fleeting to be of much use. I did determine it was a man.

Reading the license number aloud into my recorder as I drove, I glanced at the clock. Felix would not arrive at the office until seven, and DMV would not open until eight, so I was going to have to stay with this surveillance for nearly two hours before I would be able to find out whom I was following. Not a problem; as long as I had Charley with me I wasn't worried about being alone on the mean streets.

I stayed far behind the Celica for several miles. I wasn't worried about staying too close, since I knew Andrew was going to work in the adjacent larger town, and the Celica was following Andrew. As we neared Computech I drew closer to it, wondering what it would do when Andrew turned into the parking lot.

To my surprise, the Celica stopped a block away from the Computech office. I pulled to the curb several lengths back and watched Andrew ride into the lot, pause at the guard shack, then ride to the motorcycle parking area near the entrance to the building.

The Celica stayed where it was until Andrew disappeared into the building, then it drove into the lot, paused at the guard, then parked down at the other end of the parking area, well out of sight of the motorcycle corral.

I drove past the lot, watched the driver get out and lock the car then enter the building by a different entrance. Puzzled, I turned around and drove into the lot myself. The guard stepped out of the little building and asked if he could help me.

I decided the best thing to do was lie. "I was following a car in traffic and a notebook slid off the roof onto the street in front of me. I stopped and picked it up, but lost the car at the next light. I thought I saw it turn in here. It was a yellow Celica. Do you know whose it was?"

"Uh, I'm new here. Let me see if his name came up." He consulted his computer screen. A sensor gun was aimed at my windshield, no doubt for the purpose of reading parking permits. "Yeah, I have his name here. I can give it to him if you like."

"Well, this may sound mercenary, but it looks like an important notebook. Might be a reward for turning it in, you know?" I put on what I hoped was a seductive smile. "And I thought he was kinda cute, too, you know? I'd like to give it back personally. Could you tell me his name so I can call him myself?" I tried to bat my eyelashes. I've never really known why that should have any effect on a man, but in this case, it seemed to convince the guard.

He grinned. "It says it was Randy Bellamy," he said. "Good luck. You can go into the lobby there and call him on a company phone. Park over there on the right," he added, pointing.

"Thank you so much," I replied, batting my eyelashes awkwardly again. I drove where he indicated and went into the lobby where I called Andrew Field and told him who was following him.

"Randy Bellamy?" he said. "That must be Cassandra's husband … ex-husband, I mean … I think. I never did know his first name. Or maybe he's a brother-in-law?"

"Whoever he is, he came in here through another entrance. On the east side of the building."

"That's the accounting entrance. Thanks, Angela. I'll see if I can find out where he works and when he was hired. I know Cassandra's husband didn't work here when she did. Company rules against family members working here, you know."

"But Andrew, if he works here, and he obviously knows you work here, why would he bother following you to work? Surely he knew where you were going, and why."

"Good question. I can only guess he wants to intimidate me. It worked."

"That may be, especially since he's been doing it without really trying to hide the fact. Well, now that we know it isn't Cassandra following you, do you still want me to continue as planned?" I asked. "I mean, checking your background and all?"

"You bet! I still need to know what she might have found out about me. I'll call you later this afternoon."

I left Computech and drove to Cassandra Bellamy's former residence. This was located in another plush neighborhood about three miles from Andrew's. Professionally landscaping surrounded the front yard of the imposing two-story edifice. The double door to the garage was open and I could see that one stall was empty, but a car was in the second stall, a recent model light green Cadillac sedan. Cassandra Bellamy's ex-husband had good taste, at least in cars. A separate door to a third garage stall was closed.

I saw a man inside the garage – an older man with gray hair, slightly stooped, dressed in overalls and a long-sleeved blue plaid shirt. He was tinkering with something on a work bench with his back to the open door.

I drove past the house and around the block to the alley. Driving down the alley, I located the house from the rear and was greeted by a Golden Retriever with lolling tongue that galloped to the wrought-iron gate in the block fence and woofed once as I approached. Two little boys, aged about six and seven, paused and stared at me from the patio as I drove by. The back yard was neatly manicured and held a small assortment of little boy playthings – balls and trucks and the like.

I left the alley and drove back to my office, arriving shortly after eight. Felix was already on the computer, searching public records for references to my client.

"Morning, Felix," I said.

"Morning, Boss," he replied. "So have you made it with the new client yet?"

I chose to ignore the inquiry. The problem with having Felix for a secretary was that we both had the same taste in men and Felix knew it. It was clear that Andrew Field had stirred both our fantasies to an all-time high. I went into my office and put my gun in the desk. I glanced at the blank page of my appointment book and paused for a moment to be grateful we at least had Andrew Field to work for that day. And the fees we had negotiated the day before were substantial enough to make all the legwork we had to do worthwhile. After convincing me his life might be in danger, he readily agreed to my "combat pay" rates, double my usual fees.

Felix came in with some coffee. I never drink the stuff, but for some reason it's a compulsion with Felix to carry coffee to the boss every morning. As usual, I said, "No thank you, Felix. I don't drink it." And as usual, he replied, "Guess I'll drink it, then," and sat down in a chair.

It had been a ritual during the two months he had worked for me, and this morning "coffee break" was when we puzzled out our cases, I gave him his instructions for the day, and he gave me the benefit of his insight.

Felix had been raised virtually on the streets of Los Angeles and had seen all kinds. As a child, he had been branded "different" at an early age and he had to learn to fight young in order to survive. At thirteen he enrolled in Karate classes and the other kids soon learned to leave him alone.

Now anyone who called him a faggot or a sissy was in for a serious trouncing. He liked to joke about it. "Call me a sissy, and I'll hit you with my purse," he would say. "First my right purse, then my left purse," he would add, holding up first his right fist, then his left.

"Okay, Boss," he said today. "What did you learn this morning?" He made a face when he sipped his coffee. I thought it smelled a little more scorched than usual but he made no comment. He'd been battling with the second-hand coffee machine for two months and so far, the machine was winning but he refused to send it back to Goodwill where it came from.

I gave him the name Randy Bellamy and asked him to find out who he was. Then I gave him the license number of the Celica and asked him to check DMV and see if it was registered to Randy Bellamy, or someone else. I also gave him the license number of the Cadillac.

I had promised Andrew I would tail him, and his tail, when he left work at five o'clock that evening. The time in between would be spent investigating Andrew Field himself.

"Boss," Felix said. He liked to call me "Boss." "I can't find anything on Andrew Field."

"What do you mean, you can't find anything?"

"He wasn't born where he said he was born. His mother's maiden name is a phony. I can't get a hit on his social security number anywhere. It's a legitimate number and the name Andrew Field is tied to it with the birthdate he gave us, but there are no records anywhere that have that number, no school records, no DMV records, no military records, no real estate transactions, no credit history at all. You'd think something would show up somewhere."

"Why the red herring, then, Felix? He hired me to do a job. Why would he throw up such an obstacle already?" I paused for a moment, remembering my suspicion that he did, indeed, have a skeleton in his closet. "Maybe he gave me the same information this Bellamy woman had access to. He didn't want me to be any better armed than she is. Maybe he lied on his application at Computech." I handed Felix another slip of paper. "Guess we're going to have to work backward instead of forward on this one. Here's his license number. We need to start getting a picture of who Andrew Field is. See if PRICS can help."

Felix took his assignments back to his computer terminal and a few moments later I heard the contented clacking of keys as he searched the various databases available to members of the Private Resource Investigation Cooperative Service.

I turned on my own monitor and began my own search for information about Cassandra Bellamy. My first inquiry was into the credit files, searching for an indication that Cassandra was having financial problems. There was no record under that name, but a cross-check on the address yielded a record for Cassandra Elizabeth Baxter, maiden name Martin. A quick check against another part of the database told me that she had divorced a Samuel Baxter eight years previously. Apparently she had not established any credit history under her most recent married name.

Andrew Field had told me that four months had passed since Cassandra's firing. Her husband had kicked her out two weeks later and filed for divorce immediately according to office gossip. Her credit report showed that Cassandra had applied for, and been denied, three loans since then. I wondered why she was still using her first husband's last name on those applications. Her credit history up to that point had been okay, with an apparent tendency to pay her bills late, but no defaults. The loan for the Plymouth had been paid off five years ago. There was another auto loan listed, for a two-year-old Beemer. There was no recent information on its payments, so I could only assume that it was being paid off according to schedule. Maybe the husband had taken over those payments when he took the car. Odd that his name wasn't on the loan.

There was no other auto loan. The house had been purchased only a year ago, and, from what I knew about house values in that area, it appeared to be mortgaged to the hilt. The loan value was so high I doubted there had been much equity to argue about in the divorce. Again, I thought it odd that he had kept the house when the loan wasn't in his name.

I checked on Randy Bellamy. There was no credit report listed for Randy Bellamy.

And there was no divorce filing under the name Bellamy in the court records for this county. And no marriage certificate either. So what did that mean? Possibly the marriage had been in another state, but divorces have to be filed in the state of residence. According to the timeline Andrew had given me, the divorce was finalized almost exactly ninety days after he said it was filed, which is the minimum time period in Colorado, and suggested Cassandra had not contested it in any way. Why would she have agreed to his terms without any protest that would have dragged out the proceedings? I wondered if they had ever actually been married in the first place.

Felix came in with some information on my client. Somehow, with him no longer sitting in front of me, I had started thinking of Andrew Field as a client instead of a testosterone factory. Oh, well, out of sight, out of reach of my hormones. "What do you have, Felix?"

"Here's Field's DMV printout," he said, handing me a sheet of computer paper. "And the report on the Celica and that Cadillac, both registered to a Howard Bellamy at the same address you gave me for Cassandra Bellamy."

I took the documents and sent him back to his computer while I studied them, puzzled. Who the heck was Howard Bellamy? Randy's father? Brother?

Andrew Raymond Field had first received a Colorado driver's license a week before starting work at Computech. He had stated on the application that he had never had a driver's license before. *At age thirty-three?* Where had he come from, taxi-infested New York City? It was unheard of that a man his age could have survived without learning to drive somewhere along the way.

I looked at the identification section. It said he had presented a social security card and a birth certificate from a small town in Iowa as proof of his identity. Iowa? He had told me he was born in Missouri. Was he really Andrew Field at all?

Unfortunately, the IRS is not very cooperative with private investigators, or anyone else for that matter, so using Field's social security number to find out where he had worked before was going to be difficult. I decided to start with Computech. Hopefully Computech would have required some kind of assurance that a new hire was who he said he was.

At the same time, I could check on the Bellamy clan and try to figure out where Randy and Cassandra fit together. Was he her husband? And who was Howard?

I changed from my standard fare of jeans into a more feminine business suit I keep in the office for such purposes, and decided to leave Charley in the desk drawer for this trip. Before I left the office, I glanced at myself in the mirror to make sure my hair was in place and I projected the proper image of a businesswoman when I went to Computech and began to lie through my teeth.

"See you later, Felix. I'm going to Computech, then I'll call you and let you know what I'll do next. Keep searching for everything you can think of. Call me on the car phone if you need me. Don't ring the cell phone, though, unless it's an emergency." Where would we be without technology? I thought of the old mystery novels I used to read, where cliffhangers developed around the inability of the hero's assistants to warn him of imminent danger. Not today. If Felix suddenly discovered that Andrew Field was an ax-murderer, he could raise me in seconds. With my phone always set on vibrate I could get a cue to terminate an interview without the interviewee knowing I had been signaled. I carried a cell phone on me, and there was a separate phone in the car as well. The car phone would flash a light if I had a message waiting.

Car phones, cell phones, and computer terminals. Sad to say, those were my tools of the trade. Oh, yes, I had Charley, but most of my work wasn't dangerous. The days of high-speed car chases, shootouts, and undercover disguises were, for the most part, over. Unfortunately. I personally always enjoyed a good high-speed chase, which, of course was what had gotten me relieved of duty at my former position at the Myersburg police department.

I turned into the driveway at Computech and was relieved to see a different guard on duty than the one who had met me that morning. "I need your personnel office," I said, and was directed to the same parking place I had occupied that morning.

The secretary in the personnel office was most helpful after I identified myself as an officer of the National Equality Commission and demanded to see the employment applications of everyone hired in the past two years. I explained with a steely gaze that a charge been filed recently by a middle-aged Asian woman who was claiming discrimination based on sex, race, *and* age.

I soon found myself alone in a comfortable office with the requested files and a lackey who persisted in running in and out inquiring if I needed any coffee, soft drinks, something to eat, my pencil sharpened. The kid was cute, and I was tempted to ask him if he'd like to kiss my ass as well, but I remembered that this company was touchy about sexual harassment, so I resisted the impulse.

I did let the little sycophant make a lot of photocopies for me. I included a half-dozen files in which I had no interest whatsoever in case he really was there to report what I latched onto. I tried to include several applications for higher-level positions to increase the anxiety factor of anyone who was inclined to worry about my "findings." I don't know why I do these little things, but I find it amusing how quick people are to assume they're in trouble the minute someone they think is a government agent darkens their door.

The applications for Andrew Field, Cassandra Bellamy, and Randy Bellamy tucked away in my briefcase, I left the building as quickly as I could. You just never know when someone who really knows what's going on might come back from a coffee break and demand to know why some flunky let in a government agent without checking first, resulting in embarrassing phone calls and questions. In this case, there was no such agency anyway. It's illegal for a PI to impersonate a government agent so I am always careful never to use the name of any real agency. Usually by the time they give up trying to find the phone number of the agency, I'm long gone. And if I get caught, I can't be accused of impersonating a government agent if the agency in question doesn't exist, right?

Having taken the precaution of covering my license plates before driving to Computech that afternoon with a set I had found abandoned in an alley one day, I was reasonably certain that nobody would be able to trace me if they did discover I was an imposter.

I stopped in an alley and switched the plates back before driving back to the office. Magnets on the back of the false plates made this a two-second operation.

Back at the office, I tossed aside the other applications and studied Andrew's. Andrew Field had listed two employers in the ten years before he came to work at Computech. One was in Missouri and the other was in Phoenix, Arizona. *So why didn't he have a driver's license?* There was no indication that either of the former employers had been contacted by Computech to check Field's references.

Why not? Why would they have forgone a reference check on Andrew Field?

Oh, well, I supposed I would just have to do their work for them. I dialed the phone number of the Arizona firm and asked for Personnel.

Andrew Field had never worked there.

I dialed the number of the Missouri firm and asked the same questions. Andrew Field had never worked there either.

I dialed the number of Computech and asked for Andrew Field. At least he really worked *there.*

"What the hell are you trying to pull, Mr. Field?" I demanded.

"I don't know what you're talking about," he replied lightly.

"Your whole life is a lie! Your employment history doesn't check out, you weren't born when and where you said you were, and your mother doesn't exist!" Okay, so I was laying it on a little heavy, but hell, I was peeved by this point.

"Angela, if all I wanted was the story of my life, I didn't need you. I hired you because I want to know what about my life it is possible for a person to discover *without* my cooperation. I thought you understood that."

"But why did you tell me all that crap about where you were born if it wasn't true?"

"Because that's the same crap I tell everyone. Now, Angela, you're an investigator. Go investigate. Until we find out what Cassandra can find out about me, we won't know if she has any means of getting her revenge and getting us both killed in the process."

I sighed explosively into the receiver. Now the true side of Andrew Field was beginning to show through the sexy facade. He wanted to play games. What deep dark secret in his past was he so worried about? Well, he was paying me to do a job, and damn it, I was going to do it, no matter how hard he made it!

What a pleasant idea that was, my hormones taunted me.

Shut up, I replied.

"Ms Virago?" I had nearly forgotten I was still on the phone.

"Yes, Mr. Field. I'll keep checking your background like you asked me to."

"I'll make it easy for you," he said. "If we can lose my tail tonight after work, I'll take you to dinner and you can try to get me to give you whatever information you can get in normal dinnertime conversation, okay?"

"Fine, Mr. Field. But I'm not getting on that motorcycle with you."

"I shouldn't think so. I'll go home and change vehicles. I have a cell phone so we can keep in touch while we dodge that Celica. Then we'll decide where to eat."

I hung up the phone, only slightly mollified by the prospect of being able to ask him some questions, but realizing all along that he'd probably continue lying to me.

The outer door banged shut and I heard a woman's voice, talking urgently to Felix. Good, I thought, another client. Two in one week would be a first for my fledgling agency. I waited for Felix to buzz me.

"Ms Virago?" he inquired politely over the intercom a moment later. "There's a woman to see you. Her name is Mrs. Bellamy."

Chapter 3

CASSANDRA BELLAMY WAS EVERYTHING I expected her to be: sophisticated, beautiful, smooth, carefully manicured. And something I did not expect: on the verge of tears.

Fighting the telltale quivering of her chin, she sat primly in the same chair Andrew Field had occupied the day before and tugged her lime green, tailored skirt over her shapely knees. Andrew Field had said no to *that?* I was willing to bet that even Felix had done a double-take when this blonde bombshell had walked into my outer office.

Assessing her with the cold objectivity I had been taught in the police academy, I would have described her as a female Caucasian, age about thirty, five foot seven, blond hair, gray eyes, weight probably about one-thirty, much of it carried on her chest.

Her blond hair was professionally coiffed, her makeup impeccable. Her ears were adorned with tasteful gold hoop earrings and three braided gold chains hung around her slender neck, resting above her breasts against the pale cream-colored chiffon blouse she wore beneath the matching lime green jacket. Expensive-looking silk stockings clad her long legs. On her feet were cream-colored shoes with impossible spike heels.

So this was the woman whose affections Andrew had spurned so callously.

Her red-lacquered fingernails were obviously fake. I suspected the boobs were as well.

I suppose business ethics demanded that I show her the door then and there, but there was no way to do that without revealing that Andrew Field was already my client. Nothing else I could do but hear her out, and try to avoid asking her any leading questions on Field's behalf.

"I just don't know what else to do," she wailed when I asked her purpose in coming to my office that day.

"Tell me about it," I urged neutrally. "What's the problem?"

"It's my husband! He's thrown me out and taken the children and all because of some silly misunderstanding!"

Misunderstanding, huh? Is that what adultery is called in her social circle? "What misunderstanding would that be, Mrs. Bellamy?"

"Oh, it's all so silly, really." She proceeded to tell her story with a maximum of tears, hand-wringing, and heart-tugging wails. *This* woman was in charge of a high-tech computer design team? I always thought of computer people as being coldly logical, not the sentimental, emotional sops this woman was trying to convince me she was.

The story she told was at total odds with Andrew Field's tale of the day before. She had been fired from her job – that much she confirmed – but she claimed it was because she was under such stress from the emotional turmoil of her marriage that she was unable to concentrate on her work. One of her underlings, as she called him, had been talented enough to bear most of the burden of the project and it had been completed on time, but the nasty young man had gone to her superiors and complained that she had foisted the project off onto him and she had been fired!

She didn't mention Field by name.

I didn't dare inquire. Professional ethics were at stake.

"What has this to do with your marriage?" I inquired.

She nearly waxed poetic at that question. It was like a nightmare, she moaned. Her husband, Randolph, had heard a rumor that Cassandra had had an affair with the back stabber who took her job. He believed the rumor and filed for divorce. He took the children, "My babies," she wailed. "He told me I was unfit to be their mother. How could he say such a thing? I was a loving mother, a loving wife, I never looked at another man!"

A picture of Andrew Field as a self-serving bastard who would lie in order to obtain career advancement began to form in my mind. One of these people was clearly lying. Was it possible that my inflamed hormones had prevented me from seeing Andrew Field as he really was? But what could be his game?

"I'm not sure what you want me to do for you, Mrs. Bellamy. Why do you feel you need an investigator? Sounds to me like you need a lawyer, not a PI."

"The lawyer said there was nothing I can do, unless I can prove my husband is involved in fraud. That's what I want you to do, Miss Virago. He's a crook, him and that André Field. They're in this together."

Since I wasn't supposed to know Andrew Field, I couldn't ask her if calling him *André* had been an error. Something funny was obviously going on here. And how had she just happened to pick the same agency as Andrew Field to do her investigative work? That question I could ask.

"How did you happen to choose my particular agency for this job, Mrs. Bellamy? And I should tell you that I'm not certain I'll be able to take your case. I have a pretty busy schedule right now." I tugged my appointment book toward me, hoping she hadn't noticed the blank page. I picked it up and flipped through it for a moment before closing it and returning it to the desk.

"Oh, but you must! I was told to come to you!"

"By whom, Mrs. Bellamy?" I didn't realize I was already starting to get the advantages of word of mouth advertising from former clients. I thought that usually came after breaking some major case, which I had yet to do.

"Why, my postman, of course! I was explaining to him today why my mail should be forwarded to my sister's house and he told me to come see you. A friend of his had come to you recently with a problem and my postman said this friend would only hire the best!"

"Did the postman mention the friend's name?" I asked doubtfully. "I like to send a thank-you card to clients who refer other business," I lied.

"No, he didn't mention it," she replied, "and I'm afraid I won't be seeing him again, since I've moved away. I only went back because I wasn't getting my magazines, you see, and I wanted to tell him personally where to send them."

"You didn't fill out the address form at the post office?"

"Oh, of course I did! These magazines were under 'Mr. and Mrs.' and those sexist pigs at the post office assume that 'Mr. and Mrs.' means 'Mr.' when two people divorce! There should be a law!"

"What do you want me to do for you?" I asked her for the second time, realizing she had not answered the first time.

"Why, of course, it should be obvious what I want! I want you to prove that my husband and André Field conspired to get me fired from my job under suspicious circumstances so my swine husband could take the children from me!"

"These were your own children? Not his by another marriage, perhaps?"

"Of course they are my children!"

"When were you and Randolph married?" Why was I doing this, I wondered? I knew I couldn't take this case.

"Seven years ago."

"And the children, how old are they now?"

"Brian is seven and Jason is six. They're only babies, Miss Virago. They need their mother."

"Shotgun wedding?" I asked bluntly.

"Well, yes, I guess they call it that, don't they?" she admitted, blushing. "Brian was born four months after the wedding."

"He is Randolph's son?" Another blunt question, but one that begged to be asked.

She hesitated. "No."

"Whose, then?"

"I can't tell you that. It doesn't matter anyway."

"Does Randolph think Brian is his son?"

"Yes, certainly. Nobody knows the truth but me."

"So, in actual fact, Randolph has taken custody of a child who is not his by birth."

"That's correct."

"Why didn't you have him arrested for kidnapping?"

"I – can't. I can't tell anyone. I shouldn't have told you."

"I do not violate confidences. Do not worry about that. But I'm afraid I have to decline your business. I'm too occupied with another extensive investigation, and yours is a very complicated case. Had it been something simple that I could have worked into my schedule, I would have been happy to help you, but I must ask you to find another investigator to help you. I'm afraid it's impossible for me to take your case."

"Oh, please reconsider, Miss Virago!" she pleaded, and I felt bad for having allowed her to bare her soul to me on what really were false pretenses on my part.

"I'm sorry, Mrs. Bellamy, very sorry, but it's just impossible. In fact, I have to go tail someone in fifteen minutes. I'm really quite busy. You just happened to catch me in at an odd moment as it was."

I handed her the business card of another investigator who had offices in the neighborhood and suggested she call him instead.

She left reluctantly, with a maximum of sniffling and hand-wringing.

I turned to Felix, who was grinning at me from ear to ear. "So that's Cassandra Bellamy," I said dryly. "I don't know what to think now."

"Boss, I slipped out and took a look at her car while she was in there with you," he said, his grin still broad.

"What did you find?"

"It's a yellow Celica, Boss, the same one you followed this morning."

"Oh, shit," I muttered. "Now what's going on?"

The question was not to be answered immediately. I gave Felix the task of filing the purloined employment applications and drove home to change into some of my more feminine clothes in anticipation of my dinner with Andrew, feeling all along I would have been just as well off to show up in jeans and an old T shirt. Having met Cassandra Bellamy I had little hope that he would ever be attracted to me, even if I cleaned up a bit.

If he turned her down, what could I ever expect him to see in me, the perpetual tomboy?

Standing in front of my bedroom closet I thought about Cassandra's carefully coordinated outfit, perfect grooming and willowy figure and grimaced. At five foot five and some hundred-thirty solid pounds myself, I wouldn't be caught even dead in an outfit like she had worn to my office that day. My taste runs more to jeans and athletic shoes, although I occasionally have to don more feminine attire for undercover work. My mid-length dark brown hair hasn't seen a beauty parlor in nearly twenty years, and that was for my eighth grade graduation dance. My nails are manicured by snipping them off with nail clippers whenever I happen to break one on the trigger guard of my gun. As for jewelry – if I can't shoot it or talk into it, I don't need it hanging off my body. I'll start wearing earrings when they start disguising recording devices in them.

I own makeup, but only use it when I'm in disguise, and I had to ask the gum-chewing teenager at the cosmetics counter to pick which shade of eye shadow went best with my particular shade of brown eyes. I've been told I'm attractive and have nice boobs, but usually by men who want something from me – three guesses what.

The men I want something from – three guesses what – usually don't give me a second glance. Mother Nature has a warped sense of humor.

I thought about putting on my all-purpose gray pantsuit but instead pulled out my most feminine outfit, a dark blue skirt and jacket of the polyester variety with a lighter blue blouse that I kept mostly for purposes of weddings and funerals, hopefully never my own, and changed my clothes. I brushed my hair and started to put on eye shadow and mascara and lipstick, knowing full well the effect would fall far, far short of what I had seen in my office that afternoon. Halfway through the operation I gave it up, wiped it all off, and decided I'd rather fall short knowing I hadn't tried at all than give it my all and still come up second best. Or third, or fourth, or nowhere in the running at all, which was the most likely scenario.

I finished by pulling on a pair of No Nonsense Light Tan pantyhose and my trusty black flats and figured that was as good as I was going to look. Can't make a silk purse out of a sow's ear. Or a turnip.

After all, this was a business dinner, not a date. What difference would it make what I looked like? I strapped on my shoulder holster and pulled the jacket on over it, checking for bulges in the wrong places.

As an afterthought, I squirted some of my only cologne behind each ear after first sniffing the atomizer to see if the stuff had evaporated down to pure alcohol yet. I'd had the bottle for over seven years at this point. My grandmother had given it to me for Christmas the year before she'd died. Granny was the quintessential optimist. She never gave up hope that someday I would decide to act like a girl.

Satisfied that I'd gone to all this trouble for nothing, I left for my surveillance duty, not really expecting the yellow Celica to show. It didn't. I stayed well back from Andrew on the way home, watching to see if he picked up a tail anywhere along the way, but nobody followed him. Nor did he pick up a tail after changing clothes and vehicles at his house. We drove separately to an intimate but expensive restaurant several miles from his house. I let him go inside first while I circled the block twice to make sure the Celica did not appear, then I parked near the entrance and walked inside.

He was waiting in the lobby and smiled when he saw me. "You look nice," he said when I approached.

Oh, great. He was going to start out lying to me right off the bat. "Thanks," I muttered, unconvinced. "So do you." At least one of us was telling the truth.

He put his hand on the small of my back to escort me to a corner table in the rear of the restaurant. I felt a tingle run up my spine at the touch, a tingle that collided with the instinctive flash of resentment brought on by the protective gesture. I was packing heat. Did he think I needed to be helped to a table?

Knock it off, I ordered myself. He's just being polite. Polite is good.

It was a Wednesday night, and the restaurant was not very busy. There were no other patrons within earshot of our table, and I felt secure that we wouldn't be surprised by the Bellamy clan. I took the precaution, however, of sitting with my own back to the wall, facing the dining room. Not much point in carrying a gun if you're going to let someone sneak up behind you, and I make it a rule never to compromise my vantage point.

Andrew Field sat to my left, also facing the dining area. If someone he recognized entered the restaurant, he would be able to let me know in time to take whatever action might be appropriate.

But this put him in close proximity to me, and our knees occasionally brushed under the table while we enjoyed a drink before dinner. To keep a clear head, I selected a non-alcoholic wine, but Field ordered a gin and tonic, and I was glad. Perhaps with a bit of sauce in him he would open up more about who he was and what he really wanted from me.

He had changed from the black leather jacket into a tailored sport coat over a turtleneck sweater. I admired the gold chain and medallion he wore over the sweater, taking careful note of its design. It might provide a lead to his past. He declined to explain where he had gotten the medallion, or when. It was a horse's head, with flowing mane, and sapphire eyes. It appeared to be real gold and real sapphires.

He had also taken the time while changing to dab on some fresh cologne and I was both pleased and annoyed that he had selected a scent I really liked. Unfortunately, that particular scent also acted like an aphrodisiac on me, and I worried that I would lose my objectivity with him.

He had anxiously searched the dining room when we sat down, looking for Mrs. Bellamy, I presumed, but once assured she was not there, he relaxed and turned his charms on me.

"So, Angela Virago, how did you get into this business, anyway?" he asked, gazing at me over his drink glass.

I forced myself to tear my eyes away from his. "I was a cop. It didn't work out. Had to do something else. So here I am." I found myself fidgeting with my teaspoon.

"How'd you end up in Clarkdale?" he persisted. "I wouldn't think there was enough business here to pay the rent."

I glanced at him sharply. Nosy bastard. "I don't pay rent. My grandmother left me her house when she died. After I left the force, I had to leave town and this was the only place I could afford to live until I got myself established."

"I see. But why did you have to leave Myersburg?"

He was starting to hit on subjects I really didn't want to discuss. It was time to stop being the interviewee. "It's a long story, Andrew," I said with a wave of my hand, "one I don't want to talk about. We're here to talk about you, not me. What other wild geese do you want me to chase this week?"

He threw back his head and laughed, and I started to melt. Damn sexy men with sexy voices and sexy cologne and ….

He reached over and patted my hand, sending unwanted shivers down my spine. "Sorry I had to do that to you, but I explained the reason. Unfortunately, while working with Cassandra Bellamy, I'm afraid

I might have let certain things slip that I didn't mean to. I'm worried that she might be able to use those things to her advantage, assuming she is able to learn more about me than she should."

"Why the aliases?" I asked, sipping my beverage. "I can't trace you from your name, and your prior employment record is fiction. Where did you come from, Andrew? Why the secrecy?"

"Tut, tut," he replied. "That's for me to know and you to find out." Gone was the insecurity of the day before, when he had allowed me a tiny peek behind his mask at his vulnerable side. Now he was in charge, and enjoying a game of cat and mouse. But for what purpose?

"By the way," he added, "Randy Bellamy is Cassandra's husband's brother. Her brother-in-law."

I tried not to look startled. Cassandra had said Randy was her husband, but I couldn't reveal that without revealing that I had talked to her. "How did you find that out?" I asked instead.

"I asked some people at work if the Bellamy who worked in Accounting was related to Cassandra. A perfectly natural question, don't you think? Someone said he was Cassy's brother-in-law. He was hired right after she was fired. He'd tried to get work there before but they won't hire relatives."

"Cassandra was fired, Randy was hired, and today he followed you to work. Why?"

"I don't know why, Angela, and I'm telling you the truth there. I don't know why she would have had him follow me."

"Maybe she didn't. Maybe he's doing it on his own." A waiter came to take our orders before he answered. I ordered a steak, medium rare. Andrew ordered Oysters Rockefeller. Shoulda known he'd get something like that. I wondered if he was going to sprinkle some powdered rhinoceros horn on it, with maybe a little ginseng on the side. Not that he likely needed any of it. I caught another whiff of his cologne and sighed. "Andrew, is there anything you might have let slip to Cassy that she might have told Randy that would make him think you were a potential blackmail subject?" I asked when the waiter left.

He took a long sip of his drink before he answered. I thought his eyes flickered with just a hint of fear when he replied, "Possibly."

"What?" Damn it, it was like pulling teeth from a crocodile to get answers from this man.

He sighed, looked at me, looked away, looked back, then to my surprise he took my left hand in his, looked earnestly into my eyes and said, "I'm wanted by – " He broke off with a pained look when a shot rang out from the doorway.

Andrew clutched his shoulder, which was already red with blood. My hand knifed into my jacket and came out with my revolver as I rolled quickly to the floor and swung the barrel of the gun toward the doorway.

It was empty.

The doorway, not the gun! I heard a squeal of tires even as I ran toward the door, arriving just in time to see taillights disappear around the corner. "Damn it!" I shouted, holstering the gun. The smell of cordite hung in the air.

I returned to the table to find Andrew gone. In the confusion, nobody had seen him leave by the rear exit, through which I trailed him. By the time I followed the blood trail to the parking lot, his Suburban was gone.

I'd seen the blood. I knew he'd been hit. I didn't know how badly. I returned to the table and examined the wall behind the table, but found no bullet or bloodstains there. He still had the slug in him, then, and would need medical attention. Perhaps he was heading for the nearest hospital.

But though I spent the next six hours visiting every medical facility in a twenty-mile radius, I never found Andrew nor his vehicle. I checked all the emergency rooms, and called all the local law enforcement agencies. No gunshot victims had been reported all evening.

It was two a.m. before I gave up the search. Andrew had not returned home. He had not sought medical treatment. The only other outcome I could foresee was the discovery of his dead body in his Suburban the next morning on the side of some road.

I had told police what had happened. There was nothing else I could do. I went home to bed.

There was a message on my answering machine. "This is Andrew Field. I'm all right. Don't try to find me. It's just what I was afraid of. She must know everything. Forget you ever saw me, Angela. I don't want them to get you, too. I'll call … what? How did you … ?" The line went dead.

Chapter 4

I WOKE UP THE NEXT MORNING hoping it had all been a dream, but knowing in my heart it had not. The police had been unable to trace the phone call and had been unable to locate Andrew Field. I had finally gotten to sleep about four a.m.

I couldn't believe I had let a client get shot right in front of my eyes. I was supposed to be better than that, and I could only blame my hormones for letting me get so mesmerized by Andrew Field that I had stopped watching the door for threats.

The few witnesses who had seen the gunman had been no help. The gunman – or woman, I suppose – had worn a stocking mask. A long black raincoat covered the clothing. A car had been found abandoned six blocks away. I had called the police from my office first thing and wasn't too surprised to learn it was the same yellow Celica Cassandra Bellamy had driven to my office the day before.

Had she been the shooter?

Felix came in with the morning coffee and I told him what had happened the evening before.

Felix pointed out something I had overlooked. "How did Field get your home phone number, Boss? Did you two … ?" He let the question hang in the air between us like a cloud of rank cigar smoke.

"No, Felix," I said finally, "We did not …." Not that the idea hadn't crossed my mind, however fleetingly, between Andrew's caress of my hand and the gunshot. "And I have no idea how he got that number. I never gave it to him." I don't give clients my home number, and the office phone rings to an answering service, who calls me after hours if there's an emergency. Actually, they'd never had reason to call me. I'd never had a client with an emergency before.

"Well, Boss, there's another mystery for you, then," Felix said, shrugging. He picked up the coffee cup and sipped it with a grimace.

"Someday I'm going to learn to make this stuff so it doesn't taste like mud."

"It'll put hair on your chest, Felix. Improve your image." Though my tone was light, I was secretly worried. I was worried about Andrew Field, and I was worried for myself. Who was Andrew Field? How *did* he get my phone number? And who had shot him? Cassandra Bellamy? Randy? Howard?

More importantly, why? Who was telling the truth? Cassy or Andrew?

"He started to tell me something just before he was shot, Felix," I said. "He said, 'I'm wanted by … ' and then the shot rang out."

Felix took another sip of the brown mud he called coffee and said, "Boss, that's an interesting expression, when you think about it. How many endings have you ever heard for that particular expression?"

I wasn't really in the mood for riddles that morning. "What are you talking about, Felix? I don't feel like playing games."

"Think about it, Boss," he persisted. "I'm wanted by … by whom? Fill in the blank. *I'm wanted by the FBI. I'm wanted by the police. I'm wanted by the state of Georgia.* The expression usually implies that some sort of judgment has been passed, that the person is wanted for a criminal act."

"There's another way that expression is used, Felix."

"What way is that?"

"*I'm wanted by the mob.*"

Felix looked at me. I looked back at him. "You don't generally hear someone say, *I'm wanted by my accountant,*" he agreed. "How about, *I'm wanted by Hollywood for a movie? I'm wanted by IBM for their research department? I'm wanted by my ex-wife? I'm wanted by my ex-wife's lawyer?* I think we're onto something here. The police or the mob. Somehow, there's a price on this Andrew Field's head and someone tried to collect last night."

"It's not the police, Felix. Police don't come into restaurants in stocking masks and shoot people, at least not in this town." Maybe in some big corrupt city where half the cops work both sides of the street, but not in Clarkdale, Colorado.

"Then it's the mob. Gangsters. What would they want with Andrew Field?" Felix gave up on the coffee, pushing it away from him.

"And where the hell do the Bellamies fit into this?" I asked rhetorically. Neither of us had the answer to that one yet.

It was time to get into action. Felix hit the database and I hit the streets, Charley securely nestled in my armpit. I drove to the Bellamy address and rang the bell.

The old man I had seen the day before in the garage answered the door. I pretended to be a census taker doing a follow-up on the last census. Who knows? The IRS does audits, why not the Census bureau? "We had a problem with the person who took the census information in this area, and we'd like to do a follow-up to find out how many forms he falsified before we caught him," I explained.

"Come on in, little lady," he said. "I'll be glad to answer your questions."

I followed the old man into the living room, taking in the family photos on the mantle as I walked past a fireplace to the sofa. Apart from the four photographs, there was no evidence that a family with small children lived there. There were no toys, no books, no dirty socks under the sofa. I couldn't see into the kitchen to see if there was a jar of peanut butter on the counter or not.

"Your name is?" I inquired politely, pencil poised over an actual census form I had grabbed from my file before I left the office. I like to keep a supply of official forms and documents around for occasions such as these.

"Howard Bellamy," he replied.

Howard? "Uh, is that a Howard Senior, or are you one of a kind?" I asked with what I hoped was a humorous tone of voice.

Old Howard chuckled. "I'm one of a kind, missy."

"Are you married, sir?"

"No, not anymore. The wife died back in 'eighty-five."

"You live here?"

"Yep."

"Who else lives here?"

"My son Randolph and his kids, Brian, Jason, and Michelle."

Michelle? "What are their ages?"

"Brian is seven, Jason is six, and Michelle is fifteen."

"And their mother?"

"She doesn't live here anymore. The tart moved out about two months ago. Having an affair with some young punk at work, they tell me. Should'a known something like that would happen sooner or later."

"She was living here during the census, then?"

"Oh, yeah, she was here then. Hate to admit my son ever had the tramp under this roof with those kids, though."

"Weren't they her kids?"

Howard Bellamy looked at me. "She says they were."

I'm afraid my surprise must have shown on my face. It's not often that there's question about who is the mother of a child. Usually it's the father that falls under suspicion. "Is there some question about that?"

"Nobody ever saw her pregnant, Missy. Randolph told me once he was pretty sure the first boy wasn't his kid. Doesn't look anything like a Bellamy. For the second kid, Cassy had gone to live with her mother for five months before he was born. He don't look anything like a Bellamy either. And neither kid looks like her."

"What about the girl?"

"Oh, she's Randy's kid from another marriage."

"Randy has custody of the boys?" I remembered the two tots I had seen with the dog the previous morning.

"Yup. She moved out, lock, stock, and barrel and left the 'sniveling brats' as she liked to call them, with Randy. Doesn't even come to see them. Doesn't call, doesn't write."

My head was reeling with all the lies it had had to absorb in two days. Somehow, I didn't think Grandpa Howard was lying to me.

I remembered the role I was playing. "So, anyway, Mr. Bellamy, this house was occupied by you, Randolph, Cassandra, and the three children?"

"Well, I just moved in a few weeks ago to look after the kids while Randy worked. Instead of them being in that no-good child care Cassy had them stuck in."

"Where did you live before that, Mr. Bellamy?"

"Over a few blocks, in an apartment. But I filled out a census form when I was there."

"Do you know how I can get in touch with Cassandra Bellamy? I think for the census records we need to clarify the question of the parentage of these children." I hoped there was some legal basis for that lie, or that at least Grandpa wouldn't know if there wasn't.

"Sure, I've got her number. She lives over on Hidalgo Street. Shacked up with that punk she knew at work."

Hidalgo Street? That, unfortunately, was where Andrew Field lived. This was getting too strange. So far, no more than ten percent of anything anyone had told me had been confirmed by any other party. Now I was being told that Andrew and Cassy were *neighbors?*

Howard handed me a slip of paper with an address and phone number on it and I swallowed hard to keep from speaking. It was Andrew's address and phone number.

"Have you ever called her at this number to be sure she's really living there?" I asked. Perhaps she had lied about where she lived now.

"Nope. Never called, never been by. Like she never calls, and never comes by. It's for the best. The kids don't need or want her. I don't know if she's still living there or not, but that's where we send any mail that still comes here. You know how the post office is about screwing up forwarded mail. We get her stuff all the time and just write that address on it. It doesn't come back, so I guess she's there."

I left the Bellamy house and drove to Hidalgo Street. I walked up the steps to Andrew's home and pounded on the door for several minutes, but nobody answered. Glancing around to see if any neighbors were watching, I slipped around the house through an unlocked gate into the small back yard.

Somewhere in this house there had to be an answer to some of these questions, and with Andrew missing and Cassandra the prime suspect in his shooting, I knew I had to move quickly. Once the cops got around to deciding Andrew was an official missing person, my access to this house would be severely curtailed.

I picked the lock on the back door and slipped inside. I walked quickly to the front of the house and glanced through the curtains to see if anyone had observed my entrance, but nobody seemed to care about me or my car.

I looked around the living room. Andrew Field was a tidy person, and the room did not look like it belonged to a bachelor. There were no photographs anywhere in the room, which I found interesting but did not think unusual. After all, he was a computer person, and I would not expect to see evidence of emotional attachments lying about.

The kitchen I had walked through to get to the living room had likewise been tidy. I located the spotless bathroom, noted that only men's toiletries were present in the drawers and cabinets, and proceeded to the bedroom.

The place was almost too clean. The bed was neatly made, the dresser looked freshly dusted. When had he found time to clean? Perhaps he used a maid? An image of fat, ugly Dora popped into my mind, and I could picture Reginald humping away at her in our bed, his skinny white ass shining in the darkened room before I flipped on the lights and hurled an ashtray at him. Nailed him right on the left cheek, too. I suppose it left a lovely bruise, but I never saw him naked after that day so I was never sure.

I shook my head. No time to think about Reginald and Dora. Look for evidence of who Andrew Field really was.

I checked the closet, finding an array of all relatively new, fairly well-made, tailored suits and shirts. Half the closet wasn't even being used. The drawers held the usual underwear and socks, all appearing to be about the same age. No holey socks? No holey underwear? Why did all this stuff look like he just bought it a few months ago? There wasn't much there. In fact, several of the drawers were completely empty.

I looked at the clothing labels. Everything in the closet came from the same store, one that had an outlet in a mall a few miles away. Had Andrew Field arrived from Phoenix in his birthday suit and bought a new wardrobe once he got here? Oh, I almost forgot. He didn't come from Phoenix. That was another of his lies.

I supposed he could have lost his belongings in a fire somewhere along the way, and had to buy all new clothes, even down to his underwear. *Fires get reported*, I reminded myself, hoping Felix would turn up something at the newspaper morgue today.

I looked into the top of his closet, but there was nothing stored there. In fact, in my entire search of the rest of the house, including a room that had a desk and typewriter but oddly no computer, I found no personal papers at all. The house was about as homey as a hotel room, and comparably furnished. The personality of Andrew Field was not here.

I was nearly through with my search when I found a gun in the back of one desk drawer. It was a forty-five semi-automatic and from its weight I knew the clip was loaded. The serial number had been filed off the barrel, but I knew enough to take a screwdriver from my lock pick set to the handle and find the serial number hidden inside the grip. I copied it into my notebook and put the handle back together before replacing the gun in the drawer. I was careful to keep from getting my own fingerprints on the gun, not knowing if it had ever been used in the commission of a crime. But I did get a whiff of gunpowder and suspected it had been fired somewhat recently, definitely since its last cleaning.

Then I checked out front again to make sure I was still unobserved, and slipped through a side door into the garage.

Where I found the body of Cassandra Bellamy on the floor in a pool of dried blood.

Chapter 5

THERE COMES A TIME IN THE LIFE of every P.I. when you wish you could do it all over again. If I could do this again, I never would have entered that house, would never even have taken Andrew on as a client, but now that I was there, I had a decision to make. Should I call the police and report the body, or leave now and take the chance that a neighbor would turn me in and I'd become a suspect?

It didn't take me long to realize the latter option was far too risky, but at least I could look around a moment longer before calling the police.

Examining the ground carefully before stepping into the garage, I slowly approached the body. She obviously had been killed there. There was no blood trail leading to the body, and there was a small undisturbed dried pool of the stuff leading away from a single gunshot wound in the chest. Shot there, not moved, DOA.

She was fully clothed in a slinky red dress and heels, unarmed, and had been shot from the front at close range. Bending carefully over the body, I noticed scratches on her arms and a red spot on the side of her neck. I surmised there had been a struggle, she had been scraped and struck before being shot. I couldn't see if there was any skin under her fingernails that might lead to the identity of her killer.

I thought of Andrew Field and wasn't sure if I hoped any would be found by the coroner. It was his house. He had a motive. He was missing.

And he had been shot, too, I reminded myself. His fate was still unknown.

Like the house, the garage was squeaky clean, too clean. The Harley-Davidson was on the right side of the garage where Andrew had parked it before we went to dinner the night before. Cassandra's body lay on the left side of the garage. There were no tools or storage boxes in the garage. Did someone really live here? The place felt like a stage set, with only the props needed for the current scene. I almost expected someone to yell, "Cut!" I almost wished someone would.

Whoever had shot Cassandra had left no clues that I could see, and I had spent two years as a crime scene investigator for the Myersburg Police Department. Reluctantly, I left the house the way I had come in and called the police from the car phone.

Lieutenant Lombard was a gruff old fart, about sixty, gray hair, big belly. He didn't mince words when he told me in no uncertain terms that if he caught me on the premises again without his permission he would arrest me as a trespasser. I assured him that I had touched nothing in the house but light switches, and had a legitimate reason to be there since the occupant was my missing client, but he took my statement and threw me out anyway, telling me not to leave town without his permission. Sure.

Considerably miffed, I left, glad I'd done all my investigating before calling the police. I had a suspicion the cleanliness of the house was directly related to the murder and was glad I had a chance to see it for myself. And, of course, the discovery of the gun I had kept to myself. Let that smartass cop find his own clues! By the time he found the gun in that desk drawer, I'd already know to whom it had last been registered.

I put Felix onto the job as soon as I returned, and it didn't take long for him to trace the gun to a man named Vinnie Delgado, known in some circles as the Orkin Man, an "exterminator" for the mob. The gun had been registered in California and years before Delgado became connected to the mob. As I had suspected, Andrew Field had some kind of tie to the mob, but was he on the inside or the outside?

And where was he? On a chance, I called Computech and was told that Andrew Field had not called or shown up for work that day. I had Felix start checking with the hospitals again, just in case he had somehow arrived at one sometime since two a.m. No dice.

The hit had been too clean. What was Cassandra doing in Andrew Field's garage in the first place? There had been no sign of her car. How had she gotten there? In Andrew Field's Suburban? The last car she had been seen in had left the scene of Andrew's shooting and been found abandoned. Field had left the restaurant and neither he nor his car had been found. Had he picked up Cassandra, driven her to his house, killed her, and left again?

I returned to my computer terminal and began keying in names. There had to be some way to trace these people. I checked Cassandra Bellamy first. She had been raised in Scottsdale, Arizona. At the age of twenty-three, she married the son of a Scottsdale horse rancher and moved to Colorado, only to divorce a year later and return to Arizona.

She attended Arizona State University before her marriage, completing her degree in Computer Science. After her divorce, she worked for a company in Tempe installing a new computer system. She left there a year later and moved here to work for Computech.

The information I was looking at was pieced together from her credit history, court records, and her employment application. Remembering the red herrings in Andrew Field's application, I called the Tempe firm to confirm that she had actually worked for them.

I talked to a man named Olson, who barely remembered her until I described the brassy blonde to him.

"Oh, yeah, I remember now," he said. "Cassy Baxter. She worked here for quite awhile, until she got involved with that fella with the kids."

"Who was that? Randolph Bellamy?" I asked.

"Nah, his name wasn't anything fancy like that. It was Smith. Just plain old John Smith. He ran a baby place."

I had no idea what he was talking about. "A baby place? Was he an obstetrician?"

"More like a baby broker. He was a lawyer who specialized in hooking up pregnant women with people wanting to adopt. He also did some surrogate stuff, you know, where a woman has a baby for another couple?"

"How did Cassandra get involved with him?"

"I guess they were going out for a while. I don't know what she saw in him; he was old enough to be her father. I guess she figured that out because she just split, went to Colorado, and we never heard from her again."

"She didn't marry this John Smith guy?"

"Nope. Not that we heard. He's still got the baby place, in fact, he was in the news last month. Indicted for selling kids. Hasn't come to trial yet, though. Still trying to get all the evidence. Police say one of their key witnesses disappeared. Apparently Smith used some scare tactics on a couple of teenaged girls to get them to give up their babies. Told the girls they had AIDS or something and they'd be better to give the babies up right away instead of watching them die slowly."

"Didn't the babies have AIDS?"

"Nope. Neither did the girls. That's what started the investigation."

But all this had happened years after Cassandra Bellamy left John Smith, so I didn't think it had anything to do with her murder or with Andrew Field, for that matter.

You get a lot of red herrings in this business. Too many, sometimes.

I thanked the man and hung up. My problem was that I had damn little to go on. Field was an imposter. His story of his relationship with the Bellamy woman didn't jive with her story, although it did somewhat with Howard Bellamy's story. Whom could I believe, and how was I going to get more information with Cassandra dead and Andrew shot and missing?

There was one person I hadn't spoken with yet: the man I had followed in the yellow Celica, Randy Bellamy. But how to approach him, especially with his ex-wife dead? If Andrew didn't kill her, Randy was certainly the next-best suspect.

I dialed Computech again, this time asking for Randolph Bellamy. I was told by a secretary that Randolph Bellamy had come in early that morning, cleaned out his desk, and left. She didn't expect him to return. He had said something about having to go back home. No, she didn't know what he meant by "back home." She didn't think he meant his house.

I told Felix to hold down the fort and drove back to the Bellamy house. Police cars there kept me from stopping to ask questions, but I did drive around the alley again, and noted that the dog was gone. Probably in the house, I thought, but it didn't really make sense that they would have brought the dog into the house while the police were there. Then I saw that the food and water bowls were no longer on the patio, and the toys were gone.

I drove on through the alley and swung by the front of the house again, trying to see how many cars were there. As I drove by, I saw that the garage door had been opened and a police officer was standing in front of the empty garage. Another officer opened the door to the third stall, which was walled off from the other part of the garage. It, too, was empty.

I decided to take a chance and stop.

"Excuse me, Officer," I said, showing my business card. "Angela Virago. I'm trying to find Randolph Bellamy. Can you tell me if he's here?"

The first officer, Sergeant Manolo Garcia, took me by the arm and led me back down the driveway to the sidewalk. "Why do you ask?" he inquired.

"I'm trying to get information on behalf of a client."

"Who's the client?"

"Can't tell you that, Officer."

"Well, I don't know who Randolph Bellamy is."

I tried not to look too smug when I replied, "He's the owner of this house."

"Sorry, miss, you've got your wires crossed. This house is owned by a woman named Cassandra Baxter."

"She's the recent ex-wife of Randolph Bellamy," I explained. "I didn't know the house was still in her name."

He shook his head again. "Nope, she's not. She's the ex-wife of an Arizona man named Baxter, and incidentally, she was murdered early this morning over on Hidalgo Street."

"I know." I turned on my heel, since obviously I knew more about the case than this cop. "I found the body."

I could only suppose his information was faulty, since he had contradicted so much of what I already knew to be true. Or did I? Halfway to my car, I decided to choke down my pride and ask him one more question.

"Is this house empty?" I asked. "Have you been able to locate her family, her children, her father-in-law?"

"She had no family."

This cop's information must have come out of a Cracker Jack box. "You're sure the house is empty now? You've searched?"

"Yes to both questions. There's nobody in this house and indications are she lived here alone."

I shook my head, started to correct him, then decided it was not the time to tell him about my conversation that morning with Howard Bellamy. "Have you talked to the neighbors yet?"

"No," he replied. "None of them are home yet. Apparently everyone on this entire block works during the day. Even the mailman hasn't been by yet."

Professional competitiveness was one thing, obstructing justice was another. "Officer, would you let me have a look inside this house? You see, I was here this morning, talking to a man who said his name was Howard Bellamy. He said he, his son Randolph, and three children lived here. Cassandra had moved out several weeks ago."

Sergeant Garcia looked skeptical. "If that's true, then where are they? There's no sign of them inside."

"That's why I want to look around. To see if the scene has been altered in some way."

He had to consult with three other cops before they decided to let me in, and the moment I walked through the door I knew something was up. All the family photographs were gone, and the room looked, as had Andrew Field's place, freshly cleaned and polished.

"Nobody's dusted for prints yet?" I asked.

"How can you tell?"

"No powder all over the place for someone to clean up. I've never known police procedure to include cleaning up after an investigation."

"And put some poor maid out of a job?"

I could just picture fat ugly Dora cleaning up after an investigation, bitching about fingerprint powder and bloodstains. *Bloodstains?* Is that what I saw over in the corner by the lamp?

"Have you looked at this?" I asked, pointing at the floor.

"Yeah, we saw that. Looks like an old pet stain to me. We got a new puppy six months ago and I've got a stain just like that on my rug."

I bent over the stain and touched it with a fingertip. "Well, the puppy must not be far away because this is still wet. Looks like someone tried to wipe it up in a hurry, and not more than a few hours ago. And it looks like blood."

"Get away from that, then!" he shouted, his face red. "Get out of here. I shouldn't have let you in anyway."

I waited around until the chief investigator, Lieutenant Lombard, showed up. He gave me a sour look but listened while I told him I had been there that morning, with whom I had spoken, and how the room looked. I left it to Sergeant Garcia to tell him about the bloodstain, since I didn't really want to go through an ugly scene about why Garcia had allowed me into the house. Hopefully he would remember the favor if our paths crossed again.

He looked relieved when I drove away after giving Lombard my name and phone number for the second time that day. Somehow I doubted he would call me. I'd hear from him only in connection with an arrest warrant or a subpoena.

It was getting toward dinnertime and I was worried about Andrew Field. He must know, if he was still alive, that I had heard his startled exclamation on my answering machine and would be worried about him. Would he bother trying to let me know he was all right, or would he keep moving, wherever he was?

I returned to the office to find Felix in a heated discussion on the phone. He motioned to me to listen in and I picked up the receiver in my office just as Felix went into a faked coughing spasm to cover the sound of the receiver being lifted.

Felix stopped coughing and said, "Mr. Montgomery, I told you I cannot tell you who our client is. It's against professional ethics, and might even be against the law, I'm not sure. You should talk to my boss, Ms Virago."

"I know you're working for Beauchamp! I traced him to your door two days ago!"

"Even if he were a client of ours, why would you expect us to give information about him to someone who sounds like they want to kill him?" Felix countered nicely. I tilted back in my chair and propped my feet on the desk, grinning. In only two months, Felix had really learned to take the bull by the horns in my absence. Boy, was I glad I hadn't hired the empty-headed blonde bimbo who had applied first!

"Beauchamp is wanted by the police for an investigation. I traced him to your town and I had him followed to your door. I'm going to find out where he is. Obviously you're protecting him."

"I'm protecting my job, asshole," Felix retorted. "If you want any information, not that you'll get it, I suggest you talk to Ms Virago. Period. End of discussion."

"Don't you hang up on me! I'll tell the police what I know and then where will Beauchamp be?"

"Frankly, Mr. Montgomery, I have no idea. If he contacts us, I'll be sure to tell him you're looking for him."

"Don't you dare tip him off! That's aiding and abetting a criminal!"

"And just what crime has this Mr. Beauchamp committed?"

"I can't talk about that over the phone! I already explained that to you!"

"Then I guess we have nothing to talk about." Felix held the receiver over the cradle and we hung up simultaneously.

"Who the fuck was that?" I asked, laughing.

"Some jerk named Montgomery. Trying to find a man name Beauchamp. André Beauchamp."

The laughter died on my lips. "*André* Beauchamp?"

"Yes. Don't tell me you know him after all! I've been arguing with that bastard for ten minutes!"

I thought for a moment. It might have been a mere slip of the tongue, but twice Cassy Bellamy, or whatever her name was, had referred to Andrew Field as *André*. Then it struck me. "Felix!" I exclaimed. "Do you know French? Doesn't *Beauchamp* mean 'Beautiful field' or something like that?"

"I don't know. I had to learn Spanish to survive in the ghetto I came from. The only French I learned was that immortal line, '*Voulez-vous coucher avec moi?*'"

"What the hell does that mean?"

"'Do you want to go to bed with me?'"

"Didn't think I was your type."

"That's why I've never said it to you."

"Oh."

"In other words, I have no idea what *Beauchamp* means."

"Well, let's look into the name 'André Beauchamp' and see what PRICS has on him. Maybe this Mr. Montgomery knows what he's talking about."

"Boss, you sure you want to tackle this tonight? It's getting late."

"Hot date tonight, Felix?" I teased. At lunch earlier in the month, we had both had our eye on a very handsome Latin-looking waiter, but the waiter had only had eyes for my equally handsome Latin-looking secretary. I had seen them exchange phone numbers while I paid the check. Felix had been seeing him regularly ever since.

"Ricardo asked me to dinner. You know how it is. I'll stay if you really need me, but if this can wait until tomorrow …."

"Go, Felix," I said with a smile. "I'm going to call out for a pizza and stay awhile, but you can go. Have a good time for me, too. I want all the juicy details in the morning."

"Thanks, Boss," he said, turning off the computer and gathering up his jacket and keys.

"Don't do anything I wouldn't do," I called after him, knowing that he would exercise about as much restraint as I would. Which meant he'd wait until after dinner to make his move.

The pizza was barely warm and the crust like cardboard. I choked down as much as I could, washed it down with the lukewarm Coke that came with it, and signed onto the PRICS system.

André Beauchamp's name appeared exactly once. He was wanted as a witness to a crime in Phoenix, Arizona. For once, PRICS let me down. The information was confidential, and further details could only be obtained by calling the officer in charge of the investigation.

So Montgomery was partly right. Beauchamp was wanted by police, but as a witness, not a suspect.

On an impulse, I called my home answering machine to see if Field had called again, but heard only the sound of my own voice. "This isn't me, it's my answering machine, waiting here just for you. Unless you've been on another planet for ten years, you ought to know what to do. Leave me your number and maybe your name, I really don't have time for a game."

Okay, so Robert Frost I'm not, but then I never claimed to be a poet. In any event, there was no message from Andrew or André or Tom or Dick or Harry or whatever the hell his name really was.

It had been twenty-four hours since Andrew had been shot. Officially, he could now be considered a missing person. That was a moot point as far as the police were concerned, since Andrew was already wanted for questioning in the murder of Cassandra Bellamy – or whatever her name was.

It had been a long day following a short night, and as I scrolled idly through the computer files, my eyelids started to pull shut.

I keep a couch in my office for such situations, since sometimes I have to wait by the phone when I ought to be sleeping, so I turned off the light, lay down on the couch, and soon fell asleep.

I don't know what woke me up later, but the moonlight was streaming into the window overlooking the street. I lay there for a moment trying to remember where I was, realized I was at the office, then wondered why I was awake already.

I wondered if I'd been snoring and had woken myself that way. Reginald used to insist I snored, although how he ever heard me over his own grating and moaning, I'll never know.

Reginald. The weasel. I remembered the scene in my office the other day. Why the hell had he come here, anyway? Why now? I hadn't seen him for a couple of months.

Andrew had been here that day. I pictured him clearly, tall, dark, with that half-amused look on his face all the time. Well, most of the time, anyway. He was so incredibly sexy. Reginald was good-looking in a weaselish sort of way, but not physically sexy. Andrew was a walking aphrodisiac.

The last thing he had done before he was shot was to take my hand in his. It was the moment the gunman had been waiting for – a moment's distraction that took my eyes off the door.

Lazily, I rolled onto my side, facing the closed door to the outer office. *Closed?* Alarmed, I groped toward my shoulder holster, feeling for Charley and not finding him. Silently, I rolled off the couch and tiptoed to the desk, eased open the drawer and pulled out my trusty piece.

I studied the light coming under the door from the outer office. Sure enough, the light flickered slightly with a shadow. Someone was out there.

I pressed my ear against the door and listened carefully.

I heard only the sound of rustling paper for a minute, then I heard the unmistakable sound of the file cabinet being opened. It was my chance. In order to look at files in the cabinet, a person's back would be to my door.

I grasped the doorknob, gun in my right hand and cocked, and turned the knob silently. I flung open the door and pointed my gun at the intruder's back.

"Put 'em up!" I shouted authoritatively. "And I mean now, or I'll shoot you where you stand!"

Chapter 6

WELL, IT WAS BETTER THAN SAYING, "Freeze, turkey," or some such other inanity that you often hear delivered on TV cop shows. I suppose someday I'll have to come up with some sort of trademark line like, "Make my day," but for now, I settled for my old standby, "Put 'em up!" So sue me.

It was effective, anyway. Or half-effective. The intruder slowly raised his right hand into the air and I tightened my grip on Charley, waiting for the left hand to follow. Instead, the man turned around slowly, and I lowered the gun in disbelief when I found myself face to face with Andrew Field, his left arm strapped to his chest with a sling.

"Hello, Angela," he said with a smile.

"Hello, my ass," I replied politely. "What the fuck do you think you're doing?"

He pushed the file cabinet shut and started to walk across the room toward me. I gestured with my gun. "Hold it, buster. That's close enough."

"Angela, if I meant to do you harm, I could have done it while you were asleep in there. I had hoped to find what I needed and be gone before you woke up. Please put the gun away."

His eyes met mine, sincerely, disarmingly. I released the hammer and put Charley back in his holster. "What are you doing here? What happened to you last night?" I nodded at the sling. "I checked every hospital for miles. Where did you go after you were shot?"

Andrew shook his head, still smiling, but sadly. His dark eyes smoldered with suppressed pain. "I can't tell you where I was, Angela. I went to a doctor I know, not an emergency room. I couldn't take the chance of the shooting being reported."

"The shooting was reported anyway," I retorted. I wasn't sure how I was supposed to feel right then. I had been worried all day since hearing that message on my machine. Then, when I found Cassy's body in

Andrew's garage, I was sure I'd never see him again. Now I found him casually ransacking my office. "I mean," I continued, "there were plenty of witnesses to the shooting."

His smile faded slightly. "What did you tell the police about me?"

"What could I tell them?" I answered, shrugging. "Everything you've told me so far has turned out to be a lie. I gave them the name you had given me."

"Guess I was wrong when I said Cassandra didn't want to kill me. Did you tell them she might be responsible?"

"No. It wasn't until later that I figured it must have been her. The getaway car was the same car she drove – " I broke off then, remembering that Andrew didn't, and couldn't be allowed to, know that Cassandra had come to see me as a client.

"Same car she drove where?"

"Never mind. The bottom line is that I did not tell the police that she was a suspect in your shooting." I walked over to Felix's desk and looked at the files Andrew had been perusing. He had found his own file, but there wasn't much in it except a list of the dead ends Felix had encountered on the PRICS system. Since he had found his own file, what could he have been seeking in the file cabinet when I caught him?

He gestured toward the papers. "I had to know how much you had learned about me, Angela. I had to know what you might have been able to tell the police about me."

"Ha!" I laughed. "Like they'd really be interested in what I have. You don't exist, Andrew Field. What could I tell them?"

"Then you haven't unearthed my true background yet," he said, seeming relieved.

"I didn't say that. I said Andrew Field didn't exist." I picked up the papers and replaced them in the folder. "I didn't say I didn't have leads."

"What leads have you found so far?" He looked uncomfortable, standing in the middle of the room with his arm in a sling. I supposed in that condition he was harmless enough, and, after all, he was a paying client.

"Let's go into my office, Andrew," I said. "I'm going to have to ask you some questions first. You're in more trouble than you may realize."

It was already three o'clock in the morning. I wondered where he had been hiding for the past thirty hours. So I asked him, knowing full well I was about to be fed another pack of lies and half-truths. At least, by asking the question, I'd know where he *hadn't* been.

He didn't want to answer. I reminded him that I had caught him red-handed burglarizing my office in the dead of night. Perhaps he would like to explain that to the police, along with where he had been for the past thirty hours? No, no, that wasn't necessary, he insisted. Finally, he sighed and began his opening fabrication.

"After I was shot, I ran to my truck, thinking I'd follow Cassy and have a confrontation." Okay, he was half-right so far. I knew he had run to his truck. But to have a confrontation with an armed assailant who had just tried to kill him? I think not.

"Halfway down the block, I realized how foolish that was. I had a gun in my truck ..." So that's what he was going to confront her with. "... but I knew there was no way I could use it on her."

"Why not? Did your mommy teach you never to hit girls?"

He shot me a look of pure desperation and I checked my sarcasm. I kept forgetting he was a client who had come to me for help. But I couldn't get the vision of Cassandra Bellamy's dead body out of my mind. Would I ever be able to trust this lying, deceitful ... sensuous hunk? I looked into his eyes. "Sorry."

"It's all right," he said. "I suppose I deserve that after what I've done."

"So why couldn't you use it on her?"

"Well, apart from the fact that I find murder personally abhorrent, there was also the possibility that she knew something about me that she might have passed on to someone else. Perhaps to Randy, her brother-in-law."

"Husband," I corrected.

"What?"

"Husband," I repeated. "I'm not sure how everything fits together, but there is some evidence that she is Randolph Bellamy's wife."

Andrew turned away from me to study the opposite wall. In profile, I found him even more appealing than ever. His lips were full and sensuous, his nose very slightly upturned at the end, the chin and jaw strong. A stray lock of hair stuck up in the front, giving him the appeal of a little boy. I noticed a small scar on the left side of his cheek, just below the sideburn. I imagined myself tracing that scar with a fingertip, nibbling the earlobe, smoothing the cowlick. He would run those sensuous lips down my neck, across my throat, down my bare chest ... .

"Randy can't be her husband," he said suddenly, jarring me out of my hormonal daydream. "His name was Howard."

Howard? That old geezer? "Did you ever meet him, or see pictures of him?"

"No," he replied thoughtfully, gazing at the back of a framed photograph on my desk. "She never had any personal photographs in her office."

I glanced at the single photo on my desk. Blond hair hung down over dark brown eyes that held a perpetual hint of mischief in them. A laughing mouth framed a pink tongue underneath the black button nose. He'd died over a year ago, but I had never been able to bring myself to put away the photo of my beloved Sammy. He had been a darling little Pomeranian, but he was gone now.

I had kept his photo. Reginald's had been given to Felix to use as a coaster the day after he was hired. He looked real good with a big sloppy coffee ring on his face when I threw it in the trash after Felix's morning coffee break.

I remembered the Golden Retriever I had seen in the Bellamy's yard, and tried to picture the blonde bombshell framing a photo of him for her desk. No, not Cassandra Bellamy with her perfectly manicured nails and silk stockings and spike heels. She probably didn't even know she owned a dog.

But dogs weren't the issue; the question of whom Cassandra had actually been married to was. "Andrew, I met a Howard Bellamy at the Bellamy house yesterday. He told me Cassandra was married to his son Randolph."

"No way." Andrew shook his head vehemently. "Howard was her husband. I checked with Personnel."

"Andrew, Howard Bellamy is over sixty years old!"

"Randolph is Howard's brother," he insisted. "I told you that the day you tailed him. And Howard Bellamy is not sixty years old! Whoever you met must be an imposter."

"Have it your way," I said. "I've been told so many lies by so many people I'm not sure I know who *I* am anymore." I glanced at my watch. "Why don't you continue with your story of what happened after you were shot?"

"Well," he said, shifting his left arm uncomfortably in the sling, "once I realized I couldn't confront Cassy, I decided I'd better do something about the gunshot. I was bleeding, but not badly, but I knew the slug was still in me. So I drove to the house of a friend who is a doctor."

"What's his name?" I asked. "You know the police are going to have to talk to him."

"No, they're not, because you're not going to tell them about him. Or about me, either."

"Like hell. I'm not going to be an accessory...." *Shut up, you damned fool! Don't you know better than to confront a killer with the fact that you know he is one?* How many times had my former partner drilled that warning into my head?

"Accessory to what? To survival? *She* shot *me*, in case you've forgotten! The police should be looking for her, not me!"

He looked so serious I almost believed for a minute that he didn't know Cassandra was dead. But how could he not? "What happened after you saw the doctor?" I asked.

"He gave me some pain medicine that knocked me out. I've been asleep on his couch most of the day."

"And there was a witness to that?"

Andrew glared at me, making me almost wish I had kept my mouth shut. I didn't know anything about this man, and here I was, practically taunting him. Good thing I had Charley. It was probably the only thing keeping Andrew on his side of the desk so far. So far.

"No, there was no witness. I woke up alone and left the place about four o'clock this afternoon. I called my friend at his office so he wouldn't be surprised to find me gone. I didn't even dare leave a note."

"Then you went home?"

"No, I haven't been home yet. I figure if she's gunning for me already, I'm not safe there. That's why I came here tonight. I have to know if it's possible for her to have learned my secret already."

He stopped speaking. I suppose my face must have told him something, but I don't know what. That I didn't believe him? That I didn't trust him? Or did he think I knew something about him that I wasn't admitting?

"Andrew, who are you?" I asked bluntly. "Your being here involves me. I think I have a right to know who you are and why you really came to me."

"I can't tell you."

I stood up, startling him. "Damn you, Andrew Field! Will you cut the crap? This is not a game. You're wanted by the police! Do you think I won't tell them you were here? I don't have the same privileges as an attorney or doctor. I have to cooperate with the police or I can end up in jail as an accessory."

Andrew turned pale the moment I said he was wanted by the police. "You know about that? How did you –?"

It dawned on me that he wasn't referring to Cassandra's death. I decided to play my trump card and hope the few leads I thought I had were genuine. "André Beauchamp, I presume?" I said sarcastically. If anything, he turned even more ashen and I knew I was right.

"How did you figure it out?" he said finally.

"Fat lot of good it did me!" I exploded. "André Beauchamp doesn't exist either! How many aliases do you have?"

"Never mind that!" he said, leaping to his feet and staring at me as if he still couldn't believe what he'd heard. "How did you find out? How far did you have to dig?"

"Not very damn far at all! I got a phone call from someone who tailed you to my office. Felix refused to tell him if we did or didn't have a client named André Beauchamp but the man insisted he'd followed you here."

"How did you figure out it was me?"

"A little elementary French, my dear. And a little slip of the tongue by – " I broke off again. How could I continue this conversation without telling him that Cassandra had been here, referring to him as André?

I didn't have to explain. "Cassy told you my name, didn't she," he said flatly. "So you've spoken to her." His shoulders fell. "I was afraid of that. I slipped once, only once, and answered the phone by saying, 'André speaking' instead of 'Andrew.' She overheard and began to tease me about being French. Then she started calling me André when we were alone together and it became her pet name for me."

He looked so defeated it was hard for me to picture him pulling the trigger on Cassandra. "What do the police want you for?" I asked.

"You don't know?" he said, surprised. We were both still standing on opposite sides of the desk, and he looked down at me, searching my face for the truth.

My eyes met his and I felt the power of his gaze sear my soul. I wanted so much to be able to believe in his innocence, but I had been taken in by good-looking men before and I had to remain aloof until I was sure. I tore my gaze from his. "No," I replied. "I don't know … yet. The database I use said to contact the Phoenix police for information. I just discovered it this evening and haven't made the call yet." I looked up again and found that half-amused smile tugging at the corners of his mouth. "What's so funny?"

He grinned. "*That's* all you found?"

Haughtily, I tossed my head and replied, "I've barely begun looking, Andrew or André or whoever you are. I've only been at it for two days."

The smile left his face. "Cassy had weeks."

"Her search is over," I said dryly. "Mine's barely begun."

"No, I don't think she could be all the way there yet," he said thoughtfully. "But she must be close."

"Trust me. She won't get any closer."

"Why do you say that? She tried to kill me last night! That may not mean anything to you, but it tells me she doesn't know about – "

"About what?" I demanded. Time to get a few cards on the table and see if I could bluff him out of some information. "About your mob connections? About Vinnie Delgado?"

I was pleased to see his mouth drop open with surprise, just before he sat heavily back into the chair with a thump. I walked around the desk and sat on the corner of it, looking down at him. I had regained the upper hand, at least for the moment. "You trying to say if she knew about you and the mob she wouldn't have dared try to hit you?"

"How did you find out about Delgado?" Silly little amateur, I thought. To think that filing numbers off a barrel would keep anyone from tracing a handgun!

"Never mind about that," I said smugly. "I want to know why you did it."

"I was being blackmailed." I remembered something he had said that first day in my office about blackmailers needing to be shot.

"By whom and for what?"

Suddenly his demeanor changed. "If you don't know why, then you're just guessing about all of this," he said. "I think I said too much already."

"You'll say more to the cops, Andrew. I told you I'm not going to be an accessory to your crimes."

"Crimes? What are you talking about, Angela? I've committed no crimes!"

"Oh, cut the crap, Andrew! In addition to whatever you did in your mysterious past, you murdered Cassandra Bellamy yesterday morning! Don't try to deny it! I found the body myself in your garage!"

"Oh, no!" he exclaimed.

For a long moment, his eyes searched mine for some hint that I was lying, I presume, then he buried his face in his hands and sobbed.

Chapter 7

SOBBED?

I stared at him for several seconds, then became self-conscious and looked away for awhile. Reginald never cried. The scum bucket would never give me the satisfaction of ever knowing I'd gotten to him. He was about as cold as a dead fish most of the time.

I've never understood men who cried, nor do I understand men who refuse to. It was a long, awkward moment while I tried to figure out the source of Andrew's apparent anguish. Finally, I heard him sniffle a few times and take a couple of deep, ragged breaths, so I turned back to look at him.

"You okay?" I asked gently. Unless he was a pretty damn good actor, his emotional reaction had convinced me he had not killed Cassandra. Then who had? Somehow I had a feeling that we were both going to be in danger until we knew the answer to that question.

"Yeah," he said. The half-amused smile was gone from his face. Those eyes I found so mesmerizing were reddened, his cheeks damp with tears. "I'm sorry. I just didn't know. What happened? How did she die? Angela, I swear I didn't do it! Is that what you've been hinting about all night, about not wanting to be an accessory to her murder? I didn't do it!"

"The police think you did, Andrew. Motive. Means. Opportunity. And now I know you don't have an alibi, unless you were lying about being at your doctor's all day."

"I didn't kill her, Angela," he repeated. "Please tell me what you know."

I slid off the desk and paced across the room to the window. I looked down at the silent empty street and debated whether I should tell him or not. Then I saw a paperboy riding his bicycle along the street, tossing papers at darkened doorsteps and I realized there was no reason not to tell him. The discovery of the body had no doubt been reported already, but even though the woman's name may not have been given it would take Andrew all of thirty seconds with the morning edition to learn all he needed to know.

I turned around to face him. He again looked like a lost little boy, and I longed to reach out and comfort him. What had Cassandra really meant to him, that he would display such emotion over the news of her death?

"I went to your house this morning … yesterday morning," I corrected myself. "I thought maybe you might have gone home and passed out from loss of blood after the shooting. I let myself in the back door and looked through the house." I did not describe my search of his underwear drawer, nor the discovery of Vinnie Delgado's gun. "Then I went into the garage and found her dead on the floor. Shot once in the chest." I refrained from mentioning that she was wearing a slinky red dress, more suitable for seducing a lover than for killing the man who spurned her affections.

"And the police think I did it," he said in a dull voice.

"So did I," I replied matter-of-factly. "Like I said, motive, means, opportunity."

"I didn't have the opportunity," he protested. "I wasn't there. I was with you when she tried to kill me, then I was at my doctor's."

"She was killed this morning, Andrew. There was plenty of time for you to do her in."

"I've got to get out of here," he said, suddenly getting to his feet. "I can't let them find me. It would be all over," he continued, more to himself than to me.

"You're not going anywhere, Andrew Field, until you answer some questions."

"Sorry," he said, and looked like he meant it. He looked into my eyes and I felt myself start to melt when the corners of his mouth pulled up into that tantalizing half-smile. He crossed to me quickly, pulling Charley from the holster before my mind even comprehended the fact that he was moving in my direction.

I reached for the gun, but he merely danced back out of reach. I froze, not sure what he planned to do next.

With a swiftness that only comes from experience, he unloaded my gun and tossed it on the desk. "I can't stay around now that I'm wanted for something I didn't do. It would complicate things. The fact that she was killed in my garage means someone's trying to frame me. I'm the best suspect they'll ever have – and I'm the wrong one."

I took a step in his direction, then halted when a gun appeared in his hand. It wasn't Charley. So he had been armed all along. God, whatever happened to those years of training and experience I was supposed to have? Clearly I was dead meat now.

"I don't want to hurt you, Angela," he said apologetically. "I really don't. But there are things in motion that can't be upset by you or anyone else."

"You with your distaste for murder," I said contemptuously. "And you dare stand there and hold a gun on me."

"Oh, I wouldn't kill you, believe me," he assured me. "Perhaps shoot you in the foot if you pressed me. You're really no threat to me, since it's obvious you have no idea who or what I really am."

"What do you want from me?" I asked.

"I'm afraid I need your help, Angela. Just give me the keys to your car and I'll be on my way."

"How far do you think you'll get?"

"As far as I need to. You'll never find me … unless I choose to be found."

I was torn then between fear for my own safety, devotion to duty that said Field was a client needing my protection, and the raw animal attraction that kept my gaze riveted on his eyes. Someone said, "I'll go with you."

I looked around but nobody else had entered the room. Andrew looked amused, his grief of a few minutes before apparently forgotten already.

"You?" he said.

Who? I wondered. The voice spoke again. "Yes, me. I'll go with you. You're in big trouble and you need help. You're also weak from loss of blood." Damn it, that was *my* voice! *Shut up, you moron! You want to get yourself killed?*

He smiled, that charmingly disarming smile I was coming to know so well. His eyes half-closed in an appealingly sensuous manner and I felt my heart pound. He stuck his gun in his waistband then picked up my purse from the chair where I had dropped it earlier and rummaged through it with one hand before coming up with my keys.

He dropped the purse to the floor and backed to the door, gesturing once with the gun. "Sorry, Angela. I can't get you involved." He turned on his heel and strode toward the outer door.

I bolted after him, grabbing his left arm before he could turn the doorknob. "Andrew —" I started, then broke off as he turned to face me. For a long minute, he just stared at me, the hint of a smile playing at the corners of his lips again. His full, sensuous lips. I looked at the mustache, studying each individual hair as if I wanted to memorize his face. The scar again. The dark eyebrows and lashes. That recalcitrant lock of hair that still stuck out.

"Sorry, babe." He pulled away from me and slipped through the door while I was stuck in my trance.

The trance lasted for only a moment. I ran back into the office to grab and reload Charley and pick up my purse, then I was out the door myself, taking the stairs two at a time having seen that the elevator was gone.

I pushed open the door at the bottom of the fire escape and ran around the corner to where I had parked the car the night before. Andrew's Suburban was parked behind my usual spot and as I watched, he was just pulling away from the curb in my blue Firebird.

He even had the gall to wave at me as he stole my car.

I quickly learned that hot-wiring his truck did no good. It started all right, but ran out of gas ten miles later, just as Andrew pulled onto the highway, heading east.

Felix gave me a hell of a lecture that morning.

I returned to the office, frustrated and angry, in a taxi driven by a grizzled veteran who insisted on telling me several times just how fortunate I was that he happened along before some "sex fiend with a pre-version" found me alone on the streets just before dawn. I didn't bother explaining to him that I had a phone in my purse and a loaded gun under my jacket and had been a police officer for several years in a previous life. Let him keep his chauvinistic rescue fantasies.

Felix was appalled when I told him about it an hour later. "You wanted to go *with* him?" he exclaimed. "Are you crazy? I mean, with all due respect, Boss," he amended, "did you really think that was wise? We know so little about him. How can I protect you if you're going to do things like that?"

I suffered his solicitude until he got it out of his system, then I patted the desk drawer where Charley nestled. "I wasn't worried. As long as I have Charley, I'll be all right."

He finally gave up and asked, "Okay, what do we do next, Boss? Are we still on this case, or do we wash our hands of him?" He sounded a little wistful, and I recalled that the totally sexy Andrew Field had managed to turn Felix's head as well as my own.

"No way, Felix!" I said confidently. "We're just beginning, and I managed to get some more clues from Andrew. He *is* André Beauchamp, but I don't know what other aliases he might have used. He knew the name Vinnie Delgado, but I don't know if that was one of his aliases or not. I'm inclined to think not. The thing in Phoenix involved blackmail, but when I asked him who was blackmailing him and why, he clammed up. Said if I didn't know, then I was just guessing about him and really didn't know anything after all."

"Blackmail, huh?" Felix repeated. "Didn't you tell me he thought all blackmailers should be shot?"

"That's what he implied when he explained why he didn't try to blackmail Cassandra."

"Boss, it sounds to me like he must have killed someone in Phoenix."

"That's what I'm thinking. But he also said something about murder being abhorrent to him."

"Maybe he regretted doing it."

"Could be. That must be it. But I don't think he killed Cassandra."

"You don't? What changed your mind?"

"The way he broke down and cried when I told him about it."

"Oh, be still my heart!" Felix said, patting his chest. "A sensitive man! And you let him get away!"

"Oh, stop it, Felix," I said, smiling. "Or I'll make you tell me about your date last night. At least one of us didn't get rebuffed, I hope."

Felix grinned. And said nothing.

"Brat."

"Sorry, Boss. Better luck next time."

"Son of a bitch stole my car, too."

"And your car phone," Felix reminded me. "Why don't you give him a call?"

I marveled at the good fortune that had led Felix to my door. He not only was a competent secretary who amazingly *loved* filing, he was smart and assertive and loved detective work. Perhaps I'd have to make him a partner someday.

But then I'd be stuck hiring a bimbo for the front office again.

"Good idea, Felix," I said, smiling. I picked up the phone and dialed. The smile faded five rings later when voice mail picked up the call. I hung up. "I hope he didn't abandon it somewhere."

"Try again later, Boss," Felix said gently, sensing my disappointment, not at losing the car but at losing Andrew Field.

"Right. Maybe he stopped for breakfast." I tried to smile again, but found my lower lip inexplicably quivering. "Damn it."

Felix came around the desk and put his arms around me, pulling my face into his chest, patting my back. "You'll find him, Boss," he said confidently. "You always get your man, remember? Unless I see him first."

I sniffled once and giggled. "Thanks, Felix, I needed that." He gave me a final pat and released me while I blew my nose and wiped my teary eyes. It's the pits getting emotionally involved with a client. With most of my clients being women, it normally wasn't a problem, but Andrew Field had definitely gotten under my skin.

"Are you going to report your car stolen?" Felix asked when I had regained my composure.

"No," I replied. "Not unless he hasn't answered the car phone by noon. Then I'll have to believe he abandoned it."

"What will you do in the meantime?"

I took a deep breath. "I'm going to continue doing what I'm being paid for. Investigating the background of Andrew Field."

Felix reminded me gently, "He hasn't paid you for more than a few days' work, remember? Are you sure you want to keep going on that? Shouldn't you concentrate on finding out where he is now?" He hesitated a moment before adding, "Although he *is* wanted for murder, you know. It's really a police matter now. Maybe you should just let them find him."

I tossed my head defiantly. "Hah! These cops around here couldn't find their balls with both hands tied to their cocks. I had to point out that bloodstain on the rug, remember?" It was time to get back to work. I pulled a hairbrush out of my desk drawer and began to vigorously brush the hair that I knew must be a mess after my all-night ordeal. I stood up and glanced in my wall mirror. For someone who had had less than six hours sleep in three days, I didn't look so bad. I could go a few more hours before going home to shower and change clothes.

"What do you intend to do, Boss?"

"I'm going to follow my next lead. I'm going to call Phoenix and find out why André Beauchamp is wanted for questioning. I'll keep trying to raise Andrew on the car phone. If I haven't raised him by noon, I'll get a rental car, go home, change, and hit the road. He's out there somewhere and I'm going to find him."

I set Felix to the task of finding out if Andrew had ever been the victim of a house fire to explain the mystery of his clothes. While it seemed a minor point, the sterility of Andrew's house continued to nag at the back of my mind and I wanted to put it to rest by finding the explanation. Then it occurred to me that I didn't even know who owned his house, so I gave that task to Felix as well.

With my capable assistant suitably occupied in these pursuits, I picked up the phone and called the Phoenix police department and asked for the detective in charge of the case number that had been referenced on the PRICS system. Soon I was speaking to a fairly young-sounding man named Alan Foster.

"André Beauchamp?" he said, sounding like he was rustling through papers. "Yes, we're looking for him for questioning. Do you know where he is?"

"What is the nature of the case?" I responded, ignoring his question.

"I can't discuss that over the phone, Ms Virago," he replied firmly.

"I can't reveal a person's whereabouts, Detective Foster, until I know what this is about," I insisted. "Is he a suspect in a felony? Can you tell me that much?"

"I can tell you this is a felony case. I can't tell you if he is a suspect or not. Now, do you know where he is?"

"I'm not even certain I know *who* he is, Detective," I replied cagily. "Can you fax me a photo of the man you seek? There seems to be quite a question of identity regarding a certain client of mine. Someone has told me verbally that one of my clients is André Beauchamp. I have no idea if they are correct or not. I have no client who gave me that name as his own."

I heard him speak to someone about copying a photo, then he asked for my fax number. I remained on the line while the fax came through and there was no doubt at all that my client, Andrew Field, was the same André Beauchamp who was wanted by the Phoenix police department. Andrew had confirmed as much to me in the wee hours of the morning. As André Beauchamp, he wore his hair longer and sported a full beard and an *earring*? I looked twice at the photo to be sure it wasn't a photographic abnormality, but no, there really was a tiny gold earring on his right ear.

And the laughing eyes and half-amused smile were missing from the photo, too. Whenever the photo was taken, André Beauchamp had been dead serious, a side of him I had only briefly glimpsed that morning.

I repeated into the phone, "What is the nature of the case? I have to know that. Why should I help you with this if you won't do me the slight courtesy of telling me why he is wanted?"

"Then you do know him," Alan Foster answered. "Where is he? I can have you brought in, you know, for aiding and abetting…"

"Aiding and abetting what, Detective?" I snapped. "For all I know you want him for parking violations! Tell me what's going on! What is this anyway, a big government secret?"

There was a chilling silence from the receiver. Then I heard a sigh. "Trust me, it's not parking violations, and it's for his own safety – and yours – that I can't discuss the matter over the phone. I have no idea who you are or what you real objectives are. Perhaps you would be best off to simply notify your local authorities of Mr. Beauchamp's location and let them handle it."

"Sorry, Detective. I don't know where he is. And if you won't tell me why you want him, I'm afraid I won't be able to turn him in if I do find him."

"You'd be better off to stay away from him, missy." He warned.

I bristled. How dare he call me 'missy'!

"He can be dangerous," he added, like I didn't know it already.

"So can I, you chauvinistic pig!" I exclaimed before slamming down the receiver.

Frustrated by my lack of progress, I decided to call a friend for help. I dialed my old department in Myersburg and asked for Tim Reed, my former partner. A tear came to my eye when I heard his familiar voice.

"Angel! How have you been? The place hasn't been the same without you."

"I'm getting by, Tim. Busted any baddies lately?"

"Working on something that might interest you, actually."

"Really? Did you nail that drug dealer yet?"

Tim laughed. He had promised me when I cleaned out my locker that day that he would find some way to bust the guy I'd chased into the reservoir. Naturally his attorney had gotten him off without any problem once the would-be arresting officer was run out of town on a rail. "No," he said with a chuckle, "but I'm working on an inside investigation involving your old friend Francis the Mule."

"Really?" I repeated. "He's got, what, five more years in the slammer, right?"

"Not quite," he replied, suddenly very sober. "Actually, someone probably should have told you already, and I'm sorry I didn't think of it. He got released a couple weeks ago."

I felt a chill but it passed quickly. "Why is he out already?"

"That's what I'm trying to find out. I suspect something fishy's going on somewhere but haven't been able to figure out what. But don't you worry about it. We've got him under surveillance."

I relaxed. Francis the Mule was my one and only really big arrest and the man had sworn to get me when they led him off to what was supposed to be eight years, minimum, in state prison. I think he was primarily pissed at having been busted by a woman. I was glad Tim was watching out for me.

"I hate to have to ask a favor, old pal," I continued after asking Tim to keep me posted, then asked him to find out what I needed to know. If Beauchamp were really wanted for something serious, Myersburg would have received some kind of notice about it somewhere along the way.

He promised to call back within the hour with whatever he could find.

Felix had struck out with the fire idea, and had discovered that Andrew had been renting the house he lived in. The landlord knew little about him except that he had paid a year's rent in advance six months ago, so the landlord, a trusting older man, hadn't bothered with a reference check. "Seemed like a nice young fella," he had told Felix. "Didn't care much for his motorcycle, but to each his own, I guess. Not every day I find a tenant who'll plunk down twelve grand in advance for the rent of a house."

"Why," I asked Felix rhetorically, "would a man with twelve thousand dollars cash choose to rent instead of buying a house?"

"Don't know, Boss. Sounds fishy to me. With the rent prepaid like that and the income he was making at Computech, he must have been swimming in spare cash all the time. Wonder what he did with it."

"That might have been the proceeds from the last house he sold, or maybe the money he got by cashing out a profit-sharing account somewhere. It may be all the money he had at the time. He was only at Computech a few months, Felix. And he had the car and motorcycle to insure... ." My voice trailed off. "Find out who his insurance company was. If he has a history with them, they might know if he ever had a fire in his home that destroyed everything."

"Right-o, Boss." Felix turned back to the computer.

The phone rang, and I returned to my own desk to take the call from Tim Reed. "That was quick," I said to him.

"Angel," he started, using the pet name that I allowed no one else to call me, "how are you mixed up with this Beauchamp fellow?"

"It's possible he's a client of mine, using another name as an alias," I replied, knowing full well that Tim would never repeat the conversation to anyone. "Someone told me he was, anyway."

"I'd suggest you stay away from him, Angel. There's something funny going on here."

"Tell me something I don't know," I retorted. "Why do you think I had to ask for your help?"

"Well, the case is definitely under wraps, but I did get a little I can tell you. He's wanted as a witness, not a suspect. A witness for what, I don't know. There seems to be some sort of security around this case that I've never encountered before. It could be that someone is under indictment who hasn't yet been arrested. If that's who he's a witness against, they're not going to blab anything that might tip off the guy they really want."

"Tim, if there's been an indictment, wouldn't that indicate that he has already testified? Why would they still need him?"

"For the jury trial, once they arrest the accused, whoever he is."

"Then you think he testified, then flew the coop after the indictment came down. Maybe he was threatened into leaving." Or blackmailed, I thought, trying to remember exactly what Andrew had said about blackmail early that morning. I had bluffed him by asking him why he had done "it" and he had replied that he had been blackmailed. We never discussed what "it" might have been that he was wanted for.

"That's what it sounds like," Tim agreed. "Someone may be looking for him besides the police. That's why you need to stay away from him."

"I may not have any choice, Tim. He took off this morning and I don't know where he is. I doubt he'll come back voluntarily. Someone shot him the other night, right in front of my eyes."

"And you saw who did it? Shit, Angel, you're going to get yourself killed if you don't back off!"

"I didn't see the shooter, and the person I thought was the prime suspect was killed herself the next morning. I thought Andrew ... André ... had killed her but now I don't think so. And if someone's after him for some testimony he gave, that may be the person who shot both of them."

"Angel, you be careful. I don't want to pick up the paper one morning and read how you got gunned down trying to protect some sleazebag with mob connections."

My ears perked up. "What did you just say?"

Tim swore under his breath, but I had heard him plainly. "I didn't mean anything by that, Angel."

"But you said 'mob connections' didn't you? I didn't tell you that. You must have gotten it from the police." I felt my anger start to rise, a product of too much tension and not enough sleep multiplied by the fact that I seemed to be getting nowhere with this investigation. "What else are you holding out on me, Tim? I thought we were buds."

"We are buds, Angel," he said sadly, "but I've got my job to think about. I've told you everything I dare to. They really didn't tell me much more than that. They slipped out a name. It's probably the person who's under indictment but hasn't been arrested yet. I can't give it to you. You know it could mean my job."

I bit my tongue to keep from denouncing our years-long friendship. I had to believe Tim had a very good reason for not saying any more. I would just have to respect that. "I understand, Tim. Thanks for your help. I'll have to do the rest of this on my own."

"Please don't do anything foolish, Angel," he pleaded. "I'll never forgive myself if you get hurt over this."

"Wouldn't be your fault, Tim. You told me to back off. But you're not the only one with a job, you know, and this is my work now." I paused, remembering the friendship that had developed between us while we were partners. He knew me better than I knew myself. In fact, if Tim hadn't been at the hospital helping his wife deliver their first child at the time, he would have kept me from chasing that drug dealer into the reservoir that day and I'd still be his partner now. A wave of homesickness swept me and I choked back an unwelcome sob. "Gotta go, Tim. You take care. Don't let 'em win."

"Sure, Angel. You be careful too."

I hung up the phone feeling very blue. It was hard enough to hear Tim's voice, but what hurt worse was the realization that we could never again be partners the way we used to be. Now when I called Tim for a favor, there were going to be rules involved that dictated how much he could tell me.

I suppose that was when I realized I really was working solo, and would have to solve this thing myself.

Chapter 8

BUT I WASN'T QUITE ALONE, I was reminded a few moments later when Felix came into my office. "It wasn't all the money he had, Boss," he announced triumphantly.

"What are you talking about?" I asked, having already forgotten what I had asked him to do before my call from Tim.

"The insurance. There isn't any. He's self-insured. Filed a whopping big bond with the state so he didn't have to carry insurance."

"Why would he do that?"

"Don't know, but this proves he had bucks."

Tall, dark, handsome, and rich to boot. And a fugitive. Boy, can I pick 'em! I slapped my hormones into submission. I'd never get anywhere if I didn't stop seeing those sexy dark eyes boring into mine just before he left the office and stole my car.

I picked up the phone. "Think I'll try him again on the car phone. Nice to know if he wrecks it, I can put a claim in to the state and get another one." While I dialed, I remembered that I was no closer to figuring out the mystery of the new underwear than I had been that day in his house.

He answered! "Andrew, where the fuck are you?" I asked sweetly when I heard his voice.

"I wondered if you'd think to call," he replied, not answering my question.

"Of course I did, you think we're idiots around here?" Why was I acting so nasty to him, I wondered? No way to get him to bring my car back. "I'm sorry, Andrew. It's been a tough day."

"No apologies needed," he said softly. "At least, not from you. I'm the one who needs forgiveness. Angela, I hope you understand that I had no choice this morning."

"You could have let me come with you." I glanced at Felix, who was trying to get the cellular service to trace the car. "I could have helped."

"Help me do what, Angela? Get shot again?"

I felt a pang of professional remorse. "Look, Andrew, I know I let you down. That shooting was all my fault and I don't blame you for realizing it."

"That's not what I meant, Angela. I don't blame you for that. I didn't hire you for protection; I hired you to do what should have been a simple background investigation. What I meant was that the only thing I need help with right now is staying alive, and I certainly don't want you for a bodyguard. I'm not worth dying over."

Let me be the judge of that, I thought to myself. "Andrew, where are you?"

"Can't tell you that, babe."

Babe?

"Don't want you to find me," he continued. "Gotta do this myself."

"Andrew," I said, "do you know who killed Cassandra? If you'll tell me that, I can try to get the heat off you, at least from this angle." I heard a thunderous roar building over the telephone on his end, then the unmistakable sound of a large motorcycle drowned out his answer.

"What did you say?" I asked.

"I said Cassandra was killed by the same guy who shot me," he answered. "And I don't know yet who that is."

"Why would anyone want you both dead?" I practically shouted, hearing another motorcycle whiz past.

"Because I know too much!" he shouted back. "And don't ask me what I know!" The sound of motorcycles diminished suddenly as he apparently rolled up the windows.

"Thank you," I said. "That's much better."

"A whole herd of Harleys went past. Must've been twenty of them. Wish I dared risk going home for my bike, but too many people know it by now."

"Andrew, what do you expect me to do? You stole my car, damn it! I can't sit back here and wait until you get yourself killed!"

"Don't worry about me. I'll take care of myself. I just have to go back and see the man. He'll get me out of this. But Angela, I'll never see you again. It's impossible."

"Don't talk like that, Andrew," I said, my eyes misting up at the finality in his voice.

"It has to be that way. If I can, I'll send word where I leave your car. I probably won't need it much longer. Angela, I know I owe you for what you've tried to do for me. There's some cash stashed in the Suburban, under the spare tire. It's yours. In fact, you can buy yourself a new car with it if you want. Go ahead and take it. There's no way I can come back for it now, and I didn't have time this morning to get it out."

"Enough to buy a car? Is it stolen?"

"No, it's not stolen. I came by it quite legitimately, but I can't use banks yet, so I just kept it in the car. Don't worry about my needing it. I'll get more from the man." His voice was starting to fade and I glanced desperately at Felix.

"Andrew, wait," I said. "Stop the car. I'm losing you." I knew he must be leaving the service area for my bargain rate mobile phone system. That put him at least two hundred miles away already, probably in the middle of the desert. He could be in Colorado, New Mexico, Arizona, or Utah. Without knowing what direction he was heading I had no way of telling where he might be.

"Can't do it, babe. For what it's worth, I think you're terrific, Angela. I wish we'd met under other circumstances. It could have been fun...." His voice faded completely then, and I couldn't raise him again.

Tears running down my face, I looked at Felix, who hung up the phone a moment later. "Could they locate him?" I asked.

"Couldn't get it, Boss," he replied. "Sorry."

Then I remembered something. "Felix, have you heard anything from any of your motorcycle buddies about a rally this weekend? Andrew said a whole herd of Harleys passed him while we were on the phone."

"I haven't seen any of them for several weeks."

"Call someone and find out, will you? He's over three hours away from here. If we can find out what direction he's heading, we might be able to figure out his destination. He said something twice about seeing 'the man.' Maybe he was trying to give me a clue."

While Felix took care of that, I called a towing service and arranged to have Andrew's Suburban towed back to my office and gassed up. I told them to leave it in my private parking place. When it arrived, I retrieved the cash and put it in my safe. There was twenty-five thousand dollars in hundred dollar bills in a Ziploc bag in the spare tire well.

I put off calling the police. I had to report Andrew's visit eventually, but there was no reason they had to know everything right away.

Felix gave me his report. There was a huge motorcycle rally that weekend in Laughlin. Every Harley rider west of the Rockies was probably headed that way. That meant Andrew was probably heading southwest across the Indian reservation toward Interstate 40. I remembered he had said he was going "back" to see the man. There was only one place I knew he had been before and that was Phoenix. If I was right, when he got to Interstate 40 in Flagstaff, he would turn south to Phoenix. It was a very, very long shot, but I felt it was worth the gamble. If I was wrong – well, I didn't have any other ideas anyway. The challenge was going to be to get to Phoenix before Andrew did. He was three hours into a seven-hour drive so it would probably take him another four hours or more, assuming at least one stop for food and restroom. I could fly there in less than two, but only if I didn't waste any time now talking to the police about Andrew's visit.

Felix drove me home where I showered, changed, and packed in less than thirty minutes, then he drove me to the airport, where I maxed out one of my Visa cards chartering a plane to Phoenix. By the time we were airborne, I knew I would have less than an hour once on the ground to pick up the rental car (that Felix was arranging for) and get to the outskirts of town on Interstate 17 north of Phoenix. My only chance was to find him before he got to town. Once he reached the city limits, the sprawling metropolis would swallow him, and my car. I'd never see him again.

The car he would likely abandon as soon as possible. I'd probably never see it again, either, but that was the least of my worries. I closed my eyes and dozed during the flight.

Three hours later, I parked my rented beige Honda sedan at a rest stop about twenty miles north of Phoenix and waited. I had my cell phone in my purse, but I dared not try another call to Andrew. I knew my car's phone would start working again as he neared Phoenix but if he had any idea I was near, he would simply turn off onto one of the desert roads and approach Phoenix from another direction. I had to get locked onto his wake before we reached New River or I could lose him since I had no idea where in Phoenix he was heading.

I tried not to think about how much time and money I was about to waste if he was really heading for California or Nevada instead of Phoenix. Something told me my cynical grandmother was rolling in her grave while I spent a good chunk of her life savings on what may well turn out to be a wild goose chase.

I kept my eyes glued to the road for well over an hour, fighting the exhaustion brought on by lack of sleep, wishing I could get something with caffeine to drink, but not daring. It would be just my luck that he'd drive by while I was in the restroom taking a leak. While I waited, I dictated a few notes to myself into my little pocket recorder that I never leave home without. The first note was to get an alarm on the door to my outer office when I returned home. The second one had to do with installing Lojack on the Firebird.

It was late afternoon when I finally saw the familiar blue Firebird crest the horizon. He must have stopped for lunch somewhere along the way, I decided, and wished I'd been able to do the same. I'd grabbed a candy bar at the airport, but hadn't taken time for anything else. I watched him draw nearer, then shoot past the rest stop at about seventy miles an hour. I pulled onto the road behind him, about a half-mile back.

Traffic was light and I had no trouble keeping him in sight without getting any closer. As we neared the city, I inched up, not wanting to lose him, but he continued on freeway, almost all the way into the center of town, getting off finally and stopping a few miles later at a medium-priced motel down the street from a mall.

This was going to be tricky, I thought. The mall would be a good place to ditch the car. Probably he would steal another one at the same time. I'd have to keep him under continual surveillance, which meant no motel for me. While he checked in, I decided I had to eat something and looked around. The only thing in sight was a Jack in the Box. Reluctantly, I gave the clown my order and parked in the shade of a Palo Verde tree where I choked down two hamburgers with fries and a Coke without taking my eyes off the motel.

I called Felix, who had agreed to stay in the office by the phone until he heard otherwise, and told him where I was and that I had Andrew Field under surveillance.

Then I asked him if he had any plans for that night.

"Well," he replied slowly, "Ricardo had invited me to a party but I told him I might have to work pretty late."

"Later than you think," I replied. "I'd like you to catch the next plane and meet me over here. I think this is going to turn into an all-nighter, and if I don't get some sleep I'm liable to fall asleep in the middle of a high-speed pursuit. And you know how I'd hate to miss out on a good high-speed pursuit."

"I'll tell Ricardo and head for the airport now," Felix answered. "How will I find you?"

I had flown into Glendale on the chartered plane to get closer to the north side of town as quickly as possible, but told him to fly on a commercial flight into Phoenix, rent another car and call me when he had it. Then I'd let him know what to do next.

With reinforcements on the way, I had plenty of time to think. Andrew Field definitely had a past to hide, yet he had driven right to the jurisdiction in which there was a warrant out on him. Why was he here?

It still bothered me that I hadn't been able to figure out the link between him and Vinnie Delgado. I hooked my laptop computer into the cell phone and started to access the PRICS system, wishing I had a car adapter for the phone so I could keep the battery charged. Normally I don't have to worry about it since I have a phone in my car. But this wasn't my car, and I wasn't quite ready to use my spare key to steal it back until I knew what was going on. Quickly, I called Felix back and caught him just before he walked out the door and asked him to bring the AC adapter from the office.

It wasn't the best of working conditions, but somehow I managed to keep one eye on the motel and the other on the computer monitor and gradually began to piece together some information. As facts came up on the computer, I repeated key data into my recorder. I'd have Felix transcribe it into some semblance of order later.

Vinnie Delgado, the Orkin man, age thirty-nine, was born in New York City, dropped out of high school at sixteen, joined the Army at eighteen, where he was a helicopter pilot for two years before receiving a dishonorable discharge for reasons that were not recorded in the PRICS system. After numerous arrests without convictions, he served seven months in prison before being released less than two years ago after his conviction for attempted murder was overturned on appeal. Delgado had been arrested only minutes after the shooting and within a hundred yards of the victim. The victim had identified him as the shooter and he had been convicted. The problem, I read between glances at the door of the motel, was that the gun that fired the shot had never been found despite a thorough search of a full quarter mile radius of the scene. His lawyer had finally found a witness who was willing to testify to seeing another man leave the area at about the time of the shooting. He convinced a judge that this other man must have fired the shot and taken the gun away. The conviction was overturned. The gun still hadn't been found.

Of course it wasn't found, I thought with disgust. Andrew Field has it in his desk drawer at home. I was glad I had been cautious enough to keep from getting any prints on the gun during my explorations.

The attempted murder charge stemmed from an assault on a man believed to have been dating Delgado's girlfriend. The girl had disappeared, and Delgado had managed to get a slug into the boyfriend, whose name was ... *Randolph Bellamy*? Randolph Bellamy?

I tore my gaze from the computer's tiny screen and stared back across the road at the motel. Vinnie Delgado had been suspected of shooting Randolph Bellamy, the man who had been following Andrew Field, in whose possession Delgado's gun had been found.

If Andrew had the gun, did that mean he was actually Delgado? If not, why did he have the gun? And if Field had shot Bellamy, wouldn't this be a case of the mouse chasing the cat? And was Cassandra the missing girlfriend? Who had killed her? The picture of Andrew the lady killer flashed into my mind, and I wondered if the expression should be used in its literal sense.

Then I remembered that Andrew Field, as André Beauchamp, was wanted for questioning, but not as a suspect. Could they want him in order to try again to get Vinnie Delgado behind bars? Why did he have the gun?

I continued reading the computer screen but found few additional clues. Delgado's list of suspected hits was impressive, but there had been no convictions, probably because his victims usually all died. Only in the Bellamy case had the victim been left alive to testify, but now Delgado was free due to a successful appeal. As long as the gun wasn't found and traced to him, he would remain free. But I had found the gun. Surely by now the police back home had also found it and also traced it to Delgado. They probably already had done ballistics tests and established it as the gun that shot Randolph Bellamy, and maybe Cassandra as well. But who had pulled the trigger?

Randolph was missing. Somehow I'd managed to forget that fact, in my musing about Vinnie Delgado, but when I visited the Bellamy house the day before, the entire Bellamy family was gone and there was no immediate explanation for the bloodstain on the rug. I wondered what conclusions the police had reached. Perhaps Felix would know.

My eyes were growing weary from studying the computer screen in the dimming light of the now-setting sun, and I worried about the battery on the cell phone which was indicating very little juice left. I switched off the laptop and stretched, wishing I could close my eyes for just a minute....

.

I don't think I'd been asleep long – the sky was not yet dark – but I jerked awake from a dream of Andrew Field walking toward me, naked, with a gun in his hand and a sad smile on his face. I opened my eyes to see the real McCoy walking, fully clothed, toward my Firebird in the motel parking lot with a briefcase in his hand.

I fumbled to start the engine, but to my surprise, he put the briefcase in the back seat, closed the door, and walked across the street straight toward me.

My heart pounded as he approached, and for a brief moment I wanted inexplicably to flee. Then he smiled. I smiled weakly and waved, then climbed out of the car.

"I can't believe you tracked me down already," he said, shaking his head. "Why did you do it? How did you do it?" He crossed the last few feet and came to stand in front of me, looking down into my eyes in his sensuous manner, turning my knees to jelly and my heart to a pounding lump in my throat.

He had removed the sling, but was still favoring his left side, I noted, my eyes traveling hungrily over his body. He wore another stretch knit shirt, open at the collar, and had changed into shorts in deference to the warmer Phoenix climate. His long muscular legs were pleasantly tanned, hairy without being simian, and looked like the legs of someone who runs every day.

There was nowhere he could have concealed a gun in that outfit, and I wondered how he had dared relax his guard already.

I realized he was talking to me again. "Angela?" he was saying. "How did you find me so quickly?"

I pulled myself back to business, forcing myself to look up into those deep brown eyes again and reply with a haughty toss of my head, "You hired me to do a job. Did you really think you'd put me off by unloading Charley and stealing my car?"

The corner of his mouth twitched with amusement. "Charley?"

I felt my face grow warm with embarrassment. I generally didn't have reason to tell clients my pet name for my gun and I felt a little silly until he chuckled and said, "You mean like Mike Hammer's Betsy?"

"Something like that," I mumbled.

"Have you eaten?" he asked. "I'd like to hear how you got here already."

"Are you sure it's safe here?" I asked.

He laughed, and I started to melt again. How could I do a job when I couldn't even look at my client without erotic images welling up in my mind? "I'm safe here," he answered. "So are you." He touched me lightly on the arm. "Come on. There's a coffee shop at the motel. Let's go talk."

We drove the car over to his motel, my surveillance post no longer needed now that the subject had invited me for coffee. I took the cell phone in with me in case Felix called and slipped my recorder into a pocket. I had removed my jacket and holster due to the heat so I slipped Charley into my cavernous purse when Andrew wasn't looking.

It was difficult to sit across the table from him, watching his eyes, trying to concentrate on what he was saying, when all the while my hormones were doing a tap dance throughout my body. Somehow I managed to hear part of what he was saying.

"I called the man. Everything's going to be all right now."

Somehow I pulled back to reality. "What man? What about the person who tried to kill you? If I traced you here, what makes you so sure you weren't followed?"

He laughed out loud, and I didn't know if I should be relieved by his insouciance or annoyed that he wasn't taking things seriously anymore. "What's so fucking funny?" I asked.

"Babe, trust me, I wasn't followed. And unless your phone was tapped, there's no way anyone else could have figured out where I went." He smiled at me. "How did you figure out where I was going? The last place anyone should have expected me to run to was the place you knew there was a warrant out on me."

I explained about the motorcycles giving me the clue and Felix's biker buddies pointing out the direction.

"Too bad it wasn't a Gold Wing convention," he mused. "The Harleys were a dead giveaway, weren't they. I thought maybe you'd traced the car through the phone somehow. I almost didn't answer when it rang."

"Well, I'm glad you did." I tried to pretend I was really annoyed when I added, "And that took a lot of nerve for you to steal my car right in front of me like that. What made you so sure I wouldn't call the police?"

"I wasn't sure at all," he answered with a shrug. "In fact, I'm surprised you didn't. Why didn't you?"

How could I explain without sounding like a lovesick teenager? "I didn't want my car to get shot up if you resisted arrest, which I was pretty sure you'd do if you had to."

"You didn't want the car to get shot up," he repeated with a smile tugging at the corners of his mouth.

"Right."

"Sure."

He met my gaze steadily, knowingly, and I had to turn away first. "Okay, so I didn't want to have you arrested until I figured out what was going on."

"That's more like it," he said encouragingly. "And what do you think is going on now?"

I took a long swallow of my iced tea. Somehow I had to regain the upper hand. "I know about Vinnie Delgado," I stated flatly, looking him straight in the eyes as I spoke.

Was it my imagination or did that confident façade crack just the tiniest bit at the mention of Delgado's name? It was obvious from this and his prior reaction to the name that I was onto something. Somehow, Vinnie Delgado was the key to Andrew Field's past.

He recovered his composure swiftly. "What do you know about Vinnie Delgado?"

"Oh, come on, Andrew," I said sarcastically. "Let's stop playing games. I have Delgado's whole story stored on my computer. Would you like to read it? Perhaps you could proofread the file. I'm sure if there are any errors in it, you'll be able to spot them in a flash."

Now it was his turn to gulp his drink. Was his hand shaking or was that my imagination, too? "What does it say?" he finally asked.

"Delgado is a hit man. He shot Randy Bellamy because he was dating Delgado's girl. Nobody knows where the girl is. Delgado was released from prison on the assault conviction because the gun he shot Bellamy with had never been found." I couldn't help glaring at him when I added, "Until yesterday, I suspect. I found Delgado's gun in a drawer at your house."

That really hit a nerve. Andrew had tried to nonchalantly sip his Coke while I spoke but when I told him I'd found the gun, he banged the glass down on the table and blurted, "What did you say?"

"I found Delgado's gun at your house. Don't try to tell me you didn't know it was there. In fact," I started, then caught myself. Never confront a killer with the fact that you know he's a killer had always been a hard and fast rule, drilled into me repeatedly by my former partner, Tim, and here I had almost told Andrew that I suspected he himself might be Delgado.

"In fact what?" he demanded.

"In fact the police no doubt have traced it by now," I ad libbed quickly. "It only took me a few minutes myself."

His face was strangely pale, as if he had had a big shock. Surely the gun in his desk was no surprise? Or was he upset at having left it behind to be found in the first place?

"What else have you found out?" he asked in a strained voice.

I suppose I sounded smug when I answered, "Nope. Your turn. You have to tell me right now what your connection to Delgado is." My eyes narrowed. Odds were, this gorgeous hunk of aphrodisiac was a cold-blooded killer. I had to keep him off balance. "If you don't, I'll call the police right now and tell them where you are."

To my immense disappointment, the threat had not the slightest effect on him. He merely shrugged. "That's your decision," he tossed back. "The police are the least of my problems and they can't hold me anyway."

Who did this guy think he was, anyway? Houdini? It was clear by now that there was still a major piece of this puzzle missing. My brain ran through the evidence, searching for the key, but I kept coming up with more questions than answers. How could I get this man to talk?

I tried another tack. "Andrew, you hired me. How can I help you if you won't be honest with me?"

"Honesty gets people killed, Angela," he said with sudden sincerity.

"Andrew, is Vinnie Delgado trying to kill you?"

He looked into my eyes for a long moment and in that moment, I was as afraid for him as I was of him. And it was in that same moment that I first realized that I *was* afraid of him. What did I know about this man, after all, other than that my hormones had the hots for him and that murder seemed to follow him everywhere? Not much of a basis for the trust I was trying to place in him.

He jolted me back when he answered simply, "No."

"No, Delgado is not trying to kill you?" I tried to clarify.

"Correct. Delgado is not trying to kill me."

It was the first straight answer that he'd given me in a long time, but it did nothing to help me. After all, if he himself was Delgado, then of course Delgado was not trying to kill him.

"Did Delgado kill Cassandra?"

"No comment."

"Did he try to kill Randolph Bellamy?"

"No comment."

"Do you know where Delgado is?"

"No comment."

"Damn it, Andrew! This isn't a fucking newspaper interview! This is life and death!"

"My life. My death." His eyes took on a faraway look. "Again."

Chapter 9

AGAIN? BEFORE I COULD TRY TO PURSUE the matter, the cellular phone chirped. I excused myself and left the table to take the call out of Andrew's hearing. The connection was poor, but I could hear Felix say he was at the airport. I told him where I was, and that I was with our elusive client. I told him to come over, get a room, and try to get some sleep. I would call him when I needed him to take over. I made a mental note to charge the cell phone battery as soon as possible. As expected, the two-hour session on the PRICS system in the car had drained most of the juice.

My plan was to have Felix keep Andrew under surveillance later on while I tried to get some sleep myself. Of course, I thought as I walked back to the table, the easiest way to keep Andrew under surveillance for the night was if I could manage to share his room. That would kill two birds with one stone. Maybe he'd be a lousy lay, I thought darkly, and I could get down to business instead of being constantly distracted with images of Andrew Field, naked, with a gun … or anything else … in his hand.

I was ethically against the idea of sleeping with a client, but heck, I argued with myself, it would keep him from slipping away and maybe getting killed in the process.

And it might be fun.

I returned to the table. "My associate is on the way," I explained. "I told him to get some sleep and I'll call him in the morning," I lied.

Andrew smiled and I started to melt. Where had we been before that phone call? Oh, right. I remembered. "Andrew, what did you mean about it being your death again?"

The smile faded. My hormones beat a hasty retreat. Somehow he looked too serious for what I had briefly had in mind a few minutes ago. "Never mind," he said tersely. "Forget it."

I took a deep breath. There was a question of professional pride here and I wasn't about to "forget it." "Andrew, I can't forget that you were shot in front of my eyes. I was a police officer for years. I'm trained to handle these things, if you'll only trust me to do my damn job!" I paused melodramatically before adding, "A job, I might add, that you hired me to do. What do you expect me to do? Send you a bill and walk away?"

"Something like that," he said, glancing past me to the door. His eyes narrowed and I turned to see what he was looking at.

A man had entered the cafe. He was about five-foot six inches tall, stocky build, dark curly hair, clean-shaven, wearing a badly tailored three-piece suit and dark glasses. His ears stuck out like cup handles from a head that looked too big for his body. He looked straight at Andrew, nodded once, glanced at me, then back at Andrew. Out of the corner of my eye, I detected the slightest nod of Andrew's head and the back of my neck bristled. What was this, a setup? I pushed my chair back and slid my hand into my purse, reaching for Charley.

I stood up, glancing uncertainly from Andrew to the newcomer. "Who is he, Andrew?" I asked, not really expecting the truth. "What's going on here?"

The three-piece suit walked over before Andrew could answer. "Ms Virago?" he said politely while my finger twitched on the trigger of the gun in my purse.

"Who wants to know?" I demanded, ignoring the hand that he extended. I gestured with my purse. "I have a gun on you, in case you're interested, so don't try anything funny."

The suit laughed, and Andrew joined in.

"Who the fuck are you?" I hissed. "Andrew, what the hell is this about?"

"Put the gun away, Ms Virago," the suit replied. "I'm with the FBI."

"And I'm the Queen of England," I snapped back.

In reply, he reached inside his coat and extracted an ID wallet, flipping it open to show a card with his picture and the name Gilbert McKenzie. The ID appeared to be genuine FBI, but I've got one just like it in my briefcase, so I took it as proof of nothing. The accompanying shield could have been bought at a novelty shop.

At least I something to call him other than the nickname Dumbo that had popped into mind the second I noticed the ears. "What do you want with me, Mr. McKenzie, if that's really your name?"

His smile faded. "You'll have to trust me."

"I have to trust nobody," I retorted. "Especially not people who set me up," I added, glaring at Andrew. What had I ever seen in him anyway? His half-amused smile had been replaced with a look of superiority. So the bastard had been playing me for a fool all along.

Andrew moved slightly to one side and I swung my purse hand in his direction. Since neither of them had shown a weapon I was reluctant to pull Charley out in such a public place, but I suddenly realized that the cafe was empty. There hadn't been any customers but us to start with, but even the waitress and busboy had disappeared.

Oh, screw propriety, I thought. I pulled Charley out and pointed it at Andrew. "Stand over by your buddy, Andrew. I want to know what's going on."

The smile returned to his face. "Oh, come now, Angela," he cajoled. "You know you're not going to use that thing."

"For all I know, Andrew Field, or Beauchamp, or whatever your alias of the moment is, you're Vincent Delgado and you probably killed Cassandra Bellamy. You've really done nothing to convince me otherwise. I know you're wanted by the police, and I think I'm just going to call this a citizen's arrest. We'll let the *real* authorities sort this out. I'm not buying your friend's phony FBI ID. I've got one just like it. Paid a whole twenty dollars for it, so save your fairy tales for the cops."

I picked up my cellular phone and dialed 911. But I had gone to the well once too often. The battery had died.

"Shit," I muttered. "Dead battery. Not a problem. Just move over to the entrance, nicely now, and I'll use the pay phone in the lobby."

With a bored sigh, Andrew complied with my request. His complacency bothered me a little. Did he really think I was going to let him and his so-called FBI friend roust me? He knew I had a gun with me. Neither of them had made any kind of move to overpower me, they had calmly let me get the drop on them. Now they were both moving at my command toward the exit.

Something smelled, and it wasn't the Chef's Special. Where was everybody? How, and for that matter, when, had Andrew arranged to have the cafe empty when McKenzie arrived? I slid Charley back into my purse and hung the strap over my shoulder. The shoulder strap hung at exactly the right length to enable me to have my gun hand in my purse without having to hold up the purse. In this manner, I could keep Andrew covered without scaring any innocent bystanders unnecessarily.

I started to follow the two men to the doorway, still wondering what they had planned to do when I heard a noise behind me. I spun around, keeping my gun out of sight, to face another man who had emerged from the kitchen area. He was holding a gun even bigger than mine, but to my surprise, it wasn't pointed at me, it was pointed past me. "Get down!" he shouted at me. "Police!"

I whirled back to face Andrew, who had frozen a few feet from the doorway, about four feet behind me. McKenzie had made it through the doorway and was out of the line of fire. I saw the look in Andrew's eyes, that of a hunted, cornered animal. I glanced back to the new gunman and did not see the look of cold, impartial authority in his eyes, but rather the smug calmness of a hit man who knows he's about to score.

What if I was wrong?

In a split second, I gave what loyalty I had left to my client, whoever he really was, pulled Charley from my purse, and fired a single round at the gunman, striking him in the right chest, sending the gun flying from his grasp and his body crumpling to the floor.

I felt Andrew's hand on my arm, pulling me away, through the door, out into the parking lot. My feet moved as in a dream, running with him, climbing into a dark gray sedan with government license plates. I felt Andrew push me down behind the front seat, the door slammed shut behind me, the engine roared, and we were off.

Visions of the gunman's bloody body lying on the cafe floor followed me while the car sped through the streets of Phoenix. I felt it turn right, then left, then right, then right again, then left. Where the hell were we going?

I struggled to get up, but Andrew pushed me down. "Stay put, damn it," he muttered. "Do you want to get shot?"

I twisted around to look up at him. He was crouched on the back seat, one hand on my shoulder, the other resting across the back of the rear seat, clutching a gun. He watched intently through the back window for several minutes, finally content that we weren't being followed. "Get up," he said, releasing me.

Miffed, I struggled into an upright position and slid into the far corner of the seat, away from Andrew. Somehow he had relieved me of my gun, and I realized it was Charley he was holding at the ready. "May I have my gun back, please?" I asked with as much dignity as I could muster under the circumstances.

"I don't think so," he replied, pulling his hand back to his side lest I try to grab.

"I did just save your life, you know," I reminded him. "That was a hit man back there, not the police."

He studied me with apparent interest. "How could you tell?"

"The look in his eyes," I replied.

From the driver's seat, McKenzie laughed. He seemed to find everything I said funny. It was starting to piss me off, too. "What the fuck is so funny?" I demanded.

"That's almost as bad as woman's intuition," he replied, still chuckling. "The look in his eyes? Come on, sister, you trying to tell me you shot a man because of the look in his eyes?"

"I'm starting to think I shot the wrong man," I bristled. Oh, God, what if I had?

"Don't worry," he reassured me, "you didn't. And I'm glad it was you and not me. Do you have any idea how much paperwork we have to go through for every bullet we fire?"

"Of course I know, I used to be a cop," I snapped. This little short shit was really getting on my nerves. He must really be FBI, I decided.

He glanced back at me. "I know that. That's why we have to put you on ice for a while."

I turned to face Andrew, smugly declaring, "Yeah? You and whose army?" Then I saw the chloroform-laced cloth in Andrew's hand and raised both arms, struggling in vain to keep it away from my face, but failed to do so and as I breathed in the sickening sweetness I felt consciousness slip away. The last thing I heard was McKenzie's voice in the distance.

"Oh, shit, Martin, we've picked up a tail."

Chapter 10

I WOKE UP ON A BED IN A DARK ROOM and it didn't take me long to figure out that the shooting pain in my arm was caused by the rope that held my hands tied behind my back. I shifted until the pain lessened, peering vainly into the darkness, trying to figure out where I was and how I'd gotten there.

Gradually, the events of the evening before came back to me, and I remembered that Andrew Field and an elephant-eared man I believed might be an FBI agent had taken me from the scene of a shooting and said they would have to put me on ice for a while.

How could I have trusted him? I realized now that I had probably shot the wrong man back in that coffee shop. How could I have pulled the trigger without knowing for sure whom I was shooting at? What had I told Andrew? That I had decided to shoot based on the look in the man's eyes?

So much for my instincts. I should have shot Andrew instead.

I tested my bonds and found my hands and feet were tied, and my feet were also tied to the foot of the bed. Escape was unlikely unless I could free my hands. And I was too tired and groggy to think about trying to do that just yet.

Rolling over on the bed, wincing at the pain in my arms, I looked around the room. In the dim light from the curtained window I could see a dresser, chair, and closet. The closet was open and empty. There was nothing at all on the top of the dresser. Somehow I was reminded of the bareness of Andrew's home.

I discovered I was lying on a bare mattress. There were no linens or pillow on the bed. The room looked abandoned. I sniffed the musty air and surmised that the room had been that way for some time.

I listened carefully for any sounds that would give me a clue to the presence of my captors, but heard nothing but the distant barking of a dog. Somehow, the sound was comforting. If there was a dog within earshot, so, too, might be its owner. At least if I managed to escape there was a chance I could find help.

The sheer effort of concentration took a lot out of me. I stopped straining to sit up and slumped back onto the mattress, rolling onto my stomach to give my arms some relief.

I suppose I dozed again, for when I opened my eyes the room was brighter and I had enough light to see colors. I also could see the heavy cobwebs that infested the place, and the heavy layer of dust on every visible surface. Only then did I realize the mattress was as dusty as everything else. I blew across the surface of the mattress and immediately regretted it when the resultant cloud of dust made me break into a paroxysm of coughing.

I struggled again to sit up, drawing my knees to my chest for balance, bracing my back against the wall. I realized my bladder was trying to tell me something. "Hey!" I shouted. "Anybody home?" They may have had reasons for keeping me "on ice" but surely they would permit me a potty break once in awhile.

But it was apparent from the continuing silence that I was alone. Even the dog no longer barked. I began to test my bonds again, feeling carefully with a finger to see where the rope went around my hands. I found an end and began to work it carefully, but to no avail, so I studied the rope that held my feet to the bed and discovered that by kneeling with my feet tucked behind me, I could get both hands to that rope.

It didn't really take long to free my feet from the bed, and from there I used a quick Houdini trick Tim had taught me to pull my tied hands under my butt and past my feet until they were in front of me where I could work on the knots with my teeth.

I was gone before they could return, leaving the empty farmhouse behind with its dust and cobwebs. I did leave a message for Andrew in the dust on the kitchen table. It said, "The ice melted, turkey. See ya in church."

I always wondered what that meant.

Once outside, I looked around for some means of transportation and realized that my idea about the barking dog being nearby was an illusion of the still morning air. The nearest house looked at least two miles away. In the very dim distance I watched a cloud of dust follow a tractor plowing a field. Behind the farmhouse in which I had been imprisoned was a fence that separated the yard from a horse pasture.

And I suppose it would have been too easy for any of the horses to have been nearby, but the nearest one was halfway across a very large field. Nevertheless, the tractor was on the other side of the horse pasture, so I grabbed a bridle I found on the porch and a bucket I found in the yard and started across the pasture.

The bucket decoy worked, and I was about a third of the way across the field when a couple of fat white mares noticed me and sauntered over to investigate the bucket, but they scampered away when they realized the pail was empty and I was reaching for one of them with a bridle. I kept walking.

By the time I was two-thirds of the way across, I had the attention of the farmer and was gratified to see him halt the tractor at the edge of the pasture and wait for me.

He was kind enough to tell me where I was, took me to the house and let me use his telephone, and then he went outside to put the tractor away. His wife gave me clean clothes after I took a shower while I waited for Felix to pick me up. She then fed me a sumptuous breakfast and didn't even ask any questions when I explained that I was a private eye and had been on a stakeout when the drug runners I was tailing had overpowered me and taken my car, leaving me at the abandoned farmhouse next door. She did tell me that the farmhouse was owned by a Phoenix obstetrician who used to use it as a weekend retreat until the well dried up five years before. She didn't know his name, but he used to bring some of his patients' children out on weekends to ride a pony he used to have. Seemed there were always kids climbing around on an old gnarled tree in the back yard.

I listened to all this with a few polite, "Uh, huhs," not wanting to offend her but needing more to concentrate on the questions of what Andrew and Dumbo were up to, of whom I might have shot the previous evening, and of how in the world I was going to explain this to Felix without appearing to be entirely incompetent. She shut up when her husband came back in from the barn and started talking about whether they had enough fertilizer for the next irrigation or something like that. By this point I'd had enough fertilizer to last a lifetime, mostly from Andrew Field.

Finally I heard a car pull up outside, thanked them for their hospitality, and ran out to the driveway – where I found myself facing my own gun, Charley, in the hand of Andrew Field, again. He was driving my car.

Oh, shit, was nothing going to go right today? I thought of screaming but didn't want to endanger the kindly farm folk who had taken me into their home and trusted a total stranger in complete disregard for modern wisdom.

"What the fuck do you want with me, Andrew?" I demanded with a bravado I no longer felt. I heard the screen door open behind me.

"Ah, good, it's you," I heard Farmer John say. "You'd better scoot."

"Thanks, Pop," Andrew replied. "I'm outta here."

I whirled around to face the farmer. "Pop?" I demanded. "You're his father?"

The kindly farmer's face suddenly seemed less kindly. "In a manner of speaking. Go with him now. It could get ugly if you don't move soon. You were probably seen."

With that, he turned and disappeared into the house. Resolutely, I got into the car with Andrew, taking the wheel as he instructed, and pulled away from the farmhouse.

Felix was going to be in trouble. I had told him where I was and I didn't like to think of him arriving at that farmhouse unaware and possibly walking into a trap. *As I had*, I had to remind myself. But then I looked up at a road sign and realized what should have been obvious from the moment Farmer John had come out onto the porch. They had given me wrong directions. I had no idea where I really was, and had just sent Felix on a wild goose chase.

"All right, Andrew," I said after turning onto a main road that I recognized as being on the far west end of Phoenix, not the east side where I had sent Felix. "What the hell is going on? Where's your short friend with the bad attitude?"

He laughed, and I wondered how I had ever considered a romantic interlude with the snake next to me. The lying, deceitful, nonexistent Andrew Field rested my gun easily in his lap, reached an arm across the seat to caress the back of my neck, and laughed some more.

"Baby, you may not know it, but I just saved your arrogant little life," he replied.

I found his touch pleasantly distracting, which I found unpleasantly annoying. I shoved his hand away. "Get your paws off me, scumbag," I snapped. "You kidnap me at gunpoint and want me to be grateful you didn't kill me yet?"

"McKenzie is an imposter," he replied. "He's trying to get us both." He was no longer laughing.

"And I'm Richard Nixon," I retorted. "You couldn't tell the truth if your life depended on it."

"My life does depend on it," he answered soberly. "If I hadn't gotten to your gun before McKenzie did, we'd both be dead by now. He didn't figure on my being armed." He glanced over at me. "Sorry I had to do what I did. Pop thinks I'm working with McKenzie. I had to make it look good. We can stop whenever you want and call Felix. I had to get you away from there before McKenzie found out you were gone."

I pulled the car to the side of the road, and turned off the engine. I looked into his eyes and saw something there I had never seen before in Andrew's eyes. Raw fear. It touched something deep inside me, some kind of basic protective instinct, and I recalled that no matter what, this man facing me was my client, someone who had put his trust in me. Recalling my decision to shoot the night before, I realized that nothing had really changed. I had to stick with my client.

"I need the truth, Andrew," I said, holding my hand out to him, palm up. He gave me back my gun, which I immediately checked. There was only one spent round in the revolver, hopefully the same one I had expended the night before. I hated to think that my gun had been used for anything while out of my possession.

"I can't give you much of that," he answered with a shrug. "Sorry. I have my reasons."

I shot him a glare and reached for the car phone. Time to call Felix and get the hell out of this mess.

Andrew caught my hand before I could lift the receiver. "Don't," he warned. "I know it's been bugged."

I exploded. "Why the hell did you hire me in the first place, Andrew? You've put up more barriers than we had when I started this. You asked me to find out about you. Why? You're obviously capable of taking care of yourself, and anyway, Cassandra's dead. She can't be a threat to you anymore. So what gives, damn it?"

At the mention of Cassandra's name, he tore his gaze from mine and looked out the side window, away from me. Another emotional reaction. I reached out and touched him on the shoulder and he put his right hand on mine and squeezed it firmly, gently.

I remained motionless, letting him work through whatever emotions he was feeling at the time. Damn it, men weren't supposed to be like this. They were supposed to be cool, calm, collected, and above all, unemotional. For some annoying reason, I found his outward display of emotion appealing and I briefly wished I dared take him in my arms and comfort him.

Eventually, he turned back to me, dry-eyed and calm, patted my hand once, and said, "Okay, I'll level with you about what I can."

"Let's start with who I shot last night," I suggested smugly, now that I finally had him ready to talk. "Who was he and what did he want? Have I been set up for a prison rap?"

"No. You did the right thing. That was James Maxwell, a hit man probably hired by the same people who had Cassandra killed."

I digested that for a moment, along with Mrs. Farmer John's breakfast, noting that the sausages were not agreeing with my system. "Cassy was killed by a hit man," I repeated flatly. "How do you know?"

"I just know. I can't tell you everything, so just bear with me, okay?" he appealed.

"Sure. Go on." Let him tell me what he wanted to. I was sure it would be at least seventy-five percent lies, but somewhere in his tale would be a kernel of truth. My job was to try to recognize it. I thought about the logic puzzles I used to work in my youth, puzzles in which there were three natives on an island, and one of them always told the truth, another always lied, and another alternately lied and told truth. You had to figure out one question to ask them from which you could get the truth no matter whom you asked. If only I could figure out the foolproof question, the answer to which, whether lie or truth, would provide me with the answer to the puzzle, I might be able to figure a way out of this mess.

He continued. "There's a price on my head."

I snorted. "Tell me something I don't know."

"You don't know why."

"And you're not going to tell me."

"I think I need to now. I need you to trust me."

I looked at him quizzically, decided to let him take the initiative. I didn't have a foolproof question ready yet, so I wasn't going to ask anything. *Ask him no questions, he'll tell you no lies,* I paraphrased to myself.

"I'm supposed to be in the witness protection program."

That was the best he could come up with? It was all I could do to keep from rolling my eyes in disgust. Instead, I replied simply, "Go on."

"You were getting close with Vinnie Delgado." He paused, as if not sure he wanted to continue. "I'm being blackmailed."

"The Orkin man is blackmailing you?" Somehow, having read Delgado's rap sheet, I had trouble picturing him wasting his time with blackmail.

"In a manner of speaking. You see, I was there when he hit Randolph Bellamy. In fact, I intervened and got the gun away from him. Unfortunately, in the process, Bellamy wasn't really sure who had pulled the trigger. They convicted Delgado on his testimony, which was accurate, but Bellamy was on the ground when I jumped Vinnie and kept him from putting a fatal slug into Bellamy. Instead he was only hit in the shoulder. But he didn't see me and I ended up with the gun. Delgado has threatened that if that gun ever sees the light of day, he'll make sure I end up in prison for attempted murder."

"But the gun has seen the light of day," I reminded him.

"Which may be why I was shot, Cassandra was killed, and Randolph Bellamy is missing."

Since I never told Andrew about my visit to the Bellamy house, he must have gotten his information about Randolph somewhere else. I wondered if he would notice that I registered no surprise at his last statement. "Go on," I said simply.

"I think the hit on me was set up to look as if Cassandra had done it, so the natural conclusion would be that I was the one who killed her. They needed her dead because Bellamy had told her the whole truth."

"What truth was that?"

"That he hadn't actually seen Delgado pull the trigger. I was there. He was on the ground and Delgado was preparing to finish him off. Bellamy looked up at him, then turned his head away, not wanting to see the bullet that was coming. I guess he fainted after he was shot, because by the time I got the gun away from Vinnie, Bellamy was unconscious."

"So Vinnie was convicted on Bellamy's quite logical and correct belief that Delgado shot him, but with the gun in your possession and Vinnie's testimony, he could have turned the whole thing around against you."

"Right."

"So why didn't he?"

"Because I had his kid."

I raised a skeptical eyebrow. "You had his kid?"

"Yes. His son, Brian. He'd been taken from Vinnie's ex while Vinnie was out of the country. The kid ran away from his foster home and came to me. The authorities let me keep him temporarily on the condition that nobody know where he was. You see, by then they knew that Brian's dad was a mob figure and they didn't want the mob trying to get at the kid."

The image of Andrew Field as a surrogate dad was a little hard to visualize. I just couldn't see him playing catch with a little boy. Of course, I was only assuming the kid was very young. "How old was the kid, and where is he now?" I asked.

"He was six at the time –"

I cut him off. "Six? You're trying to tell me a six-year-old kid ran away from home and came to you for help? Come on, Andrew. I know you've been lying through your teeth ever since I met you, but give me some credit!"

His eyes narrowed and I wondered if I'd gone too far. Should have kept my mouth shut. After all, there still was a chance that Andrew was a killer. I didn't need to piss him off, but it was too late for that.

He gazed at me coldly for a long moment, then he smiled and chuckled. "I guess it does sound a little far-fetched, but this was no ordinary six-year-old. The kid spent most of his life on the street with his mother, which is why the authorities took him away from her. He came to me because there were a few times when I took them in and fed them a meal."

"Shades of Oliver Twist," I murmured by way of apology, trying to picture this streetwise youth, wondering what sort of life he must have had, and wondering, as I'd already asked once, where he was now. I asked again.

Andrew turned abruptly and looked out the window, not answering for a moment. When he finally spoke, even his answer wasn't an answer. "I can't tell you."

"Why?"

He turned back to me and sighed. "It's a long story, one I can't go into, but the truth is I frankly don't know any more. But that's why Delgado will never kill me. If he does, he knows he'll never find the boy."

"Is he safe?"

"I don't know that either. The only thing I know is that Delgado hasn't found him yet." His handsome face clouded over with anguish. "That crazy fool screwed everything up."

"Who?"

"Never mind."

This conversation was going about like most of our past conversations had gone. I'd had about enough. I restarted the car and flipped a U-turn in the middle of the road without saying a word.

"Where are we going?" Andrew asked.

"I'm going to find a phone and call Felix. Then Felix and I are going home." I stopped for a red light and turned to glare at Andrew in what I hoped was a chilling manner. "I can't work under these conditions, Andrew. Not with bullets flying around wherever you go." Guiltily, I realized that the last of those bullets had come from my own gun, but, what the hell, it was to protect him, wasn't it?

His brown eyes met my gaze without wavering. "I thought you had professional pride."

"What's that supposed to mean?" I sputtered. What the hell was he trying to suggest? That I was wimping out on him?

"You're supposed to be an investigator. Don't tell me you've never had to dig for answers before." He sighed. "I suppose it was a mistake, coming to a woman. I really thought you were tougher than that."

Naturally, the feminist in me rose to the bait. The light turned green and I mashed the accelerator, killing the engine in my annoyance. I could feel my face redden as I restarted the engine and moved out at a slightly more decorous pace. "I am tough," I spat out as we drove through the intersection. "I'm also not stupid. One person has already been killed, and another shot. I'm not going to be next and if you can't play straight with me, I'm not going to play at all."

Andrew didn't reply, and we drove back into town in stony silence. God damn him, anyway. Who the hell did he think he was, telling me I wasn't tough enough? My foot pressed harder on the gas pedal as my ire rose. Thinks just because he's thrown up a few brick walls in my path that I couldn't solve the problem if I wanted to. I just don't want to. That's all.

I felt better once I convinced myself that I was quitting just because I didn't feel like continuing with this lying swine. Lying, handsome swine. Lying, handsome, sexy, attractive, appealing, sensitive, desperate, hunted swine. I flicked a glance in his direction. His face was turned slightly to the right, away from me, looking out the window. It was a troubled face, looking like he was wondering what to do next.

What would he do next? He said McKenzie was an imposter and was looking for both of us. Andrew had come to Phoenix, expecting that "the man" would make everything all right. Was McKenzie "the man"? What had gone wrong? If I left him now, how would he protect himself? Whom could he trust?

Why should I give a damn?

I stopped at a pay phone and reached Felix on his cellular. We agreed to meet back at a coffee shop near the motel. My rental car was still in the motel parking lot, according to Felix, but the police investigating the shooting wanted to talk to me.

Great.

I hung up the phone with disgust. I didn't need to become part of an investigation right then, but there really wasn't any way out of it. I walked back to the car and jerked open the driver's door.

"Thanks to you, the police want to talk to me about that shooting yesterday," I spat out unfairly as I climbed behind the wheel.

It was then that I noticed I was talking to myself. Andrew was gone. I looked around but didn't see him anywhere. Maybe he'd gone to the restroom, I thought uneasily. It didn't seem likely that he would have taken off on foot, but when another man emerged from the only restroom about three minutes later and said that nobody else had been in there, I realized my elusive client had pulled another fast one.

At least he had left me my car this time. And his briefcase, I saw, lying on the rear seat. Cursing myself for getting out of sight of the car while I made the phone call, I pulled the briefcase into the front seat and toyed with the lock. Rifling a client's private possessions was not my style, but there were too many unanswered questions and I was on the hot seat for that shooting.

I picked the lock.

Inside were several fake ID's – big surprise – and some legal papers, subpoenas, copies of depositions, and twenty thousand dollars in cash.

And a passport for one André Jacques Martin, now aged thirty-four, born in Mill Valley, Missouri to Sandra and François Martin. The name François Martin seemed familiar for some reason, but I couldn't place it. The passport had never been used. I peered at the picture. It was definitely the man I knew as Andrew Field. I fished my recorder out of my pocket and began making notes to myself.

In the dim recesses of my memory, I recalled the last words I had heard before losing consciousness to the chloroform. Something about picking up a tail, but the significant thing was that Dumbo the elephant, a.k.a. Gilbert McKenzie, had called Andrew by the name of Martin. I had forgotten that until now.

If McKenzie knew him as André Martin, and McKenzie was a bad guy, according to Andrew, could it be that McKenzie knew his secret? Perhaps McKenzie had been assigned to provide Andrew with his new identity and had been bought off by Vinnie Delgado's people?

No, Andrew had called McKenzie an imposter, not a turncoat. There's a big difference and I suspected Andrew knew that. McKenzie was not "the man" he expected to meet, but someone masquerading as "the man." And something else didn't make sense.

Why hadn't Andrew testified about the Bellamy shooting? He said he had had Delgado's kid, but what power could Delgado have had over him? Something didn't smell right. If given promptly, Andrew's testimony would have corroborated Bellamy's, and powder residue would have established for the police which of them had actually pulled the trigger. Why hadn't he come forward with the gun and his testimony at the time of the shooting?

No, there was something else going on, and perhaps the answer was in the briefcase. I looked at the legal documents and debated about reading them on the spot, but Felix was waiting. Reluctantly, I put everything back in the briefcase and tossed it into the back seat again.

I had no idea where Andrew was, or why he had left his briefcase behind, but I couldn't sit in front of a mini-mart all day speculating. I had to meet Felix and give a statement to the police about the shooting. I just hoped I wouldn't be arrested.

Chapter 11

FELIX WASN'T VERY HAPPY WITH ME when I caught up to him at the coffee shop down the road from the motel where the shooting had occurred.

"Do you have any idea at all how worried I've been?" was his first comment after greeting me with a solicitous hug and kiss.

"Yes, mother, and I'm sorry I was out all night," I replied.

"That's not funny," he answered, and I could see he had really had a bad night of it. "I've been looking for you all over town."

"Sorry about the wild goose chase," I apologized, and told him about my ordeal and my breakfast with Farmer John the mobster. At least I guessed he was a mobster. He hadn't seemed that way at the time, though.

He ordered coffee. I ordered a large Coke.

"We're sticking together from now on," Felix stated when I was through, and I was frankly too tired and depressed to pull rank and argue with him about it.

"So what have you done while I was being drugged, kidnapped, fed lousy sausage, and kidnapped again?" I asked lightly.

"Other than looking for you in all the wrong places, I scored a hit on PRICS."

I resisted the inevitable urge to make a pun.

"I know what Andrew was wanted for."

"He's a witness to an attempted murder," I answered for him. "I know. He finally told me something resembling the truth for once."

"Wrong-o, Boss. He's a witness to a baby-selling racket."

"Huh?" I must be more tired than I thought.

"Baby selling," Felix repeated. "You know, where they kidnap kids and sell them to couples who want to adopt. Sometimes they trick unmarried girls into giving up their babies when they're born, then they sell the kids. They can get fifty grand or more per kid, depending on the age and how blue its eyes are."

"I know what baby selling is, Felix, but I can't quite see Andrew Field in that role." As soon as the words were out of my mouth, I recalled thinking similarly about him keeping Delgado's son in hiding. Could it be that I had been so blinded by my thoughts of him as a sex object that I had overlooked a gentler side to the man?

"He did cry," I said aloud.

"What?"

"Never mind."

Felix looked at me oddly but I decided not to tell him what I was thinking. Sensitive or not, I had a hard time accepting Andrew/André Field/Beauchamp in the role of child protector. Too many bullets had recently flown because of him.

I drained half the Coke in one long draft, not that I needed the caffeine with all the adrenaline I'd pumped out lately. Felix handed me a sheaf of papers, notes on what we knew so far. All the relationships, the aliases, the names were listed. How many red herrings had we caught in our little dragnet?

He had listed the Bellamy clan: Howard, Randolph, Cassandra and an assortment of children of questionable parentage. It occurred to me then to wonder just whom the cops had notified as Cassandra's next of kin. Were they trying to find Randolph? Had they contacted her ex-husband the horse rancher? Were her parents still alive? There were a lot of possibilities.

"Felix," I said, "did you turn up any information on Cassandra's family, her parents, any relatives? Everything I know about her has to do with her life after she became an adult."

"Her mother is still alive. She divorced her father over twenty years ago. I couldn't trace him. The mother has since remarried. I don't recall her new name. Want me to try to find her?"

"Yes, and any siblings." We had done about all we could using computer technology. Not knowing who Andrew Field really was (presupposing that the information in the briefcase was as fictitious as anything else we knew) I knew it was pointless trying to find his kin, but Cassy's family was another story. It was time to get off the computer and start talking to some human beings. It was a long shot, but maybe her mother had attended the wedding and could tell me whether it was Howard or Randy she had married.

I also decided to look up the first ex-husband.

I suppose I was getting desperate. Andrew was gone; I had no idea if it was by choice or force; I had to do something. Cassandra was my only other clue.

Felix caught a waiter's attention and ordered a sandwich to go with the coffee. I declined to eat, still feeling the effects of the sausages rolling around in my gut.

I read on.

There was little on Felix's printout regarding Andrew Field himself, or rather, André Jacques Martin if his passport and the other information in his briefcase could be believed. I penciled the name from the passport onto the printout.

Martin? I glanced back to the information on Cassy. Cassy's maiden name was Martin? Could it be a coincidence? Or could Cassandra Elizabeth Martin be related to André Jacques Martin? Could that explain Andrew's emotion over her death? Could it also explain his reluctance to become physically involved with her? Could he have hired me in order to know if it was possible for Cassandra to learn he was related to her? He knew who she was, but she didn't know who he was?

"Felix," I started, "let me try an idea on you."

"Sure, Boss."

"According to the passport I found in Andrew's briefcase, his real name might be André Jacques Martin."

"Right. But that could be as phony as his other aliases."

"True. But Cassandra's maiden name is also Martin."

"You think they're related, Boss?" Felix asked. "Martin is a fairly common name. Could be a coincidence."

"Yes, yes," I conceded with a sigh, "but right at this point I don't feel inclined to dismiss anything as mere coincidence." I studied the printout a few more minutes. Something else on the printout was nagging at me. I read through the Bellamy names again. Howard Quincy Bellamy – the old man I had met, who claimed to be Cassy's father-in-law, but who Andrew believed was her husband; Randolph Bellamy – Howard's son and possibly husband of Cassandra; Brian, Jason, and Michelle Bellamy – two of them supposedly the children of Cassandra, although nobody had ever seen her pregnant.

I finished my Coke. "Keep at it, Felix," I said as I stood up. I handed him my recorder. "Go get another motel room, get on the computer, and find out all you can. And transcribe this. I guess it's time I turned myself in over that shooting. And while you're at it," I added sadly, "check the want ads and see if you can buy me another gun. I have a feeling the cops are going to want to impound Charley. And one other thing – Andrew says the car phone is bugged. Do something about that, would you, please?"

I turned toward the door just as two Phoenix policemen walked in and took me into custody for questioning.

Chapter 12

"I CAN'T TELL YOU THAT," I SAID for what had to be the forty-ninth time. "It's privileged information."

"Damn it, Miss Virago, this is not television! When are you going to realize you're only hurting yourself by refusing to cooperate?" They had started playing good cop-bad cop with me early on in the interrogation, but had gotten nowhere. In fact, I had long ago stopped listening to their questions, merely replying, "I can't tell you that. It's privileged information," every time Dimple paused to take a breath.

I did think it incongruous that they had assigned the role of bad cop to a baby-faced apparent rookie with the cutest dimple on his left cheek, but he had a somewhat gravelly voice that might have been intimidating to some. To me, the whole thing was a major bore.

Goldilocks (good cop) motioned to Dimple and they stepped outside the interrogation room. I suppose next Goldilocks would come in, tell me he wasn't sure how much longer he could keep Dimple from really getting rough, and encourage me to tell him what they needed to know so they could release me to go on about my business.

The problem was, they thought they needed to know who I was working for, where he was, where Randolph Bellamy was, did I know who had killed Cassandra, and did I know who had hired the hit man I'd shot the day before.

What I had told them were my name, address, phone number, that I had no idea who hired the man I shot, and that everything else was privileged information. Not knowing whether they were straight cops or if they were on someone else's payroll, I was disinclined to even let them know if I knew Randolph or Cassandra Bellamy or anything about them. So far, they had not mentioned Andrew Field/Beauchamp/Martin so I had to suspect they had made the connection to the Bellamy case through the hit man I'd shot, James Maxwell.

The door burst open and Goldilocks came in, saying over his shoulder, "No, leave me alone. I'll handle this now. You always go too far, Steve."

Right on cue.

He closed the door and sat opposite me. "Angela, Angela, you really should cooperate with me. I don't know how much longer I can hold him off, you know. He wants to charge you with attempted murder for the shooting of James Maxwell last night, and accessory to the killing of Cassandra Bellamy. If Maxwell dies, you'll be facing murder one."

"It'll never stick and you know it. You haven't got squat on me. You know I shot Maxwell in self-defense last night. I took off because I didn't know if he was alone or not."

"That's not how a jury will see it."

I sighed with as much disgust as I could muster. Felix was getting me a lawyer but apparently hadn't found one as quickly as I would have liked. This had been going on for over two hours already and I was starting to grow weary of the bullshit. Of course, I knew that was exactly what Goldilocks and Dimple were counting on, so I repeated my stock line, "I can't tell you that. It's privileged information."

"I didn't ask you anything," Goldilocks protested.

"I can't tell you that. It's privileged information."

"Damn it, who are you protecting!" Goldilocks exploded.

"Tsk, tsk," I chided him. "That's Dimple's line. You're supposed to be the good cop."

"Do you want to go to jail? We can hold you, you know. We don't even have to charge you. We've got a nice, cold, rat-infested cell out back just waiting for you."

"I should have guessed all the rats in Phoenix would be at police headquarters. Why does that not surprise me?" Delivering that line was a little harder than I thought it would be. After all, I used to be a cop once, and did not consider myself to be a rat. So far, Goldilocks and Dimple didn't seem to realize that I was a former cop or they would have known that their games were completely obvious to me.

"I – " Whatever he planned to say next was cut off when the door burst open again and Dimple walked in with a scowl on his face and a lawyer on his ass.

Well, not quite literally, but in any event I was released, uncharged, about five minutes later.

Chapter 13

THE COPS WERE SURPRISINGLY UNDERSTANDING after the lawyer finished threatening them with charges of false arrest and harassment. Actually, the fact that the hit man I'd shot had actually been armed and had a rap sheet as long as John Holmes' dick helped. It clearly was a case of self-defense.

And they impounded Charley before telling me I was free to go.

All in all, it worked out about as well as I could have hoped for. I was off the hook, and I hadn't had to tell the cops about Andrew or McKenzie. They reluctantly said I could have Charley back in a few days if the ballistics tests came up negative on Cassandra's murder. I suppose it was their last arrogant effort at harassment. I already knew from PRICS that Cassy had been shot with a forty-five, not a thirty-eight, so who were they kidding?

I was still on my own, except for Felix. I called him on his cell phone and learned where he had moved to, and that he had already acquired a gun from a local resident. I was relieved. I felt naked without Charley nestled in my armpit.

The new motel was about five miles from the first. I drove there in my own car after getting my stuff and calling the rental agency to come pick their car up at the diner where just about twenty-four hours earlier, I had pulled the trigger of my gun to protect a client. For some reason, probably pure incompetence, Dimple and Goldilocks had not managed to connect me to either the rental car nor the Firebird that had sat in the motel parking lot all night before my missing client retrieved it.

Once again, I questioned whether my faith in that client was misplaced. Where was Andrew Field? I had left his briefcase with Felix to keep it out of police hands. Perhaps the answers lay in the unread legal briefs I had found that afternoon.

Felix had rented two adjoining rooms at the new motel, probably the only "suite" in the whole place. He had selected an inconspicuous dive called The Bunkhouse located about fifty yards from a busy railroad track. From the looks of the furnishings, the place originally catered to down-on-their-luck cowpunchers in the 1800's. I wasn't surprised to see hitch rails in front of the rooms which faced a common courtyard. The rooms were tiny and the furniture was heavy, wooden, and had probably been carried in by covered wagon a hundred years ago, but at least the mattresses were the modern kind, not stuffed with corncobs like I first suspected.

The "magic fingers" device didn't work. The shower dripped continuously.

Outside the building, a green neon horse bucked in front of a pink saguaro cactus. I found the steady flashing of the neon horse somehow comforting. I wasn't real happy that the hitching rails were in front, while the parking spaces were around in the back, but apart from that one inconvenience, I felt safely anonymous there.

Andrew had thoughtfully left my purse behind the seat of my car and I was relieved to find everything intact. The cell phone was still as dead as a doornail and I plugged it into the wall to recharge it. Communication is so important in my line of work. With Charley gone and the cell phone dead, I had felt as naked and vulnerable as if I'd been standing in the middle of a freeway at rush hour in my birthday suit.

I was still staring out the window, wondering why the horse was green instead of the cactus when Felix tapped on the connecting door.

"Come on in, it's open," I called, pulling the drapes closed.

"Hungry, Boss?" he asked. "I ordered a pizza. Should be here any minute." He tossed me another thirty-eight Special and a box of shells.

"Famished, actually," I answered gratefully, checking and loading the gun. Lucky for me Arizona still believes in the right to keep and bear arms. I slid the piece into my holster and patted it contentedly. "All I've eaten today is what I had at the farmhouse – and my gut has been complaining about that ever since." I sat on the edge of the bed. "How'd you make out with Cassandra's family?"

"Not bad," he replied with a shrug. "Her mother's name is Sandra Baker now. Lives in Las Vegas. No siblings. Cassy had a brother but he died when she was a baby. Even the mother doesn't have any siblings, and both sets of grandparents are dead."

"Sandra Baker," I murmured absently. "Cassandra must have been named after her mother. What happened to the father?"

"Don't know, but it seems he's been out of the picture more than twenty years. The mother has been remarried for the third time for seven years now."

"That means Cassy's father never got to meet his grand kids," I concluded, then immediately wondered why I thought it mattered anymore. For some reason, the various children in this case were weighing heavily on my mind.

"I don't think Sandra Baker has met them either, Boss," Felix answered. "I called her house. She wasn't there, but a servant answered the phone and was more than willing to share a bit of gossip with a stranger, which I found interesting. The police did contact Cassy's mother about her death, but according to the servant, Sandra Baker disowned Cassandra several years ago and wants to have nothing to do with her or her death. Didn't even ask about the kids."

I mulled this over for a moment, my gaze wandering idly about the room, wondering where Howard and/or Randolph had taken the kids. Suddenly I found myself staring at a print on the opposite wall, a pastoral scene of a solid white mare with a spotted foal lying in a patch of moonlight, with a proud bay stallion looking on. The foal's white spots contrasted sharply with his black coat. *What's that stallion got to be so proud about*, I found myself wondering. *With those spots, it obviously isn't his baby.*

The significance of what Felix had just said hit me. "Baby," I said aloud. "It's not his baby."

"What?" Felix said.

I turned my gaze back to Felix. "That horse. It's not his baby." I nodded at the print. "Howard said he thought the kids weren't Randy's. Then whose were they?"

Felix had no answer, but it didn't matter because we heard a knock on his door in the next room. The pizza had arrived.

I glanced out the window of my room while Felix dealt with Domino's, my new gun drawn in case it was a trap. It wasn't Charley, but it would do for now.

Felix returned with a large pepperoni pizza and a six-pack of Dr Pepper. My stomach growled audibly and I forgot about Cassandra and her missing kids while I dealt with the first item on Maslow's hierarchy of needs.

Twenty minutes later I was ready to work again. "We were talking about the kids, Felix. If Howard Bellamy didn't think the kids were Randolph's, probably Randy didn't either. In fact, Howard didn't even think they were Cassy's. Why did they take them? Whose kids were they? Why did Cassy have them?"

"Good question, Boss. Maybe she couldn't have kids but always wanted them? Lots of women adopt, or use surrogates, if they can't have their own."

"But why would Randy fight her for custody if he knew they weren't his?"

"Who says he did?"

"What?"

"I said, who says he did? How do we know he has custody? You said before, everything Andrew told you was a lie. Everything Cassy told you conflicts with what Andrew says. How do we know any of them, Andrew, Cassy, or Howard, told you anything but a crock?"

For the thousandth time, I thanked God I had hired Felix. "That's it, Felix!" I exclaimed. "I have to assume that everything is a lie. That's where I've been going wrong, I keep trying to believe what they tell me, instead of finding my own facts." I jumped up from the bed and began pacing the room.

"But Boss, how can you find any facts on these people? We don't even really know who Andrew Field is."

"Oh, jeez, how could I forget? Felix, where is that briefcase I gave you today? Andrew's passport is in it!"

"Sorry, Boss, I left it in the car. I'll go get it."

Felix pulled his car key out of his pocket and walked outside to the parking lot behind the building.

The sudden wave of apprehension I felt as I watched him go was justified a minute later when he returned, empty-handed. "It's gone," he said simply. "I'm really sorry, Boss. It's all my fault. I should have brought it in with me."

Chapter 14

IT WAS GONE, ALL RIGHT. THE SIDE WINDOW had been smashed. I doubted it was random burglary, either. I noticed a video camera on the rear seat of the car in the next stall. It was untouched, and Felix assured me that the other car had been there before he parked. It could mean only one thing. Someone knew we were there.

And I was willing to bet that only Andrew Field knew what was in that briefcase, and knew which car was Felix's. That belief kept me from feeling like we were personally in danger, and it also comforted me to know that if Andrew was able to retrieve his briefcase, he must be all right.

And that knowledge made me instantly angry.

"Damn him!"

"Who, Boss?"

"Andrew, that's who! That louse, that son of a bitch, that asshole, that lying, scheming, motherfucking – "

"Okay, okay, I get it," Felix cut me off, grabbing my arm and steering me back to the room.

"Damn him! That son of a bitch!" I was starting to repeat myself, but the frustration and stress of the preceding twenty-four hours were starting to catch up with me.

"Boss, I'm really sorry about this," Felix began, but I stopped him, guiltily realizing that he was blaming himself unjustly.

"Stop it, Felix. It's not your fault. We should have been safe here. I can't imagine how he found us. I am sort of relieved to realize it must have been Andrew, though. Although if I ever lay eyes on the sonofabitch again, I'll shoot his balls off."

Felix smiled. "No, you won't. I know you better than that."

And he was right, of course. We decided to call it a night since there was nothing else to be done at the moment. Felix retired to his room and I was left alone with my dripping shower.

I didn't know what time it was when he arrived. I had fallen asleep having noticed that the dripping of the shower was timed perfectly with the flashing of the neon horse. It was like a Chinese water torture with a simultaneous light show. Only by covering my head with a pillow did I finally fall asleep.

He awakened me gently, prodding my shoulder with the barrel of what turned out to be my own gun before my catlike instincts bothered informing me that danger had arrived and already had the upper hand. He had apparently lifted the pillow from my head and relieved me of my gun while I had continued snoring.

I groggily rolled to face him. "What the hell do you think – " was all I got out before a masculine hand that smelled faintly of Ivory soap covered my mouth. A flashlight shined into my eyes, preventing me from seeing his face. I tried to push him away, but found he was sitting on one hand, and the other was tangled in the covers. I was stuck.

I did the only reasonable thing, under the circumstances. I bit his hand as hard as I could, which wasn't very hard considering all I could do was graze my teeth across the flattened palm. In the process I bit my own lip.

"Damn it, Angela, it's me!" he hissed. "Shhhh. I don't want to wake everybody, for pete's sake."

"Mell, yi stoo," I blubbered through his hand.

"What?" He pulled his hand back slightly.

"I said, well, I do!" I blurted. The hand smooshed back against my lips.

"Are you going to shut up or do I have to gag you?"

Finally my brain finished waking up and I recognized the voice. "Manfrew?" I mumbled.

"Yes, it's Andrew," he replied.

I finally freed a hand and pushed the flashlight aside. Around the edge of the blind spot I was left with, I could see it really was Andrew. When he realized I recognized him, he removed his hand from my mouth. I debated briefly whether I should kiss him or kill him, couldn't decide, did neither, and finally opted to simply sit up and abuse him verbally.

"Just what the fuck do you think you're doing," I hissed. "How dare you break in here like this!"

"Angela, shut up. You're in danger and I couldn't leave without warning you." He switched off the flashlight and set the gun on the foot of the bed.

"How the hell did you find me, anyway?"

"The same way they would have. These aren't amateurs you're dealing with, sister. There was a tracking device on Felix's car. The only reason there isn't one on yours is that they didn't realize the car I came to Phoenix in was yours. They put a tracker on both the rental cars, but not the Firebird. They probably followed your rental car all the way back to the airport where you rented it."

"Why didn't you tell me this earlier? You were obviously here a few hours ago, retrieving your briefcase. Why didn't you tell me then?"

"I followed Felix. As soon as he parked and came inside, I had to grab the briefcase and get the tracking device off his car and take it for a ride. If I'd let it stay still too long, they would have known where you were. Actually, it's probably in the next county by now. I stuck it to a freight car about five miles up the line. I had to leave them a trail of crumbs to follow so I'd have time to come back and warn you."

"Andrew," I said, looking at him intently now that the spots were gone from my vision. "Who the hell are 'they'? What is going on?"

"Angela, you've got to trust me. You have to get out of here. Go back home, leave tonight, right now. Take Felix with you. And forget you ever met me. I think I'll be okay, but you won't if you don't drop this case right now. I never should have gotten you involved. I know that now, even though I still don't know if Cassy knew that I – " he broke off without finishing the sentence.

"That you what? What is this big secret you're keeping, Andrew? How can I help you if you won't tell me the truth?"

He shook his head, and in the light from the flashing neon horse, I once again saw that little half-smile that had so captivated me just a few days before, only this time it held sorrow, not amusement. "You can't help me, Angela. Not anymore. There's no turning back now. I don't know if I'll live through it, but enough have died already. First Cassy, then – " He stopped again and turned his face away from me. I saw his shoulders convulse once.

I reached out a hand, touched his shoulder, felt him stiffen, then relax. Without turning back to me, he stood up. "I have to go now. Please, do what I said. Get out of here. Now. Before it's too late." To my complete shock, he turned back, bent to kiss me quickly, then with the silence and grace of a cat, he crossed the room, cracked open the door, glanced out, and was gone.

I threw back the covers, planning to follow him, but immediately remembered that I slept in the nude. Client or not, I wasn't going to run after him in my birthday suit. Shivering slightly in the night air, I pulled on some clothes and pounded on the door to Felix's room.

"Felix! Wake up!" I turned the knob and peeked in. Felix had somewhat more decorum than I do – he was wearing pajamas. He rolled to face me, groggily.

"What? It can't be morning already."

"Andrew just left. Get up. Something's happened and we need to find out what." I turned back to my own room, giving Felix time to waken and get out of bed. I switched on all the lights and turned on the laptop, which had been quietly charging itself for the whole three hours I had been sleeping before Andrew's arrival.

Felix shuffled through the door in bare feet, rubbing his eyes. "What happened?"

"Andrew let something slip that I think we can follow up on. He said something about too many people having died already. He said 'First Cassy, then – ' and he stopped. I think he almost cried again. Someone else must have died since Cassy, someone he cared about. We need to find out who. There has to be something on the system." I didn't mention that he had kissed me goodbye. I was starting to wonder if I'd imagined it.

Felix was now wide awake. "Gotcha. Let me at it." He sat on the lone chair at the edge of the dresser, pulled the phone cord off the telephone and plugged in the modem. With the laptop on his knees, he signed onto PRICS and started a search for deaths reported in the past few days.

I felt it only appropriate that I help him out since I had just roused him from a much-needed sleep – so I found the tiny foil packet of instant coffee the motel so thoughtfully provided for its tired travelers, ran the bathroom faucet until the water reached a temperature three degrees above tepid, and made Felix a cup of coffee in the glass I found by the ice bucket.

He actually drank it.

About five minutes later, after I had paced a path between the bathroom and the front window about ninety times, he beckoned me to the laptop to see what he had found.

My stomach turned when I read the brief report of a shooting death. A seven-year-old boy whose description matched that of the older boy I had seen in the Bellamy yard had been shot and killed two days ago by a sniper at a gas station about three miles from the Bellamy home. He had just used the restroom at the Shell station and was killed as he came out of the bathroom at the rear of the building. The gunshot had been heard, but was presumed to be a backfire from the service bay. A station attendant saw a man he assumed was the boy's grandfather walk around back, then return to his car and drive away in a big hurry without getting his change. The attendant found the body a few minutes later and called police. By that point, five minutes had passed since the gunshot and the assailant was long gone. There were no clues and no suspects. They didn't even know who the boy was. All the attendant remembered was that there was a Golden Retriever in the back of the Cadillac sedan with another little boy.

Was Brian Bellamy dead? First Cassy, now her son? Or was he her son? I glanced up at the picture of the horse family again. Whose kid could he be, if not Cassandra Bellamy's?

"Oh, hell, Felix!" I exclaimed. "Why didn't I make the connection before? Cassandra used to date a baby broker! She must have gotten the kids from him! And Andrew is caught up in this because he has evidence against the guy!" I started pacing again, agitated, something was right on the tip of my brain, but I couldn't shake it off. There was something I knew, but I hadn't yet put it together. "Felix, we need to focus on the kids. All the kids in this case. There's got to be a connection between Andrew and the kids!"

Felix worked on making a list of what we knew about each of Cassy's children while I racked my brains, still fuzzy from lack of sleep, trying to remember – something. It continued to elude me. I started packing. We weren't going to be there much longer, and it looked like I was done sleeping for the night anyway. Felix grimaced once when he saw what I was doing and understood the implication. At least he had had a full night's sleep last night while I was trussed up like a turkey in that farmhouse.

Farmhouse. Farmhouse. What was it Farmer John's wife had been babbling about while I ate her sausages? Something about the farmhouse where I had been tied up belonging to an obstetrician. Kids playing on the old tree all the time. Riding ponies. Something like that. I had ignored her while she talked about it, but apparently my subconscious had picked up enough for me now to wonder why a busy doctor would entertain patients at his farmhouse often enough for the neighbors to notice.

Farmer John had ties to McKenzie. McKenzie had orchestrated my abduction. McKenzie had taken me to that farmhouse. The locks had been intact. He didn't break the door down to get in. He must have had a key. Could he be the "obstetrician" who entertained the kids at the farmhouse on the weekends?

Andrew had said McKenzie was an imposter. Andrew also called Farmer John "Pop." What was going on?

Felix had the list ready, showing what we had learned, whether truth or fiction, about the three Bellamy children, Brian, Jason, and Michelle. It was quickly obvious that most of what dear old Grandpa Bellamy had told me must have been untrue. I wondered if he had suspected I was an investigator and fed me a meal of red herring. Had he known Cassy was dead? Had he told me she was living at Andrew's place in order to get me over there to find the body and set up Andrew as a suspect more quickly?

How had they vacated the Bellamy house so quickly -- lock, stock, and Golden Retriever? For that matter, had the living room been staged for my arrival with a few pictures and props that could easily be whisked away when it was time to move on?

Was that why I felt so much like I had been on a Hollywood stage set at both Andrew's house and at the Bellamy house?

Who was the director of this drama? I had already realized it certainly wasn't me, and didn't appear to be Andrew, either.

"There's another kid involved, Felix," I remembered. "Andrew took care of Delgado's kid for a while. But he says he doesn't know where he is now. He'd be about seven, same age as Brian."

"Don't see what it has to do with Cassy, but we ought to put him on the list, too," Felix concurred. "Did he tell you the kid's name?"

"Yeah, you had the recorder. Did I think to mention it?"

Felix switched the computer to another screen where he had transcribed the notes. "Ryan," he answered. "You said it was Ryan Delgado."

"Ryan? That doesn't sound right, Felix. Are you sure it was Ryan?"

"Well, that's what it sounded like, but you were driving while you dictated and there was some engine noise in the background."

Duh. I couldn't believe I'd been so dense. "Felix, it wasn't Ryan. It was Brian. Delgado's kid is also named Brian."

Chapter 15

THE SUN WAS JUST COMING UP when we arrived at the office of John Smith, Attorney at Law and suspected "baby broker." The office was in a small complex, with each office door opening onto a common courtyard. According to the sign, the hours were nine to four, Monday through Friday. A quick stroll through the complex revealed that none of the other tenants were early birds. I felt safe jimmying the lock and entering the office.

The office next door was an OB/GYN. I hoped we would find what we were looking for without having to also rifle the office of the man who might be the doctor who provided the babies.

Felix turned on the copy machine so it would be warmed up if we needed it, then sat at the computer while I took the old-fashioned approach, rummaging through the file cabinets. It did not take me long to find what I was looking for: records of adoption of two children by Cassandra Baxter. Contrary to Grandpa Bellamy's red herring, they both were adopted at the same time. Cassy had never "gone home" to Mother to have any of her children. Nobody had seen Cassy pregnant because Cassy had never pretended to be pregnant. The adoptions predated Andrew's employment at Computech by only a few weeks, which I felt somehow helped confirm the suspicion that Brian Bellamy and Brian Delgado were the same child. Which also meant that Cassy's alleged marriage, to whoever really was her alleged husband, had been childless until just a few months before it allegedly ended in divorce. By now I was convinced that the older daughter had been the husband's, not hers, and this was why she had only mentioned two children the day she came to see me.

Why had the ex taken the children? And, who really was Cassy's ex? Howard or Randolph? According to the adoption file, Cassy was unmarried at the time of the adoption. The marital status box was checked "Divorced" and listed the rancher's son as her ex.

Felix made a noise, some sort of gasp, and I spun around from the files. He was staring intently at the computer screen, which amazingly enough had not required a password to access it. "What did you find?" I asked.

He hit a few keys and walked over to the printer instead of answering. Then he handed me a single sheet of paper which turned out to be a copy of a letter written the day we had all come to Phoenix. I scanned it quickly, then grabbed the file I had found and photocopied the contents. "Let's get out of here," I said, returning the file to its place, closing and locking the cabinet as I had found it while Felix turned off the equipment.

We slipped quietly through the door and left the complex without being seen. As we pulled out, we realized we had had a fairly close call, as a pickup truck loaded with lawn mowers and tools pulled in just as we turned the corner. Another two minutes' delay and we would have been caught by the gardeners.

"Can you believe it?" Felix asked once we were underway.

"I have to believe it. It's the only thing so far that has made any sense." I pulled into a parking lot a few blocks from the office we had just rifled and stopped the car.

I took another look at the letter that had bolted us from the building. It was actually a fax memo, addressed to "Gilbert," that stated that "Andy" had been located and needed to be "dealt with" before he had a chance to learn the location of "the child in question." It gave the description and license number of *my car* and said that he was clearly on his way to Phoenix. It also said that the matter needed to be taken care of quickly, as "Fred" was arriving at six a.m. Monday to bring the money and "Andy" had better not be in a position to interfere.

It had been five forty-five a.m. on Monday when Felix and I had bolted from the office.

Who could have known Andrew had my car? I hadn't even reported it to the police. The only possibility was that someone had been tailing Andrew back home, and had phoned ahead with his whereabouts.

"Felix, it's obvious that this John Smith is the baby broker that Andrew planned to testify against."

"Right, Boss," Felix replied.

"But if that's the case, why would the writer of this fax have expressed concern that Andrew be iced before he learned the location of the child, which I presume must be Brian Delgado? Wouldn't he have been more concerned about wiping Andrew before he could testify?"

"Yes, unless they didn't need to worry about his testifying as long as the kid was hidden. Maybe they were holding that over him to keep him quiet."

I considered that for a moment. "Yes, that would tie in with the blackmail angle. Andrew said he was being blackmailed. Somehow they must have gotten the kid out of his custody and threatened to ice the kid if Andrew testified."

Felix snorted. "Then why did they kill the kid the other day? Now Andrew has no reason not to testify."

That threw a new light on things, and I did not have an answer immediately. Then I thought of another angle. "Felix, that kid was Delgado's kid. Delgado was a mobster. Maybe the kid was iced, not because of Andrew, but because of Delgado."

"Not the mob's style, Boss," Felix argued. "The mob doesn't usually hit kids to pay back their daddies."

"No, just chop the heads off their horses, I suppose," I retorted. "Just because it isn't generally done doesn't mean it couldn't be done."

"Anything's possible," Felix conceded. "It's also possible the kid was hit by accident. Maybe the target was Randolph or Howard and the kid got in the way. I know the police report didn't read that way, but it didn't sound like they had any real witnesses."

I glanced at the dash clock, started the engine, and drove back toward the office complex. The only vehicle in the lot was the gardener's truck. The gardeners were not in sight. I drove down a half block and parked in a location that gave me a view of the driveway into the office complex.

I didn't have to wait long. Exactly at the stroke of six a.m., a vehicle turned into the driveway. It was a blue Ford pickup truck, and it was driven by "Farmer John," whose wife had fed me lousy sausages for breakfast just the day before. A minute later, Gilbert McKenzie arrived in the same gray government sedan in which I had been kidnapped the night before that.

I filled Felix in, remembering that he had not seen either man before. "Now all we need is John Smith himself and we'll know who all the principals are."

I suppose I should have been more surprised that when "John Smith, Attorney at Law" arrived for his six a.m. meeting in a light green Cadillac, he turned out to be the man I knew as Howard Quincy Bellamy.

Chapter 16

"GRANDPA HOWARD," I MURMURED. "I should have known."

"Howard?" Felix responded, puzzled. "You mean as in Howard Bellamy?"

"Yup." I nodded toward the Cadillac. "That's the man who fed me that meal of red herring the other day. That's the car that was in the garage there."

"What do you suppose it all means, Boss? Why would Howard Bellamy be hooked up with McKenzie and Farmer John?"

"It's the kids, Felix. As John Smith, he placed those kids with the Bellamys. We think we know where Brian came from, but we don't know where he got Jason, the six-year-old. When Cassy was killed, he was on the spot to pick them up. Maybe he killed Cassy, or knew it was going to happen, or knew right after it happened."

"But where is her ex-husband? How did Smith get the kids away from him?"

"He's probably mixed up in this, too, if he exists at all. After all, nothing has come up on PRICS suggesting that he reported the kids missing, has it? But I've never seen him. In fact, we really don't know if he exists. He might be as phony as the rest of them. Maybe he's Andrew," I added with a short laugh.

Felix was watching the three men shake hands, lock their car doors, and walk into the courtyard. After they disappeared from view, he said thoughtfully, "Boss, if Howard Bellamy a.k.a. John Smith took the kids from Cassy's house after her death, and Brian was killed that same day, and now Howard is here, doesn't that mean that Jason and the Golden Retriever must be here, too?"

It was an angle I hadn't thought of, but had to admit was likely. Where would Howard have stashed the kid and dog? If he was really John Smith, Attorney, he must have a home somewhere in the Phoenix area. "Check the directory, Felix. Under John Smith. God knows how many you'll come up with, but maybe one or two will say 'attorney' and we can cut down the search that way."

"Righto, Boss," Felix replied, and pulled out the laptop, plugging it into the car phone system. I kept watching the building. A few minutes later he had the results. "There are three John Smiths listed in the greater Phoenix area that have an attorney designation in the file."

"Any of them live in this area?"

"There's one in Scottsdale and another one in Paradise Valley."

"How far are they from this location? He probably wouldn't live too far from his office."

"The Paradise Valley address is about six miles away. You think that could be it?"

"Try running all the license plates first. Chances are, they're all lease cars anyway, but you never know."

Felix dug out the binoculars and quickly jotted down all the license plate numbers before returning to the keyboard. "No luck," he said. "John Smith's plate is registered to Howard Bellamy with the Colorado address, so that's definitely the same car you saw in the garage. Farmer John's plate is registered to Fred Gaines at an address that sounds like that farmhouse, out on the west side. McKenzie's plate doesn't come up at all. Could be bogus or could be government. Could be a stolen plate, too. Wouldn't be hard at all to pinch one off a government vehicle in a storage yard somewhere."

"Tough part is deciding which car to follow when they leave. I think my money is on Bellamy/Smith. Maybe he'll lead us to the kid."

"And then what, Boss?" Felix asked. "What will you do if you find the kid? You have no evidence that a crime was committed. You don't really even know for sure that the kid who was killed is the one you saw at Cassy's."

"It has to be, Felix, but you're right, I'll never be able to prove it to the cops." I started the engine, as the three men had returned to their cars and were preparing to drive away. "But if we find the kid and dog, at least I can tell Andrew when I see him again. As much as I know he's lied through his teeth to me, he's the only one of this bunch that I'm reasonably sure hasn't killed anyone yet."

Where the certainty came from, I'll never know, but as the words left my mouth, I knew I believed them with all my heart. André/Andrew Field/Beauchamp/Martin, or whatever his name was, might be a liar, thief, kidnapper, and great hunk of beefcake, but he was not a murderer.

I didn't get a chance to follow the Cadillac because it pulled out first and I didn't dare pull out behind it since I knew I would be seen by McKenzie, who knew my car. I was in no mood for that short piece of bad news in a bad suit. I didn't need to follow Farmer John, so I turned the opposite direction and drove around the block before setting out for the Paradise Valley address of John Smith, attorney.

It wasn't hard to find, but the Cadillac was not in the driveway when I got there. I supposed it likely could be in the four-car garage, but I had no way to find that out. I wasn't quite ready to knock on the door, since I had no idea what I would say to him. "Grandpa Howard? Fancy seeing you again. I was just auditing the census records of this neighborhood and wanted to ask if there are any children or dogs living with you right now." Right.

Instead I circled around to see if there were an alley in the exclusive neighborhood, and found to my amazement that there was. I guess rich folks aren't that keen on having garbage cans in front of their homes. Of course, this alley was paved and clean. The trash cans were all primly displayed on concrete slabs. All the fences were identical block fences, painted a uniform shade of southwestern beige.

I drove down the alley with my window down until I reached the correct house, third from the end. Two dogs barked at me, but the yard I was most interested in was silent. Of course, Golden Retrievers are such friendly dogs anyway, and this one wouldn't have had time to feel territorial about this yard yet, so I knew I was going to have to look over the fence. The challenge was going to be to do it without drawing suspicion from occupants or neighbors.

Luckily there was a hedge growing up over one corner. I turned to Felix. "Shall I boost you up, or do you want to boost me?"

He snorted. "Are you kidding? I'll boost you, thank you very much. If I show this ethnic face over the top of a fence in a neighborhood like this I'm liable to get arrested, if not just shot outright. Just say 'Here, kitty, kitty,' while you look over and nobody will blink an eye at you."

Sounded like a good enough ploy to me. He interlocked his fingers and braced them against his thigh and I stepped up. The fence was only six feet high, so I was able to look over without any trouble. Peering through the oleanders, I was just able to catch a glimpse of the Golden Retriever, sleeping on the back steps. He didn't even look up at me.

I quickly jumped back down and we climbed in the car and left. As far as I knew, I had been unobserved.

"Well," I said after we emerged from the alley. "Now we know where the kid and dog are. We know Howard is John Smith. I'll bet money that if we were to check the ownership of that farmhouse they left me tied up in, we'll find it belongs to that obstetrician with the office next to Smith's, unless Mrs. Farmer Gaines is also a liar."

"Wouldn't it be a hoot if it turned out it belonged to Andrew Field?"

I gave him a sour look. "Not very funny, Felix," I chided him. "But on the outside chance you're right, get on the computer and find out."

He switched the laptop back on and logged onto PRICS. How did investigators ever get along in the days before PRICS, I wondered? A few minutes later, Felix said, "Well, you were almost right. It belongs to Smith."

"So how did Andrew and short shit get in there to leave me the other night? There's no way that Howard Bellamy a.k.a. John Smith could have been there. If he was, they know who I am and why I'm here." I thought hard a moment. Like everything else about this case, nothing made any sense. Howard must have known I was not a census auditor that morning, or how would he have known exactly what lies to feed me to get me to Andrew's house? Most likely he knew exactly who I was, also that I was working for Andrew.

Dumbo had shown up at the coffee shop that morning and was immediately accepted by Andrew. Later, after he and Andrew had collectively kidnapped me and left me in the farmhouse, Andrew came to pick me up, supposedly to save me from McKenzie, whom he said was an imposter.

If McKenzie was a "bad guy," why didn't he kill me, and maybe Andrew, at the farmhouse? Andrew had said McKenzie was trying to kill us both. Why was Andrew left free to move around and come to my rescue?

Or had he escaped from McKenzie himself? He did have my gun to help him.

Assuming Andrew was telling the truth about McKenzie, Farmer Gaines had helped Andrew save me from McKenzie. Why was Farmer Gaines now meeting in perfect amity with McKenzie and John Smith, a.k.a. Howard Bellamy?

And why did Andrew call Gaines "Pop"?

Suddenly I remembered something that made me veer the car to the side of the road and stop.

"What's up, Boss?" Felix asked.

"Felix, we just witnessed a payoff of some kind, right?"

"Based on the letter we found, yes."

"What was being paid for? What is it Smith buys and sells?"

Felix stared at me. I held his gaze for only a moment before checking traffic and making a U turn. "Kids," Felix finally said. "He sells kids. And we know he has one."

"Right. And he was supposed to have two of them."

"So who's the buyer?"

"Probably a nice rich couple in Scottsdale. Or Boston. Who knows how well connected these guys are. Maybe McKenzie is an agent for a buyer."

"Then what was Gaines doing there?"

"Who knows," I said, wondering what I was going to do when I got back to Smith's house. "Keeping them honest? Maybe he gets a finder's fee? Maybe he's partnered with Smith?"

"Maybe he hands off the kids?"

"If that's the case, Felix, he should have followed Smith home."

"Would you transact business like that at home?"

I turned onto Smith's street in time to see a green Cadillac drive away from Smith's home. I couldn't see Jason, but in the back seat, I could see a familiar blond head. A moment later, a window was lowered and the blond head stuck out the window, ears blowing in the breeze, tongue hanging out, while inside the car an excited tail wagged.

Dogs love to go for a ride. As I tucked into traffic to follow, I wondered where this ride would end.

Chapter 17

I STAYED WITH SMITH UNTIL HE TURNED onto a farm road on the west side of town, the road leading to the house where I had been held captive. Surely he wasn't going to leave a six-year-old boy there alone! I found a place to park where the car would not be seen from the farmhouse and turned off the engine.

"What now, Boss?" Felix asked.

"We wait." I pulled a pair of binoculars from my purse and trained them on the house. I watched John Smith lead a small boy inside the house after tying one end of a rope to the dog and the other end to a post on the porch. He was inside for about five minutes, then he came out and got into the car.

As soon as I saw him start to turn the car around, I started the engine and pulled back onto the road. I drove in the direction of Gaines' farmhouse until I saw Smith's Cadillac emerge from the driveway behind me and turn back the way it had come. I stopped.

"He left the kid, Felix, but did he leave him alone, or was someone waiting?"

"There weren't any other cars," Felix noted.

"I know, but Gaines could have brought his wife there earlier, maybe to clean the place up."

"Do you think she's in on this?"

I remembered that she had been babbling on about the kids next door while her husband wasn't in the room. Maybe she didn't know what was going on. It was Gaines who had given me the wrong address, and his wife had not been present when I used the phone.

"Maybe, maybe not. She could be in on it without knowing there's an 'it' to be in on."

"Huh?"

"She could be helping them without knowing they're doing something wrong. Like, maybe she's been asked to babysit Jason for an hour. She may not know he's being sold. Chances are the kid doesn't know it. Smith probably does enough legitimate adoptions that nobody would question it unless someone reported an abduction. If the kid is an orphan, who's to complain that he gets a home and doesn't have to be institutionalized like a lot of them? This is a little blond boy. Probably has blue eyes, too. Worth a fortune to someone, no doubt. But there's nobody to look out for him."

"Except us?"

I looked at Felix, torn between conscience and duty. "We have no evidence, Felix. We don't know there's anything wrong with Jason being here. Other than Smith lying about who he was when he was masquerading as Howard Quincy Bellamy, what proof do we have that he's anything but a legitimate lawyer, transacting a legitimate adoption? It might not even be an adoption. Maybe it's a custody battle."

"So you're going to do nothing?"

"I didn't say that. I just want you to understand that if we move in and take the kid, we are the ones who will be going to jail if it turns out this is legit after all."

"Can't we call the police?"

"And tell them what? That we broke into a lawyer's office and found a note with no last names on it that talks about someone picking up money? That we saw two kids and a dog in Clarkdale, think one of the kids is dead, and have found one kid and a dog here and we think – what is it we think, Felix? I don't even understand this myself. How can we explain it to the police?"

Felix sighed. "Got it, Boss. We need more info."

"We can keep that house under surveillance, though, and try to see if the kid is alone. If we can establish the kid is alone, that's child endangerment, and we'll call the cops and keep an eye on the kid until they get here. Is that fair enough?"

Felix seemed satisfied with that plan and I turned the car around. I needed to find a place to hide it, but short of running it into an irrigation ditch, I didn't see any way to get it out of sight. The Valley of the Sun is pretty much flat as a pancake, with no hills to hide behind, and the roads are mostly all straight as an arrow. A car parked on the side of a road could be seen for miles. A half-mile down the road, a side street leading to another farm appeared. I turned down it, drove about a quarter mile and parked as far to the side as I could. We were now less than a mile away from the abandoned farmhouse where little Jason was being kept.

The cotton crop in the field wasn't much cover, but it was better than nothing. A nice tall corn crop would have been better cover, but we weren't in Kansas, Toto. In Arizona, cotton was king.

An irrigation ditch ran along one edge of the field leading toward the abandoned house. Luckily, it was empty and dry, and Felix and I had no trouble using it for cover as we quickly made our way to the farmhouse. Weeds growing up at the far end of the ditch provided a camouflage while we surveyed the scene and tried to decide what to do next.

The house was about thirty yards from the end of the ditch. The dog was still tied to the porch, but had lain down in the shade. It was a warm day and he was panting. I noticed there was no water provided for him, and I wondered if that was a sign that John Smith didn't care about the welfare of the animal, or if it was a sign that he didn't expect the dog to be there very long.

We could hear no sounds from the house, but I took that as proof of nothing due to the distance. Unless Jason was screaming, I wouldn't expect to hear anything. Sweat ran down my brow and I wished Andrew had picked some place other than Phoenix to get involved in … whatever he was involved in. It may be only April, but it had to be nearly a hundred degrees already. I watched the dog pant and began to wish I had some water – for him and for me.

"Well, Boss," Felix finally whispered. "What are we going to do? You want me to try to get up to the house?"

"Too much risk you'll be seen, Felix. There's nothing between here and the house but an empty driveway."

"Wait a minute," he said. "Other than Andrew, none of these people have seen me, right?"

"As far as we know."

"What if I just drove in there, like I was looking for the way to the farm we're sitting on? Either someone will come out to see what I'm doing, in which case I'll play dumb tourist, or nobody will come out, which will give you a chance to use the cover of the car to get to the house while I'm turning around in the driveway."

I looked at Felix, who was seeming like more of a partner and less of a secretary all the time, and said, "You know, it just might work." After all, I would be right there with a gun in case anything went wrong. "Cover the license plate, just in case they think the car is familiar. I have several sets in the back. Use the Nevada plates."

"Right-o, Boss. Be back in a few minutes." With that, he was jogging back up the irrigation ditch while I continued to watch the house for any signs of life.

It was about twenty minutes before I saw the car turn into the end of the driveway. The only sign of life from the house so far had been the dog standing up, turning around three times, then lying back down on his other side.

Felix approached the house slowly and I watched the windows for any sign that someone was watching his approach. One curtain parted slightly, then dropped again. Had it been Jason? Mrs. Gaines? Someone else?

I held my breath while Felix pulled alongside the house. Would anyone come out onto the porch? The dog stood up and started barking, wagging his tail as if hopeful that whoever was in the car might give him some attention, or at least some water.

Felix has balls, I'll say that for him. Apparently not satisfied with the lack of response, he stopped the car in a position where I could no longer see the windows, but which also meant nobody in the house would be able to see me, and got out.

He walked boldly to the front door and knocked. While he created his diversion, I crawled out of the ditch and crept along the ground until I was next to the car. Felix had thoughtfully left the windows down, and I was able to hear when the door was opened and Felix asked, "Is your mommy or daddy here?"

Jason. Jason must have answered the door. At least he wasn't tied up or in a closet somewhere.

I heard a child's voice answer but couldn't make out the words. I decided to make a run for the house and started to emerge from behind the Firebird, crouched over, ready to dash to the side of the house.

Then I was brought up short by the sight of someone else creeping around from the rear of the house, gun drawn, sliding stealthily around to the porch.

While little Jason distracted Felix at the door, a man was about to get the drop on him from the side of the porch.

There was no chance to warn Felix, and by this point I wasn't sure what to warn him about.

The man creeping toward him was none other than Andrew Field.

Chapter 18

I STOOD UP AND LEVELED MY OWN GUN. "Put 'em up. And I mean now," I said loudly.

He froze, turned toward me, saw who it was, and put his gun down. "Oh, it is you," he said. "I thought that was your car, but when I didn't see you driving it, I thought maybe McKenzie got you."

As if I would ever let Dumbo get the drop on me again. With my ego appropriately bruised by Andrew's lack of confidence in me, I twitched my gun. "Get them up. You know the routine."

He half-complied, holstering the gun and holding his hands up about shoulder high. "You need to get out of here or you're going to ruin everything, Angela," he said.

"Felix!" I called. "Look who I found."

Felix left the doorway and stuck his head around the edge of the porch. "Just like a bad penny," he commented. Behind him, Jason emerged from the house and sat on the porch, hugging his dog.

"You've got to get out of here now," Andrew repeated. "You can't be here when they get here and they're due any minute. And put that gun away. You'll scare the kid."

"Who are 'they,' Andrew?" I asked, leaving my gun where it was. "John Smith, attorney at law, a.k.a. Howard Quincy Bellamy? Or Fred Gaines, a.k.a. Farmer John, a.k.a. 'Pop'? Or maybe Gilbert McKenzie, whose real name I have yet to discover, Mister André Martin, a.k.a. Andrew Field?"

"I guess you've been doing your homework," he conceded. "I don't have time to explain. Just get out of here now. I'm trying to save this kid from his brother's fate…." He broke off, suddenly realizing he had given me some information.

"This kid Jason is Brian Delgado's brother?"

"Geez, you even know the kid's name?"

"There are still lots of things I don't know. Right now I'm inclined to take the kid, call the cops, and have them come pick up you and the kid. They can sort it out down at the station. I have reason to think Jason is in danger, especially seeing the company he's being forced to keep."

"Angela, I'm trying to get Jason out of danger, but if you don't get out of here, you're going to blow the whole thing."

"You're not handing that kid off to some baby buyer, Andrew."

"I'm planning to hand the kid off to his own mother, Angela."

"Yeah, right," I said with disgust. "Tell me another one. Your nose is gonna grow."

"I'm telling the truth."

"If you are, it's the first time, ever, so don't expect me to believe it. I think there's room in my car for all four of us and the dog, so let's get out of here. You can leave the mother a note, if you're telling the truth, and give her my car phone number. She can call when she gets here. If you can convince me you're telling the truth, maybe we'll let her take the kid. Maybe not. This whole thing smells pretty fishy right now, and I don't think it's because I just crawled out of an irrigation ditch."

We sped away from the farmhouse a few minutes later, Felix, Jason, and the dog crammed into the back seat, Andrew in the front with me.

After turning onto the main road, I drove back toward town, stopping at the first gas station I found, where I turned the car so I could watch the road from both directions. I left the car running so the air conditioner would work and faced Andrew. "Okay, Andrew, spill it. What's going on? The whole truth."

"I can't tell you."

"Fine," I said, putting the car in gear, "we'll go to the police."

He pushed the gearshift back into Park. "Okay, okay."

"How much does you-know-who know about what's going on?" I asked, twitching my head toward the back seat.

"He's been taken care of by people who care about him until his mother could come for him."

"He know about his brother?"

"Yes."

"Who hit his brother?"

"Enemies of his father."

"How do you know this one will be any safer?"

Andrew sighed. "The feds are involved."

"Like they were involved with you?"

He nodded.

"And you got shot. Oh, yeah, he'll be safe."

"It's too complicated to explain, Angela."

"Oh, I know it's complicated, Andrew. I could make a career out of figuring out how many aliases you all use, and that's just the beginning. Try me anyway."

"Angela, if I tell you too much, you'll be in danger, too."

"If you don't tell me enough, I'm in more danger already," I retorted. "Shoot. Or I will," I warned. Charley Number Two was in my lap and had been since we left the farmhouse.

"Okay, okay. I told you the truth about Cassandra originally. All that was true, about her coming on to me, getting fired, threatening me, the whole thing. What I didn't tell you is that I knew she was lying about having a husband and kids. I knew where her alleged kids had come from."

"John Smith."

"Yes. She didn't know that I was working with John Smith on a couple of very tricky placements."

"Involving Delgado's kids."

"Yes."

"You arranged for her to get Delgado's kids, then you arranged to get a job in her company so you could keep an eye on them."

"Right."

"Why did you blow the whistle on her at work?"

"If I didn't do something to stop her, she would have gotten me fired, and I needed to keep that job for a while. It would have been far more suspicious for me to have done nothing."

"Why didn't you just sleep with her?"

"I couldn't, Angela. I can't tell you why, but I couldn't."

From the back seat, Felix had been silent through this entire conversation, but suddenly he spoke up. "She was your sister, wasn't she."

Andrew twisted around in his seat, but Felix was on his side of the car and he couldn't make the eye contact he no doubt wanted. "How did you figure that out?"

"Her maiden name was Martin. Your passport is in the name Martin. Doesn't take a PhD in quantum physics to put two and two together and make four."

"So that's why her death shook you so much," I mused thoughtfully. I'd suspected she must have been a relative but had figured she was a cousin or niece.

Andrew sighed. "She was my sister."

"Did she know that?"

"No. We hadn't seen each other since I was about five."

"Why was that?"

"I was sold, through John Smith, to a couple in Phoenix."

"Don't tell me, let me guess. Fred Gaines and wife."

"Yes."

"Why are you still so friendly with Gaines?"

He shot me a look that told me the answer should have been obvious. "He's the only father I've known since I was five. He raised me."

"Sorry. You probably had no idea at the time."

"No. That's how these guys get away with it for so long, you know. The kids are usually so young they have no idea of escape. They give the kid some story about the parents being killed in a car accident or something. Usually the parents they end up with are fairly normal, loving people. It's their desperation to have children that drive them to people like John Smith. Usually, they think it's a legitimate adoption. The kids usually come from some kind of disrupted family, one without the resources to do any investigating, sometimes from parents who are relieved to get rid of the kid."

It was the most information he had volunteered in one breath since I'd met him and I wondered if he was finally being straight with me. "So what was your situation?"

"My situation is irrelevant," he replied. "But you may be screwing things up for Jason. His mother is scared to death, you know."

Something didn't feel right about this whole scenario and I didn't care if he knew it. It was time to ask the hard questions and hope to get some hard answers.

"You told me Brian was taken from his mother," I started. "Why would you give Jason back to her?"

"Her situation is straightened out now. The reason they took the kid is because of Delgado. With Delgado out of the picture now, she'll be safe. I told you the feds are involved. They're ready to move her and Jason somewhere safe, as soon as we get them back together."

"Somehow, Andrew," I said as I reached for the cell phone, which was ringing, "I don't think we'd find your idea of 'safe' in any dictionary. Hello?" This into the phone.

It was a female voice on the line. "Who are you?" she demanded rudely. "Where is my son?"

"Your son is safe, maybe for the first time in months, lady. Are you alone?"

"I'll answer no questions until I know who you are."

"My name is Angela Virago, and I'm a private investigator. I have your son with me right now. He's fine. I have reason to believe his life is in danger."

"Where is Andy? Andy was supposed to be with him."

"He's right here." I pushed the phone against Andrew's ear and said, "Say hello, Andrew."

"Hello, Sylvia," he said. "Jason's fine. I just have to convince this crazy lady that he'll be safe with you."

I pulled the phone away. "Sylvia, huh? Nice to meet you," I said. "I'll ask you again, are you alone?"

"Yes."

"Then come meet me." I asked what she was driving, then gave her directions to the gas station where we were and told her to drive there and wait. Then I pulled out and drove down the road, parking on the side of the road where I could watch the gas station.

A few minutes later, the white Dodge minivan pulled in and parked by the restrooms. I watched a blonde woman get out and look around. From where we were sitting, we could see both roads that made up the intersection for some distance. We were still pretty much on the outskirts of Phoenix, and there had been little traffic. I wondered idly how the gas station could afford to stay in business while I examined the few passing cars to see if the drivers showed any interest in Sylvia, or if they gave more than a casual glance my way when they reached my car.

Finally convinced that Sylvia had been telling the truth about being alone, I drove back to the gas station. "Jason," I said to the little boy who had been silently hugging his dog ever since we left the farmhouse, "do you know that woman?"

Felix released the little boy from his seat belt so he could stand up and see out the window. "Mommy!" he screamed. "That's my mommy!"

I shut off the engine, got out and pushed the seat forward so he could climb out of the tiny back seat. Felix restrained the dog from following. Jason ran straight to the woman, who bent down and swept the little boy into her arms. "Jason, oh, Jason," she sobbed.

"Mommy, where were you?"

"I've been looking for you, sweetheart. And now I've found you again."

I hadn't noticed Andrew getting out of the car, but now he approached the woman with a smile. "Hello, Sylvia. I'm glad to finally see you again."

"Thank you," she said softly, wiping tears from her eyes. "I know I never would have gotten him back without you."

I stood there silently, feeling like a complete fool by this point, but feeling a tug of tenderness toward the little boy. Too bad there had been nothing I could do for his brother.

Andrew patted Sylvia on the shoulder. "It was the least I could do, Sylvia. I wish I had known sooner how close they were. Is everything arranged?"

"Yes. I drive straight to – " she broke off, looking at me. "Who is this woman, Andrew? And why is she interfering?"

"She's all right, Sylvia. She's one of the good guys. She saved my life the other day. Anyway, she doesn't need to know anything else, so you better get going. I'll get Max."

It was the first time I had known the dog's name. "No, wait a minute," I said. I walked to the car and took the dog's leash from Felix, then led Max over to a faucet where I gave him a drink, using my cupped hand as a bowl. He drank thirstily for over a minute before he was satisfied. "Bless the beasts and children," I murmured, stroking his head once. Then I led him back to the minivan and handed the rope to Sylvia. "I hope you all make it, Sylvia."

She smiled at me for the first time. "I hope you do, too."

Andrew had buckled Jason into the back seat of the van while I watered the dog, and now the dog hopped in and licked the boy's face while Jason giggled. "Take care, Sylvia," Andrew said. "You know how to reach me if you need me again."

"Thanks for everything, Andy," she replied. Then, while I looked on in shocked jealousy, she put both arms around Andrew, kissed him full on the mouth, then got in the driver's seat and drove away without a backward glance.

"Fed them a meal once in awhile, huh?" I muttered when he walked over to my car. "I'll bet."

He didn't hear the comment. "Come on," Andrew said. "I need to go back to the farmhouse."

"Why?"

"Because I'm not supposed to have wheels, remember? Sylvia was supposed to come get the kid at ten o'clock, then thirty minutes later Gaines was going to come pick me up and take me back to McKenzie. I made a deal. If I'm not where I'm supposed to be, they may go after Sylvia. I need to be back in that farmhouse in ten minutes."

We got back in the car and I apologized to Felix, who had remained in the hot car mostly because it was such an ordeal for an adult to climb in and out of the narrow back seat area. "S'all right, Boss," he assured me. "At least now I can use the whole seat." He had turned sideways and was now sitting on my side of the car, the better to keep an eye on Andrew, I surmised.

I turned the key but to my dismay, the car refused to start. I tried repeatedly, while Andrew became increasingly agitated. "Damn it, Angela, I have to get back to that farmhouse!"

"Sorry, Andrew. It does this sometimes when it's hot. It'll start. Give it a minute."

"I don't have a minute," he replied. He looked over to the gas pumps, but there were no other cars there at the moment. I suppose he would have tried to bum a ride, but I was the only game in town at the moment.

I tried the key to no avail several times over the next five minutes. Finally, it fired up. "I told you it would start." I pulled out of the station and headed toward the farm.

Andrew looked at his watch. "We're going to be late. I can only hope they are, too."

I stomped the gas and the car shot ahead. I pushed it easily to eighty-five, where the speedometer pegs out, and held it there. We were only about four miles from the farm, but we were definitely cutting it close. Andrew breathed a sigh of relief when the farmhouse came into sight. "Thank God," he said as I swung into the driveway. "They're not here yet. Drive up there, drop me off, then keep going straight on the dirt road. Don't try to go back out the driveway or they'll see you when they pull in. There's another road down there, just keep driving and you'll –"

His voice cut off with a gasp. I slammed on the brakes, skidding to a halt on the dirt road, nearly sliding into the irrigation ditch that ran along the right edge of the drive. In the adjacent pasture, the two fat white mares galloped as fast as they could toward the other side of the field, fleeing from noise, smoke, flames, and flying debris.

The house had just blown up.

Without Andrew in it.

Chapter 19

I LOOKED OVER AT MY CLIENT and found him predictably as white as a sheet. I probably looked a little pale myself, and I usually enjoy this sort of thing. I flicked a glance at Felix in my rearview mirror. "Everyone okay?" I asked.

"Fine, Boss," Felix replied, rubbing his shoulder. Because he was sitting sideways on the rear seat, he had been using only the lap portion of the seat belt and his left shoulder had knocked against my seat back when I hit the brakes.

Andrew was staring mutely at the smoke and flames and did not answer my question. Debris floated gently from the sky, and a few splinters of wood settled onto my hood. Part of a door frame had landed in the road a few feet in front of the car. Had the car stopped straight instead of skewing to the side, I likely would have had a broken windshield.

"I trust you and the kid were the only ones in the house before we left," I said to Andrew as I put the car in gear and backed in a reverse U-turn across the dirt road.

"Yes," he replied numbly.

"Then we're out of here," I said. I hit the gas, spraying dirt and gravel from the rear tires as I drove back toward the main road. I turned left at the end of the driveway, toward the farm owned by Fred Gaines and his wife the bad cook.

Andrew realized where I was going and began to panic. "Where are you going? Are you nuts? They probably triggered the bomb from there."

"Just doing a quick drive-by to see who's here and who's not," I explained. The Gaines driveway was visible from the main road and I wasn't surprised to see Gilbert McKenzie's car parked by the house. Since it was facing the rear of the property, I surmised he had no suspicion that anyone would connect him to the bombing. Otherwise, the car would have been facing the road, ready for a quick getaway, and he would have already been in it, uh, getting away.

Andrew groaned when he saw the car. "I can't believe Pop would have been part of this," he said. "I knew McKenzie was gunning for me, but how did he get Pop to cooperate? He raised me!"

I drove about a half mile down the road and pulled over. "Maybe he didn't," I replied. "Maybe Gaines is…." My voice trailed off. Gaines was on a tractor, plowing a field behind the house. "Maybe Mrs. Gaines? Did she raise you, too?"

"The woman who raised me died three years ago. Are you saying there's another wife?"

"I assume so. She fed me breakfast the morning after you and short shit dumped me in that tinderbox back there."

"What does she look like?"

"Your basic elderly fat farm wife," I replied. "Plump, gray haired, matronly. Chatterbox. Went on and on about the farm next door, how the doctor who owned it used to bring kids over to ride a pony he had. Said the well went dry and they didn't see him much after that."

"Not her." He groaned again. "And Gaines is mixed up with her?"

"Appears so. I assumed she was his wife. Of course, at the time I was also assuming they were just a kindly farm couple who were playing straight with me. I wasn't looking for subterfuge, you know. I didn't know they were double crossing me until you showed up and took me away at gunpoint."

A fire truck roared by, siren wailing.

"So if she's not a farmer's wife, Andrew, who is she?"

And suddenly, he was the old Andrew Field once again. His face changed and I could almost see him closing a door in my face. Whatever he had let slip during the shock of realizing he had just survived a second attempt on his life was all I was going to get. The library was closed.

"Sorry," he said, and he almost sounded like he meant it. "You already know too much." He glanced back over at McKenzie's car, which remained arrogantly parked in plain sight by the farmhouse. "I have to get out of here," he continued. "I have to get a car."

I put my car into gear and turned north without speaking.

"Where we going now, Boss?" Felix asked. He had been uncharacteristically silent since the explosion.

"Home."

"Home?" he repeated.

"Home?" Andrew echoed.

"Home," I confirmed. "I think our work here is done. The kid is safe. My client is still alive. I have my car back. I'll have to do without

Charley, I guess, at least for a while longer. But while we're still all in one piece, I'm going home." I glanced over at Andrew. "Anyone who has a problem with that can get out and walk. Just say the word and I'll pull over."

There were nothing but cotton fields in various stages of growth for as far as the eye could see. I was pretty sure I would have no takers on my offer.

I continued driving for a few miles, then found a road that would lead to the interstate and turned right. At the interstate, I stopped at a gas station and filled the Firebird with Premium for the ride home.

"What's it going to be, Andrew?" I asked as I shut off the pump and closed the gas cap. "You with me or not?" I hung up the nozzle.

"I have to stay here," he replied. "I'm not going to steal your car again, Angela, but I'm asking you please to take me back there."

"Where? The farmhouse where I found you? You want to go back and wait for your ride to show up?"

"Not to the farmhouse. To Smith's office. It's on Tatum in Paradise Valley, the other side of town from here. I know it's asking a lot, but Angela, there's a lot more involved here than getting Jason Delgado back to his mother." He sighed. "And I'm still not safe." He shook his head. "I have to go contact … I can't tell you who." He touched my arm. "Please," he said, "I need your help."

I looked at his hand, lightly resting on my forearm, then up at his face and found in his eyes the same hunted look I had seen moments before I pulled the trigger in that diner two days ago. I felt the old feeling, that hormonal rush that had captured me the day I met him. I didn't know why I felt so protective of this man who only a few days ago had been a stranger. But I recognized a need in him, and in myself I felt a need to stay with it. I still didn't know the answers to too many questions. If I quit now, I would never know.

He was right. I had professional pride. And I couldn't walk out on him.

As I contemplated that reality while his hand lay on my arm, I heard a car backfire somewhere and flinched. The sound was too like a gunshot and was followed by a metallic ping somewhere to my right. The warmth of Andrew's hand on my arm was replaced with a tingling, burning sensation. I heard Andrew groan and looked down to see that his hand was no longer on my arm, and my arm was bleeding. Andrew clutched his hand, which was also bleeding, to his chest and gasped, "I've been hit."

Well, so had I, but the first order of business was to locate the gunman. Without thinking, I had already grabbed Charley II from my shoulder holster and spun around to face the direction the shot had come from.

"There he is," I heard Felix call from the car. He pointed across the street to where – big surprise – I saw Gilbert McKenzie's car. He must have pulled out to follow me almost as soon as I was out of sight of the farmhouse. I pointed my gun across the roof of my car, but my target hit the gas before I could return fire and drove back the way we had come, back toward the farmhouse.

The danger gone for the moment, I holstered my gun and turned my attention to Andrew. "How bad is it?" I asked. "Do you need a doctor?"

"Let's get out of here and talk on the way," he said through clenched teeth.

I opened the hatch and pulled out the first aid kit before getting back behind the wheel. I tossed it to Felix. "Find me something to clean this blood off with," I said. I pulled out, holding my bleeding left arm out the window so I didn't get blood all over the car. I got on the freeway and turned east, back toward Phoenix. Andrew had won this round.

Felix handed me an antiseptic cloth, and I wiped the blood from my arm. It was only grazed, and I held my arm up behind my head so Felix could wrap it with gauze while I drove. I'd been shot worse before, in my prior life in Myersburg, and knew I could function. It would take an hour or so for the real pain to set in. For the moment, adrenaline was keeping it pretty much at bay.

After he finished doctoring my arm, I put both hands on the wheel and said, "See how bad he is."

Out of the corner of my eye, I saw Andrew pull his hand away from his chest and hold it where Felix could examine it. He used some more wet wipes to clean the blood away. "Just a graze again, Boss," he reported. "You're lucky neither of you ended up with the slug. Looks like it went over the surface of his hand and across your arm," he said. He wrapped Andrew's hand and threw the bloody wipes and gauze wrappers over the back seat into the tiny trunk area.

"I heard a ping. The slug must have hit the gas pump. We're lucky it didn't cause another explosion."

"It probably was supposed to," Andrew replied. "I told you he's trying to kill us both."

"Well, for a hit man, he makes a pretty good FBI agent," I retorted. "That's four attempts on your life now – two within the last hour – and he missed every time."

"You sound disappointed."

"No, just glad we're dealing with an unworthy adversary. So far, all this guy has managed to do is knock off a seven-year-old kid and an unarmed woman."

"Don't underestimate him. He's not working alone, you know. And he didn't kill Cassy or Brian."

"How would I know that? When are you going to start telling me the truth, the whole truth, and nothing but the truth, Andrew? Don't you realize how hard it is to help you when I don't know what I'm dealing with?" I changed lanes to pass a slow-moving semi loaded with hay.

"I didn't ask you to follow me to Phoenix."

"If she hadn't, wiseass, you'd be dead by now," Felix spat out from the backseat. "And don't you forget it."

Andrew glanced back at Felix. "I haven't forgotten it. Look, I'm sorry I've had to do it this way, but I can't tell you anything you don't already know. I know you'll never believe it, but it's for your own good."

"Fuck my own good, Andrew. I can take care of myself. But I need some answers and I need them now. For example, Andrew, the day you picked me up at Gaines' house after kidnapping me the night before, why and how did you disappear while I was making that phone call to Felix?"

"Geez, I thought you would have figured that out by now."

"Obviously I didn't. Since you think I already know, it shouldn't hurt you to tell me."

"Smith picked me up. He was following us the whole time, waiting for a moment when you would be out of sight. He knew you'd recognize him, so when he pulled up next to the car, I jumped out and went with him. I couldn't wait around to leave you a note."

"Why did you leave the briefcase?"

"Would you believe in my haste to get out of there before you came back, I simply forgot about it? Then when I realized I had, I knew I better get it back quick before you went through it and reached some wrong conclusions about me. Or some right ones, for that matter."

"So you stole it from Felix's rental car."

"After tracking it to the motel. You're lucky I did. McKenzie was going to kill you when he found you again. He knew you'd know he wasn't really FBI after he left you tied up in that farmhouse."

"So what is he? And why didn't he kill us both that night?"

"As I said before, I had your gun. I don't think he figured on my being armed."

"You taking notes?" I thought to ask Felix.

"Yes, Boss."

"Let's understand something, Andrew. You seem to think John Smith is a 'good guy' in this scenario, right?"

"No. But he doesn't kill people. I trust him that far."

"Andrew, John Smith, pretending to be Cassy's father-in-law, lied through his teeth to me a few days ago, then set me up to find Cassy's body. I would conclude from that that he either killed Cassy or knows who did. He also knew where the body was. How do you explain that?"

"He told me about that. You caught him just as he was getting ready to leave with the kids. He was waiting for Randy to show up, then they were all going to leave for Phoenix. He sent you over to my place to get rid of you. He didn't want you spending any more time at the Bellamy house."

"How did he know Cassy was dead?"

"Randy told him."

"How did Randy know?"

"He was there when it happened."

"Who killed her, Andrew?"

He sighed. "That's the one I don't know. Randy isn't talking."

"Are you sure Randy's alive?"

I think I drove a full mile waiting for the answer to that one. "Well?" I finally prodded.

I felt his gaze on the side of my face and turned briefly to face him. "That's why Randy isn't talking," he said at last. "I think he's dead, too."

Chapter 20

WELL, THIS WAS VERY NICE. We were racking up quite a body count by this time. Let's count them up: Cassandra Bellamy whom I now knew was Andrew's sister; Randolph Bellamy, who might be Cassandra's husband or brother-in-law; Brian Delgado, who first Andrew, and then Cassandra had said was Cassandra's son but Grandpa Howard a.k.a. John Smith had said was not her kid (and he would know); last and probably least, the hit man James Maxwell, whom I had shot in the cafe who might die at any time. At least Jason and the dog Max were still alive, as far as I knew.

As for attempts, we could count four on Andrew's life and at least one on my own, two if we counted the assault on my innards perpetrated by Mrs. Gaines' sausages. So far only Felix was unscathed.

"So how did Randy get dead?" I asked.

"I don't know. Smith said after you left the Bellamy house, he collected the kids and dog and packed everything up in the car, mostly just the kids' clothes and some toys to keep them occupied on the trip. He left Randy to wipe the house clean and took the kids out for ice cream so they wouldn't know what was going on in the house. He said he returned to the house an hour later, expecting to pick up Randy, and found him gone and a puddle of blood in the corner of the living room. Needless to say, he got the hell out of there with the kids."

"And while he was filling the car with gas, Brian was killed by a sniper."

"Yes. Sad thing was, the boy needed to go to the bathroom at the house, but Smith couldn't let him go into the house because it had been wiped clean. Then when he found the blood, he certainly wasn't going to let the boys back into the house. If he had, Brian might be upset from seeing the blood, but at least he'd be alive."

"I wouldn't count on that, Andrew. If someone wanted him dead, they'd have found a way."

He shrugged. "Maybe. Maybe not. We saved Jason."

"Andrew, who was Randolph Bellamy?"

"He was pretending to be Cassy's husband. Cassy's real name is not Bellamy."

"I know. It's Baxter," I retorted.

"You knew that already?"

"Of course. What do you think I've been doing the last several days?"

"I have no idea, other than showing up in all the right places at the right times." He paused. "I guess I should thank you for saving my life a couple of times, shouldn't I."

"You're welcome. And I think you owe me more than that."

"I can't give you any more than that, Angela. Sorry."

I fumed silently for a few miles, slowing with traffic as we reached the main part of town. I wasn't sure I was willing to go to Smith's office just yet. We had left Felix's rental car at the motel that morning. I turned off the freeway and headed for the Motel of the Neon Horse. Time to let Felix out of the back seat. And I was realizing that with all three of us in the same car, it would be too easy for the baddies to get us all at once.

I would play along with Andrew but I needed Felix on the outside, watching my back.

I pulled into the parking lot and climbed out, pushing the seat forward to let Felix out of the back seat. He crawled out awkwardly, stretched, and rubbed his lower back. "Thanks, Boss. Next time we need to haul four people and a dog all over town, let's use my car, okay?" He grinned.

Andrew stayed in the car. I shut the door. "Sorry about that. Maybe we should have made Andrew sit in the back, but I'd rather keep him where I can see him."

Felix snorted. "Is that all you ever think about?"

I grinned. "Not always. Just most of the time. And you're a fine one to talk." Another car pulled into the lot, parking several spaces away next to Felix's rental car. I glanced anxiously at the driver, who remained in the car, and was relieved to see it was nobody I recognized. I was starting to get very, very paranoid.

"So what now, Boss?" Felix asked.

"I'm going to take Andrew to Smith's office, I guess. Maybe he'll answer some more questions. You are to tail me, far enough back that Andrew won't see you. If you see anyone else following me, call me on the car phone, not the cell phone. I'm going to leave that in my pocket in case there's any need to make a run for it."

"Right, Boss. I'll act like I'm going to my room for a minute to give you time to get out of the parking lot."

I got back in the car and Felix disappeared through the breezeway toward the rooms. "So," Andrew said as I pulled out of the parking lot, "what did you decide? Where's Felix going?"

"I told him to check out, return the car, and fly back home," I lied. "I don't want him to get hurt, and I don't like there being nobody in the office during the week. Might miss out on some business if nobody's there to answer the phone, you know?"

I have no idea if he believed me or not but he made no comment while I drove toward Paradise Valley for the second time that day. Hard to believe it was less than twelve hours ago that Felix and I had been rifling the office of John Smith, Attorney at Law. Since then, I had seen two attempts to kill my client in front of my eyes. Other than the fact that at least he was still alive to talk about it, my ego might have been suffering a bit over my current batting average.

"Are you taking me to Smith's office?" he finally asked.

"That's where you wanted to go, wasn't it?"

"They know I'm not dead."

"Apparently."

"They'll try again."

"You said Smith isn't a killer."

"He may be with McKenzie."

"So what are you saying? You don't want to go there? I'm perfectly willing to drive back to Clarkdale right now. That's where I was headed before we got shot."

He looked down at his bandaged hand. "Wish I knew a doctor over here I could trust."

"Well, we could always drop in on that OB/GYN next to Smith's office. Maybe he could fix you up."

I couldn't help feeling a bit smug when out of the corner of my eye I saw his jaw drop. "Have you been there?"

"Of course I've been there." I sighed. "Jesus, Andrew, why are you constantly surprised when I know something you haven't told me? I figured out a long time ago that you've told me nothing but lies. You hired me to investigate you. All right, I've been investigating you. The meter is still running, too, by the way. We'll settle up later with the cash from your Suburban."

"The money doesn't matter," he said quickly. "What matters is, how much do you know?"

I turned onto the parkway, heading for Paradise Valley. "I haven't exactly been sitting on my ass the last few days, Andrew. I've been doing the job you hired me to do, in between finding dead bodies, shooting hit men, and getting first chloroformed, then shot, myself." I recalled that the case, as presented by Andrew in my office last Tuesday, had started out a simple case of harassment gone sour, a stalking case at best. Who knew I would have to follow a trail of bodies to get to the truth. A truth that, come to think of it, still eluded me. I still hadn't found the "skeleton" in Andrew's closet.

"I have to know what you've found out," he insisted. "It's crucial."

I shrugged. "Let's see if I can summarize the highlights. You don't exist. Your mother doesn't exist. Your entire work history is fiction. You're wanted by the police. You may or may not have been sexually harassed by your own sister; I have only your word for that, so who knows if it's true. I find it highly unlikely. Cassy herself confirmed that you got her fired, but she claimed it was over work jealousies, not sex." I paused. Had I ever confirmed that Cassy had even worked for Computech? I realized that while I had a copy of her employment application, I had never confirmed whether she ever actually worked there. But what reason could she have had to lie? For that matter, what was the real reason she had shown up in my office that morning at all? She clearly had been lying about the kids. I felt a chill as I wondered if she had been checking me out for some reason. Then I remembered Reginald's unlikely visit the day before. Coincidence?

"I knew you must have talked to her," Andrew was saying. "How did that happen?"

"She came to see me, ostensibly to hire me to get the goods on you. I couldn't tell her you were my client, so I told her I was too busy to handle her case and gave her the name of another PI in Clarkdale. I suspect she demonstrated as much capacity for telling the truth as you have, Andrew. I don't think either one of you were telling me the truth about the other."

"What did she tell you about me?" he asked tensely.

I glanced over at him. "That you and her husband Randolph conspired to get her fired so Randolph could get the kids. But there's one other thing I never found, Andrew. I never found any proof of her marriage or her divorce. Of course, I didn't look for any proof, but the only corroboration I have for her marriage is that pile of baloney John Smith, pretending to be Howard Bellamy, served up to me the day she was killed. He was lying about everything else, why not that? So if I take the rational way out here, and assume Cassy was not married to anyone, then what was that bullshit you fed me the first day you came to my office?"

"Understand, Angela, I knew from her only what she told me."

"Bullshit. Are you forgetting you already admitted to helping place the Delgado kids with her?"

"I understood she was married. To Howard Bellamy. That's what I was told. I just learned yesterday she wasn't married."

"And have you ever met Howard Bellamy?"

"No."

"How do you know he exists?"

He sighed. "Maybe I don't."

I snorted. "I thought as much. Now, you want to hear another good one? Howard Bellamy exists. The cars were registered to him. But Randolph doesn't exist. Didn't," I corrected myself, remembering that he, too, was dead. Then I also remembered that there had been no notice of his death on PRICS. He had died the same day as Brian Delgado. I wondered where his body had ended up. Or was the news of his death greatly exaggerated? I glanced at Andrew. Had it been another of his lies? Why?

"So that's what he meant," Andrew said, more to himself than to me.

"What's what who meant?"

"Something Gilbert said once. Said something like, they went to all that trouble to set everything up and the idiot got the name wrong. It was a few days ago when I called him in his office to tell him everything was falling apart and I might need his help again."

I stopped at the red light at Shea Boulevard, glancing in my rearview mirror to see if Felix was anywhere in sight. It thought I saw his car about five back, but couldn't be certain. It was the right color, anyway, but half the cars in Phoenix were beige. I looked at Andrew. "You told me once you were supposed to be in the witness protection program. Was Cassy?"

"No. But Randy was."

Suddenly a lot of things made sense. The false pasts, the confusion with the names. Identities had been set up for Howard Quincy Bellamy, including links to Cassandra Bellamy as his wife. But the person for whom that past was concocted used the name Randolph instead of Howard. Maybe it was supposed to be Randolph but some bureaucratic moron set everything up as Howard in error. Or maybe Randolph was being perverse by using Randolph when he was supposed to be using Howard. Or, I thought, remembering that his application at Computech showed the name Randolph, maybe half his past was set up as Randolph, the other half as Howard. I had found the name Howard only on the car registrations. I had not run a driver's license on Howard or Randolph, but both the Celica and the Cadillac had been registered to Howard. Nor, I remembered, had we checked either of them for a police record since it was Andrew Field who was the true subject of my investigation.

Lord knows what else we had missed. But at the moment, I suspected that Randolph Bellamy was probably very much alive, and likely using the name Howard by now.

The light turned green and I turned right, heading toward Tatum Boulevard.

"And what about you, Andrew? What's your cover story? Who are you supposed to be?"

"Andrew Field is the name they told me to use. They got me the job at Computech with that name."

"That's the only place that name works, Andrew."

He sighed. "That's the whole problem, Angela. That's why I hired you. My background was never filled in. Remember my saying I couldn't use banks yet?"

"Yes."

"I got into the witness protection program partly because of Delgado. I told you about that. They were supposed to set me up a new identity, history, job, bank account, the whole nine yards. They started the process as far as getting me a job. I asked them to set me up at Computech because of Cassandra. You see, they didn't know at the time that I was still protecting Delgado's kids. Unfortunately, I was working with Smith closely enough to get picked up on the radar when he came under investigation. Somehow they found out the name André Beauchamp, the name my father used for me when he sold me to Smith, even though I had grown up as and was using the name Andrew Gaines, although it had never been legally changed to that. I suspect they found my adoption record. Anyway, the Feds backed off the rest of my history once that want was issued on me in the name Beauchamp. They set me up another identity – don't ask me the name – and were getting ready to move me when I became suspicious that Cassy had figured it all out. That's when I came to you. I think John Smith told her some things he wasn't supposed to about me."

And then I knew that Cassy had found the skeleton in Andrew's closet before she died. The question now remained: who else knew?

Besides Reginald, that is.

Chapter 21

I ALSO KNEW THAT TAKING ANDREW to Smith's office was going to get us both killed. I drove past Tatum, ignoring Andrew's protests. "I know where I'm going," I explained, without really explaining anything. The truth was, I didn't yet know what I was going to do.

I'd gone about two miles when the car phone rang. I glanced quickly in the rearview mirror but did not see Felix anywhere. I picked up the receiver hoping it was a wrong number.

"Hello?"

A vaguely familiar voice growled back at me. "You missed your turnoff, lady."

"Who is this?"

"I've got your little fag friend here."

I pulled over to the side of the road, scanning the rearview mirror again. Felix's car was not behind me. Several cars went past, then the roadway was empty. I swung across the road in a U turn and went back the way I had come from.

"Where are you? What did you do to Felix?"

"He's fine. For the moment, anyway. I'm not interested in him. It's your client I need. Put him on the phone."

Andrew had heard only my side of the conversation. I switched the phone to hands-free and hung up the receiver. "It's for you," I said to Andrew.

"Where's the kid, André?" the voice growled. Andrew turned pale.

"The kid's where you'll never find him, Gilbert," he replied. So it had been Dumbo all along. "The feds have him by now. The real feds."

"You double-crossed me, André. I don't like that."

"Get over it."

"We had a deal. You for the kid."

"You're right, we did. So sue me."

I was scanning the road ahead and spotted Felix's rental car in a parking lot at the corner of Tatum and Shea. I didn't see Felix, and there was only one person visible in the car, talking into what must have been Felix's cell phone. He didn't notice me as I drove past and turned left. I turned into the parking lot behind him, parked with the motor running so the car phone would pick up the sudden silence indicating that I had stopped moving.

I left Andrew arguing about the finer points of contract law and approached Felix's car from the right rear blind spot, grateful he had rented a cheap compact car that did not have a right hand mirror. The broken window had not been repaired or covered, so I was able to sneak right up to the car, unseen, and listen to Dumbo's side of the conversation.

I picked a moment when he was shouting at Andrew and I knew he was distracted to glance into the back seat, expecting to find Felix's body there. But the back seat was empty, and once I saw that there was no reason not to, I pointed Charley II right at Gilbert's head and cocked the hammer.

He froze, then slowly he turned and saw me. "Hang up the phone, dirt bag," I said calmly. He complied and I tested the door handle. It was unlocked. I opened the door and moved to where I could see him, and he could see me. "Out of the car," I ordered. "This side." I stepped back while he swung his legs one at a time across the console before sliding into the passenger seat. The seat belt receiver gouged his left cheek and I grinned when he winced.

"Turn around. Hands on top of the car. You probably know the routine." I patted him down, relieving him of one gun in a shoulder holster and a second one strapped to his right ankle. "Okay, asshole," I said. "Where's Felix?"

"In the trunk."

"Dead or alive?"

"Alive unless he's committed suicide in the last ten minutes."

I slammed a fist into his kidneys, not too hard, just hard enough to get his attention. He gasped and doubled over, retching. "Don't be a wise ass," I warned him. "Open the trunk."

I allowed him to reach into the car for the keys, and he opened the trunk. Felix was alive, awake, but tied and gagged. And livid, I might add, which I found out as soon as Gilbert untied him. Felix was still in the trunk when he shot a foot into Gilbert's solar plexus, knocking the wind out of him. For the second time, he doubled over, this time gasping for air.

Felix climbed out, took a moment to limber his arms and legs, then without warning, slugged Dumbo in the stomach. "Call me a fag, will you," he muttered, drawing back his left "purse" for another blow. I caught his arm in mid swing. "That's enough," I said. "There are probably witnesses calling the cops by now. We have to get out of here. What happened, anyway?"

"He was waiting at the corner," Felix replied. "When I stopped for the light, he jumped out of his car over there and shoved a gun in my face, but not so anyone else would see it. He made me move over, drove into that alley over there and put me in the trunk."

"He hurt you?"

"Just my feelings," he replied.

"Go steal his car," I said, pulling Gilbert's car keys out of the pocket where I'd felt them earlier. "Take your phone. It's on the dash. Resume tailing me. I'm going to get –" I broke off when I looked back to where I had left Andrew in my running car, talking on the car phone.

Naturally he was gone.

So was my car, of course.

"Shit. He did it again. Come on," I said to Gilbert. "Get in." I kept my gun trained on him while he got in the passenger side. "Fasten your seat belt," I ordered him, not wanting to get stopped on a misdemeanor. I pulled out the handcuffs I keep in my hip pocket and tossed them to Gilbert. "Cuff yourself to the door handle, asshole. Both hands."

With a strangely silent Gilbert McKenzie cuffed to the door and Felix trotting across the street to steal his car, I pulled out of the parking lot, relieved that nobody had bothered getting involved enough to call the police.

But damn that Andrew Field! Stealing my car again, when I obviously had the situation under control. Why had he run? And where had he run to?

On a hunch, I drove past the office of John Smith, Attorney at Law, but did not see the Firebird in the parking lot. Then I pulled out my cell phone and called the car phone number. "It worked the last time," I muttered to myself.

But this time, my client did not answer the phone, and it was with great annoyance that I glanced at this albatross I had been stuck with. What the hell was I going to do with Dumbo? If I'd still been on the force, I could have taken him to headquarters and dumped him in a cell for twenty-four hours while I took care of business. But with no official standing, and not really even knowing who he was or how he fit into all this, I was at a loss. I considered parking him in the trunk, just so I wouldn't have to look at the little jerk.

"Why did you capture Felix?" I asked him.

He sneered at me without answering and I backhanded him across the chops without thinking. "I asked you a civil question, dirt bag."

He glared at me again, but twitched his head away as if anticipating another blow. "Why do you think?" he spat.

"Hostage to trade, I'm guessing. I figure you were going to trade him for Andrew. Like you did with the kid."

"You figure right. You're not as stupid as you look."

I raised my hand to smack him again, then considered something and put it down. "For someone who's been taken at gunpoint and handcuffed inside a moving car, you're being pretty nervy. You think someone's going to come rescue you?" I asked.

"You have no idea what you're mixing up in, lady," he replied, shaking his head. "You're in so far over your head you probably can't see daylight anymore."

"Such imagery. What were you, a liberal arts major? No, that can't be. A liberal arts major would have a personality, something you're sorely lacking."

"You should talk, bitch."

"Tut, tut," I chided him. "Such language. First *fag*, now *bitch*. You shouldn't be antagonizing the people who have taken you captive, you know. We might make you eat at Jack in the Box if you don't change your attitude real quick. Assuming we feed you at all," I amended.

I was driving aimlessly at this point, mostly trying to give Felix a chance to see if we were being followed by anyone else. I picked up my cell phone from my lap and called Felix. "Everything okay?" I asked.

"Fine."

"Felix, this creep is acting like he knows something I don't know. I don't trust him. I think we're going to abandon this car and take his until we catch up with Andrew. I'm pulling off the side of the road up here. Catch up and we'll join you."

After Felix caught up to us, I uncuffed Gilbert, then decided I'd rather have him out of the way, so we tied him hand and foot, gagged him, and put him in the trunk of his own car. After we got underway, I folded down half of the split rear seat so I could keep an eye on him.

Then I had Felix turn around and drive back the way we had come, stopping on a side street with a view of Felix's car.

Sure enough, we hadn't been there three minutes when another gray sedan with government plates stopped behind the rental car. Two men got out, looked inside, pried open the trunk, then drove off in apparent disgust.

"I had a feeling there was a tracking device on it," I said as we pulled out. "Follow them, Felix. Let's see where they go."

We stayed back far enough that they couldn't tell it was McKenzie's own car behind them. They turned east and drove through Scottsdale, out into the desert past some mountains, then turned down a dirt road leading to the middle of nowhere, from what I could see. The sun was just setting. We waited at the side of the road, watching the dust cloud proceed in a straight line for about two minutes, which I estimated to be about a mile or less, then turn back to the west toward the mountains. About a minute later it stopped but it was too dark once the dust settled for me to see if there was a building. I supposed there must be, but it would have to wait for now.

I tried my car phone again, but Andrew still wasn't answering.

"Well, Felix," I said as we turned back toward town. "What do we do now?"

"Go home?"

"What do you think?"

"Dump the jerk in the back?"

"That's a good idea, but do we kill him first?" I said that rather loudly, for Dumbo's benefit.

"You know, Boss, this is his car we're in. Didn't you say he chloroformed you? Maybe there's some more of that stuff."

"Not a bad idea, in fact, maybe we can find an abandoned barn or something to dump him in. It is a rather nuisance having to drag him everywhere we go."

"Boss, what did he want, anyway? Why did he take me in the first place?"

"Who knows, Felix? I've been lied to so often by so many people lately I'm not sure I'd know the truth if it bit me on the butt. He said he wanted to trade you for Andrew, but he put a tracer on your car knowing full well Andrew wasn't in it, so I suspect there's more going on. And I figured out a few things, but let's not discuss them in front of the jerk. Turn here," I said, pointing at a dirt road leading out across the desert. I had spotted a tractor shed.

We left McKenzie there, tied up, handcuffed to a tractor, but not gagged. We did chloroform him, just to put him to sleep. After my own experience, I figured that would keep him quiet until morning. We would be back by then and could decide what to do with him then.

Too bad he didn't give me an excuse to shoot him. He really was more trouble than he was worth.

We ate dinner at Taco Bell and rented a room for the night. I tried the car phone again, redialing over and over until it had rung at least thirty times, hoping the annoyance of the ringing would drive Andrew to answer it, but all I heard was ringing. I didn't even know if he still had my car or had abandoned it.

I also was assuming he had driven off of his own accord. If Dumbo had an accomplice there, surely they would have liberated him, wouldn't they? Or had Gilbert been a pawn, just a distraction to enable them to get Andrew while I was busy rousting Gilbert? The idea made me uneasy.

"Okay, Boss," Felix said after we settled into a single motel room with two beds. Screw decorum, I had reasoned. There was safety in numbers and I still wasn't completely sure what we were dealing with. "You said you had figured some things out that you didn't want to talk about in front of the gentleman with the bad attitude. What did you figure out?"

"Felix, how did Reginald get in the office that day?"

"Walked in, I guess. The door wasn't locked."

"When I came into the lobby, you were between him and the exterior door. Meaning he was on the ground between you and the desk. Were you at your desk when he came in?"

"No, Boss, I had stepped into the restroom to dump out my coffee cup. I was running water and didn't hear him come in. When I came back in the room, he was reaching for your door knob."

"So you don't know how long he was in the office, do you."

"Well, couldn't have been too long. Oh, wait, I did take a leak while I was in there. I guess I might have been gone two or three minutes."

"I thought that might have been the case. Felix, what was on your desk when he got there?"

"Well, Andrew Field had just come in. I had taken some preliminary information on him, name, address, things like that. To set up a billing file in case he hired you. The usual stuff. It was lying out on the desk still."

"I think Reginald saw it. I don't think he was there to see me at all. He was following Andrew."

"But why? Why would Reginald have been following Andrew Field? Why would he even have known him?"

"Did I ever tell you what my ex-shithead did for a living?"

"No, you don't talk about him much at all. What did he do for a living?"

I sighed. "Well, mostly he sponged off me, but sometimes he'd turn up with cash and wouldn't say where he got it. I didn't know this when I was with him, Felix, I only found out after we broke up, but he was some kind of flunky for the mob. Mostly delivered numbers from what I understand. Nothing physical or dangerous of course – the weenie couldn't fight his way out of a paper bag."

"Sweet guy. I'm glad you saw him first. The mob, huh? You sure can pick 'em."

I smiled. "He was strictly small potatoes, Felix, that's why I never gave another thought to his coming to my office that day. But I'll bet he wasn't drunk at all, and he was there to find out something about Andrew. And I'll bet you anything he planted a bug."

"And that's how word got to Phoenix that Andrew was on his way."

"Right."

He groaned. "Jesus, they must have known everything, then. Everything we learned about him got fed straight to – to whom? Who could have been behind this?"

"I suspect John Smith. I think Cassy was out of control, about to blow the whole game, so they iced her and set it up so Andrew would be the prime suspect."

"Then why did Cassy come to your office?"

"She was sent there to set her up as the suspect in Andrew's shooting, which then set him up as suspect in her killing."

"Why would she go along with it?"

"Because she really was mad at Andrew. He really had gotten her fired. So Smith had her mailman suggest she come to me, knowing that Andrew had already been there. She didn't know it was a setup. But I'm sure she did know something about Andrew that she had told someone, hoping they would help her get her revenge on Andrew."

"Well, what did she know, and who did she tell?"

And before I could answer, the door burst open and two men in what appeared to be Phoenix police uniforms entered the room with guns drawn. And for the second time in three days, I was shoved in the back of a car and chloroformed.

Chapter 22

IT REALLY WAS STARTING TO GET TIRESOME. I opened my eyes to realize it was still the middle of the night. Again I was tied and gagged and again I had been left in a place sorely in need of housekeeping. I could smell the dust – and something else. Was that horse manure? I was able to make out a few shapes as my eyes grew accustomed to the darkness. I could see half-walls, topped with vertical bars. Groping with my hands, I could feel twigs – or was it straw? I moved as much as I could and figured out I was on the floor of a horse stall. A bucket hung on the wall above my head, and the sight of it brought on an immediate thirst.

I thought about Max, the dog I had watered the day before, and wondered if anyone would be as kind to me.

I doubted it.

I wondered if Felix was all right. I had no idea if he had been taken, too, but I was certain he would not have been left there alive. I hoped he was somewhere nearby.

I moaned as loudly as I could through the gag, hoping if he were there that he would hear me and respond. I listened for a minute and was relieved to hear rustling on the other side of the half wall. Then I heard a loud equine snort. Apparently I had awakened only a horse.

But at least that meant I hadn't been left in some abandoned building to die. Someone must be caring for the horse so I knew they couldn't leave me there too long. Horse people are known for being up at dawn, especially in Phoenix in the warmer months, trying to beat the heat to the horsekeeping chores.

There was nothing to do but wait. I made myself as comfortable as I could in my bed of straw and tried to sleep.

The sun was just peeking over the horizon when the same two bogus (I assume) cops dragged me out into the barnyard and shoved me in the back of a windowless camper – with Andrew Field. There still was no sign of Felix, and I prayed he was all right, but wherever he was, there was nothing I could do for him. I had to save myself first. And, apparently, Andrew as well.

They left us tied but did remove our gags and give us a drink of water, which made me hopeful that they didn't need us dead. Why keep us alive if they were only going to kill us anyway?

"When did they get you?" I asked after they closed and padlocked the door and started driving out of the yard. The camper was nothing but a shell on the back of a full sized pickup truck and there was no boot opening into the cab. At least we could talk without being overheard.

"While you were getting the drop on McKenzie. Apparently it was all a setup."

"I was afraid of that. They had a tracker on Felix's car again. Once I figured that out, I switched cars and took McKenzie's."

"I suspected as much. You know they probably had Lojack on it."

"So that's how they found us."

"Us?" he asked. "Was Felix with you when they found you?"

"He was," I replied. "I have no idea where he is now, though. I hope they didn't kill him."

"Probably left him tied up in another barn somewhere. So what did you do with McKenzie?"

"He's in a barn of his own."

He chuckled. "You're really something, you know?"

"So are you," I retorted. "I just haven't figured out what yet."

We were facing each other in the truck, each leaning against an outside wall, and even in the half-light filtering in through the cracks around the door, I found myself mesmerized by his eyes. I stared at him hungrily, realizing that much of my anxiety had gone once I saw that he was still alive. I hoped he would stay that way -- that somehow we would get out of this together, get to the right people, and put an end to this nightmare.

And live happily ever after in a house in the suburbs with two-point-five children and a cocker spaniel.

I shook the fantasy out of my head. What was the matter with me?

"Where are they taking us?" I finally asked.

"I'm not sure, but I'm afraid it's somewhere I don't want to go," he replied and I saw with a sinking feeling that he was scared.

"Where is that?"

"Back home."

"Where? To Gaines' farm?"

"No."

"Where then? Where is your home?"

He looked straight into my eyes for what seemed like an hour before he finally answered, "Myersburg."

My jaw dropped. "We're going to Myersburg?"

"Looks like it."

The sickening feeling in my stomach might have been an after effect of the chloroform but somehow I doubted it. All of a sudden, everything fell into place with a resounding crash. This was not going to be a homecoming I could look forward to either. "Shit," I said. "I should have known. How could I have been so stupid?"

He didn't answer. After all, how can a question like that be answered?

"What do they need me for?" I asked nervously.

He shook his head. "Angela, you've been a part of this all along. Did you really think I picked you out of the phone book?"

"So you know who I am," I said dully. "And now I know who you are. You're Francis the Mule's son." I felt sick. Per my old partner, Tim Reed, Francis the Mule was no longer safely in prison.

"Yes. How much do you remember about my dear old dad?"

"I knew him as a mob figure named Frank Martinelli. Busted him three years ago for robbery and attempted murder. His priors included suspicion of murder, assault and battery, drug charges, grand theft auto, extortion, spousal battery, and child abuse. Probably a few things I never knew about. He had done time on the assault charge several years before but other than that, he was never prosecuted for anything, or if he was, he got off on some technicality or other."

"And now he has again."

"How the hell did he get a name like François Martinelli?"

"My grandmother was French. He started using the name Martin before I was born just to throw people off from his family connections. My birth certificate is in the name Martin, but he never legally changed his own name which is why you know him as Martinelli."

"So what does all this mean to you? And me, for that matter."

"I was the child he abused, but more importantly, I once saw him kill a man. Right after that, he sold me to Smith. Told him to make sure I never knew where I came from or he'd have to kill me. Gave me the name Beauchamp, which was his grandmother's maiden name. I was five at the time. I quickly forgot my real name, and I grew up not knowing who I was, but I've always had a very clear memory of the killing. About two years ago, I finally managed to trace my background. I'd always assumed that the memory I had was a dream until I learned who my father was, and that he was in prison. Only recently did I find out you put him there."

I was silent for several minutes, my mind racing with a million unanswered questions, but one loomed larger than the others. I decided to ask it. I looked him square in the eyes and asked, "Are we going to live through this?"

He looked back without answering for a long minute, then turned away. "Probably not," he finally said. "Probably not. I'm sorry."

Chapter 23

IT WAS AN EIGHT-HOUR DRIVE from Phoenix to Myersburg and the back of the truck was noisy and hot. Now that I finally knew what I was up against, it seemed I was going to be powerless to do anything about it. I hated to put too much stock in it, but my one and only ace in the hole was that I knew where Gilbert McKenzie was. The problem was that he would probably be dead in a day or two unless someone found him and brought him some water pretty soon. Dead hostages usually aren't worth much.

There was also the chance that Felix had already been forced to take them to McKenzie. With a sinking heart, I had to recognize that McKenzie's location was the only information Felix had that he could use to keep himself alive. Once he took them to that tractor shed, his usefulness would end.

The only glimmer of hope I could cling to was that Felix was smart enough to realize that, and he would use that knowledge to keep himself alive as long as possible.

"There's something I don't understand," I said. "The only want that was out on you was for the John Smith investigation. You told me you were being blackmailed over that. Why?"

He looked over at me. "We were blackmailing each other, Angela. I told Smith I wouldn't testify against him if he'd help me with Brian and Jason. Their mother was in jail and Delgado was looking for them. To make sure he had a good hold over me, Smith made me turn over the boys in front of a witness, with a camera rolling. If I'd testified against him, he would have implicated me and I'd have gone down with him as an accessory. I had them placed with Cassandra, knowing she was my sister, expecting to get to know her and eventually tell her the truth. I also hoped to learn through her where my real mother was, but I guess that will never happen now."

"I know where your mother is, Andrew," I said quietly. "She's in Las Vegas. She refused to have anything to do with Cassandra and she thinks you're dead."

He sighed. "I thought as much."

"But why did Cassandra want two kids? What was in it for her?"

"Through Smith, I paid her a lot of money to take them. But she was also with Randy, and he was highly motivated to cooperate with us too since Delgado tried to kill him. He was put in the witness protection program too as soon as Delgado was released. We hoped that if we kept the kids with him, the Feds would help keep Delgado from finding the boys. But Cassy turned out to be completely neurotic and I knew I could never trust her. She was supposed to be living with Randy, but she moved out and left the boys behind, then tried to shake down Smith for more money. After Cassandra and Brian were killed, I knew Randy's cover was blown and I had to get Jason back to his mother. Delgado wants me bad and hired McKenzie to get me. So I made a deal. I knew Delgado's gun had been found and that case would get reopened. I promised to confess to the attempted murder of Randolph Bellamy if they'd let me get Jason somewhere safe." He sighed. "I never figured they planned to kill me at that farmhouse. I hope they don't go after Jason now. I don't think I'll ever forgive myself if anything happens to him, too."

We talked for what seemed like hours, and after Andrew and I had shared with each other everything either of us could think of, the situation seemed very bleak indeed. Figures that the one time he decides to tell me the truth it's when we're on our way to our own execution. There was a certain psychological satisfaction in finally understanding some of this mess, but it didn't sound like I would get much chance to revel in my new information before being dispatched to the Great Beyond.

I managed to slide across the truck to his side so we could try to test each other's bonds but neither of us could manage to make any headway at all on the ropes. I was leaning against him, feeling his fingertips caress my hands as he picked uselessly at the end of the rope, when the truck halted.

Quickly, I slid back to my place. A moment later I heard someone fumbling with the padlocks and the back door was opened. The taller and skinnier of the two men who had taken me the night before stood there. "Boss said we have to feed you. You hungry?"

I blinked against the sudden glare of the sun. Through the open door, I could see we were in Las Vegas. Why would they stop for lunch with Myersburg only a couple hours away? "A little," I admitted truthfully. I wondered what our last meal would be. "Mostly I'm thirsty. Are you allowed to give us water?"

"I suppose," he grunted. He glanced at Andrew. "You, too?"

"Not very hungry. But water would be nice."

"Back in a sec." He slammed the door.

"Why are they being nice?" I asked. "Something's not right."

"They're just flunkies. Following orders. They have no beef with either of us. If the order came down to kill us, they'd do that just as cheerfully and never look back."

A few minutes later, Beanpole was back with a sack from Burger King and a couple large cups of water. He climbed in the back with us and shut the door. I felt the truck start to move again, and we drove for what felt like a couple miles before the truck turned off the road and parked again. The driver, a shorter man with wide hips, opened the back door again and stood there, holding a gun on us, while Beanpole untied me and gave me a couple of minutes to eat a cheeseburger and drink some water. When I was through, he tied me back up and untied Andrew so he could eat.

The whole stop lasted less than ten minutes, then they got out and left us there in silence. I wondered why we didn't leave immediately, then suspected they were eating their own lunch. They probably had French Fries, I thought darkly. And milkshakes.

"Hate to think that the best they could do for a last meal was a lousy cheeseburger from Burger King," Andrew said.

"At least it wasn't Jack in the Box," I retorted. "They have some class, anyway."

"It was probably convenient. I'm sure they would have fed us sawdust if it were available. The boss said to feed us, but I'm sure he didn't tell them what."

"Why would they keep us alive just to kill us later?"

"Maybe they want us strong enough to be able to talk. Before they kill us, they'll need to know how much we know and whom we've told."

"What could we know that they'd be interested in?"

"The location of Delgado's gun, for one. The whereabouts of Jason Delgado for another. And whether you told the cops anything the day you shot that hit man."

"And the location of Gilbert McKenzie."

"That, too."

We shut up for a few minutes when we heard voices and footsteps approaching the truck. The engine roared to life and we started moving again.

"We'll be in Myersburg in about an hour and a half," I told Andrew. "The only thing we have in our favor there is that if we have any chance to escape, at least I know the whole town inside and out. I also know at least one cop I'd trust with my life."

"Hope you get a chance to call him."

We were unloaded inside an enclosed garage and led into a house through a door leading to a laundry room. We were shoved at gunpoint down a hall and into a large office at the rear of the house. The house somehow seemed familiar, but I couldn't quite place it.

Why was I not surprised to see Reginald there?

Before I had the chance to greet him in a fitting manner, Andrew and I were ordered to sit in two chairs facing a bay window. The drapes were open and the sun was shining in. It was a very old ploy. With the light at his back, it was nearly impossible to see the facial features of the burly man seated behind the desk. Meanwhile, we got to squint into the glare.

"Hello, son," Frank Martinelli said. "How have you been?"

I glanced quickly at Andrew. His normally arrogant expression had long ago been replaced with a look of despair. At the moment, I saw only raw fear. He did not answer the question.

Andrew was terrified of this man who had abused him as a child and killed a man in front of his eyes. From my own dealings with him, I knew his fears were far from groundless. Francis the Mule was a pretty ruthless character. And I had sent him to prison. And his son could again.

I suppose I should have been scared myself, but I had been taught at the academy many years ago never to show that fear.

Nevertheless, I needed to pee.

"Excuse me," I said. Frank turned to glare at me. "Can I use the john?"

His face turned in my direction but I could not see his eyes due to the backlighting. He shrugged and turned back to Andrew. "Take her to the bathroom," he snapped to Beanpole, who had been standing behind me holding a gun on us.

He took my arm and led me back down the hall to a windowless bathroom. He even untied my hands and let me go in alone, although he kept the door blocked open with his foot. Somehow I managed to do my business with a minimum of embarrassment. I glanced around the room for possible weapons but found only a wooden-handled toilet plunger in the corner behind the commode. I supposed there might have been cleaning chemicals in the cabinet under the sink that might have been helpful in making an escape but I didn't think Beanpole would tolerate my taking a peek.

He left me untied while he walked me back at gunpoint to the office. When we got there, he tied my hands again, but apparently, having delivered us to his destination, he was less concerned with my escape and he tied my hands in front instead of in back.

I had been gone probably less than two minutes. Andrew continued to look terrified. Reginald, sitting on a chair at the side of the room, looked smug. I wondered how much he had been paid for his part in all this, and, for that matter, why he was here at all. As far as I knew, he had no ties to Myersburg.

Frank took his gaze from his son and turned to look coolly at me. "So we meet again, Detective Virago," he said finally.

It had been years since anyone had called me that, and nobody had ever said it with quite the sarcasm this man managed to deliver. But the voice was the same and I did remember it. Hearing the words made me remember the promise he had made to me years before, a promise hissed at me as he was led out in shackles to begin serving what was supposed to be his eight- to twelve-year sentence. The snarled words, "We will meet again, Detective Virago," had been followed by, "and then I will kill you."

I wondered if there was any chance he had forgotten the rest of the sentence, but he quickly put my curiosity to rest on that point when he continued, "And now I will kill you."

Yup, he had remembered. "I don't think you want to do that, Mr. Martinelli."

"Why not? You took three years of my life."

"You're lucky. It was supposed to be eight to twelve."

He laughed, a nasty, sarcastic laugh. "It is not lucky to be put in that place for even three years, Detective. I have waited for this day a long time. Imagine my surprise when I learned that my step-nephew here," he nodded to Reginald, "had been so intimate with the only cop who ever managed to make it stick. Yes, that was a very fortunate discovery I made when I learned that."

I shot a glare at Reginald. Worm that he was, I never would have thought he'd have the balls to do anything like this. Apparently I had been wrong about his "small potatoes" status with the mob. Apparently he knew some of the very large spuds in this outfit. I wondered if he had known all along that he was signing my death warrant by cooperating with these thugs.

Maybe I shouldn't have hit him with that ashtray after all. Maybe I should have shot him instead. And made Dora clean up the resulting bloody mess.

"Look, Mr. Martinelli," I started. "I was just doing my job. There's no reason to take it personally. It was just beginner's luck." The collar had been made the first month after I managed to get promoted to detective. Tim had helped me with it. I wondered if Tim was also on this creep's hit list. I hoped not. Tim had a wife and kid. I remembered that Tim had not testified at the trial. With any luck, maybe I was the only target and Tim would be all right.

"Beginner's luck." He snorted. "You expect me to believe that some rookie police dick just happened to stumble onto my operation?"

"I'm sorry you don't believe it, but that's what happened. If you hadn't tripped over the door jamb and fallen, you probably would have gotten away with that job, too." It had been his full handprint on a freshly cleaned wooden floor that had connected him to the armed robbery. There had been no clever detective work involved at all, just a competent job done collecting the print. The match up had been done by computer. The arrest had been uneventful. Once we knew who we wanted, a paid informant tipped us to his whereabouts. Tim and I had driven over with an arrest warrant and a couple backup patrols and arrested Frank Martinelli as he lounged poolside. Come to think of it, I realized why the house seemed familiar. The pool, I figured, must be on the other side of the office wall, the one without any windows.

After Frank Martinelli had been taken to jail on the arrest warrant, Tim and I had returned with a search warrant to look for the cash that was taken. We had torn the place apart but never did find the money.

"Doesn't matter how you did it," he growled. "You put me away, and now you're going to pay."

"Killing me won't get you anything," I said with a shrug. "I can do you a lot more good alive than dead."

"That's what they all say." He nodded to Lard Butt, the other "cop" who had arrested me in the motel the night before and who had been the driver on today's little journey. "Go kill her," he ordered. "But not in here. It will make too much mess."

"Sure thing," the man replied, stepping forward to take my arm.

"Just a minute, Frankie," I said. "Don't you even want to know why I think I'm more good to you alive than dead?"

He put up a hand to hold off Lard Butt, who was trying to drag me bodily off the chair. "Fine. I spent three years waiting for this moment, another minute won't matter. I can afford to humor you. Why are you more good to me alive than dead?"

"I know a few things you don't." Out of the corner of my eye, I could see that Andrew was absolutely panic-stricken with worry about what I might say next. I wished I could reassure him that I knew what I was doing, but the fact was, I wasn't sure I did. I was trying a bluff because that was all I had.

"What might that be?"

"Oh, sure," I snorted. "You think I'm an idiot? I tell you what I know and you have no reason not to kill me. First, I want some answers."

"Answers to what?"

"Questions."

"What questions?"

"What are you going to do with my friend here?" I replied, nodding toward Andrew.

"André? I'm sorry to say the gene pool is about to be purged of my own genetic material. I guess I am not fit to reproduce. My own son is a bigger threat to my existence than anyone else is so I fear I must order a very late-term abortion. I should have done it when he was five but his mother did not approve. She's gone now, I have no idea where, so there's nobody to interfere anymore."

"You plan to kill him. Why? What can he possibly do to you?"

"He knows something he shouldn't know. And now I know he knows who I am. It's that simple. If only he hadn't done that snooping around while I was unjustly incarcerated, but, unfortunately, his adoptive parents never taught him to mind his own business. His sister was the same way, though, so maybe it's more my fault than theirs. Those genes I mentioned, you know. At least I didn't have to kill her. Someone else did that for me. She found out her brother wasn't dead like we'd told her he was and in doing so became as big a threat to me as he was. I was surprised to learn I am not my son's only enemy. Many others need to see him dead. Actually, one of them is paying me a high price for the opportunity to kill him for me. Perhaps I'll let him kill you, too, as a bonus. Two for the price of one."

"You would let someone kill your own son? And how do you know he hasn't already told the police whatever he knows?"

"Doesn't matter what he told anyone. There is no recorded, sworn testimony or I wouldn't be free right now. He could have taken out an ad in the paper telling all and it wouldn't matter until he goes to a grand jury. Pardon me, I mean unless he goes to a grand jury. And he won't. I simply can't let him."

And in that moment the final piece of the puzzle fell into place. Andrew wasn't in the witness protection program because of Delgado, and it wasn't because of John Smith and Delgado's kids. Andrew had needed the extreme measure because he was about to testify against his own father, a known mob figure. And based on the fact that he was actually in the Witness Protection Program, it was a grim certainty that he had already told what he knew, and probably under oath and on the record. Francis the Mule was already screwed. He just didn't know it yet.

I certainly wasn't going to tell him. And, since Andrew had kept this one nugget of truth from me during his three-hour confession in the truck, I suspected he wasn't going to tell his father either.

There was a noise outside and Martinelli glanced out the window. A helicopter flew past, toward the freeway that I knew was only a mile away. "Damn traffic reporters. Fucking choppers have been flying over me day and night all week." He muttered something to Reginald that I didn't hear, but Reginald stood up and closed the windows and drapes behind his uncle's back.

For the first time I was able to see the face of the man I had sent to prison three years before. I could barely see the resemblance to Andrew. The image was distorted by a scar that ran from Frank Martinelli's left ear to the tip of his chin. He had not had the scar when I arrested him so I surmised it had happened in prison. I decided not to ask how. Clearly he had survived the attack; I wondered if his attacker had fared as well.

Somehow I suspected not.

"So, Detective Virago, any more questions before you tell me why you think I should let you live?"

"Just one. How badly do you want Gilbert McKenzie?"

He startled, and I fought to hold my own facial expression from revealing anything. I had assumed he knew that Dumbo the elephant had been dogging my tail for a few days, but his reaction told me that he had no idea that I knew anything about the short former FBI agent with the big ears and bigger ego.

"How do you know McKenzie?" he finally asked.

"Usual way. He picked me up in a bar." Well, a coffee shop, anyway, but it was close enough for my purposes.

"Do you know where he is?"

"Usually right behind me," I replied with just a trace of smugness. Maybe it had been a stroke of genius stashing him in that tractor shed. He was probably still alive, too, at least for the moment.

"Don't be a smart ass, Detective," he snarled. "Don't forget who has all the guns today." Beanpole, standing in the corner, shifted his gun slightly to emphasize the point.

"Sorry," I replied. "No offense intended, but that is where he's spent much of the last few days. I finally got him off my ass yesterday, but I wouldn't be surprised if he followed me up here."

Frank Martinelli's face wavered just a bit and I knew I had hit a nerve. Francis the Mule was actually afraid of Gilbert McKenzie. Not only that, he was believing every word I was saying.

Suddenly, he was composed again. "If he comes here, I'll be happy to kill him too." He shrugged as if McKenzie's whereabouts were of no interest to him. I recalled a similar attitude shift in his son a few days before, who had been tense and agitated when he learned I had found the want on him, then shrugged the whole thing off a moment later when he must have realized I had tipped to the wrong want.

"I doubt he'll be alone," I replied. "How many men do you have here? Just these two goons? And that twerp?" I added, nodding toward Reginald.

I caught the flicker of doubt in Frank Martinelli's eye and realized something I should have figured out the moment we arrived. This so-called mob boss … wasn't. He was a lone wolf, simply trying to avenge a personal score. Despite his grandstanding, it would seem that his only purpose here really was to off Andrew and me, one to avoid going down for a murder rap, and the other just to settle an old score.

Chances were the mob wasn't backing him up at all, and Beanpole and Lard Butt really were all he had at the moment. Oh, and Reginald the Weenie. I already knew the extent of Reggie's courage. His primary method of self-defense was to turn tail and run.

With that realization came a glimmer of hope. But, whether he had two henchmen or a hundred, the score was still at least two to zip as far as guns were concerned. And Frank Martinelli no doubt had one or two tucked away in that massive desk somewhere.

"We've wasted enough time. I should have had you killed and dumped in the desert on the way up here, but I wanted to meet you again, Detective. I wanted you to know who was behind this, who had ordered your execution. And I wanted to see my son one more time before he died. Now I have seen you both. Time is up. Take them away." He nodded to Beanpole and Lard Butt and turned to talk to Reginald. I couldn't hear what they were saying.

We were dragged back through the house. I noted a phone on the kitchen wall as we passed through but there was no way to get to it with Lard Butt's gun digging into the small of my back.

To my surprise, we were loaded back into the truck and again left alone while our captors rode up front where the air-conditioning no doubt worked. I tried to remember the layout of the Martinelli estate while the truck backed out of the garage and pulled around in the circular driveway, heading toward the main road.

I wondered where we were going. Frank Martinelli had said someone was paying for the privilege of killing Andrew. I supposed I was being thrown in as part of the bargain just to keep Frank's hands clean.

We did not drive very far, maybe ten minutes total. The last five or more minutes were over a dirt road, and dust drifted into the truck when we finally lurched to a stop. I listened carefully, but did not hear any voices other than Beanpole and Lard Butt. I was pretty sure they weren't authorized to kill us, so I decided our best bet was not to antagonize them into committing any unauthorized acts.

The door was yanked open and Beanpole gestured with his gun. "Get out."

I climbed out, followed by Andrew. We had stopped in front of a shed of some kind, out in the middle of nowhere. "What are we doing here?" I dared to ask.

"You wait. In there." I felt Lard Butt's gun digging into the small of my back, shoving me toward the windowless shed.

There wasn't a lot of point in arguing, so we complied. The shed was dusty and empty except for a couple dozen or so old salt licks. The area didn't look much like cattle country to me, and judging from the dirt on the salt licks, there was a good chance the area hadn't looked like cattle country to anyone else, either, for many, many years.

The problem with being locked up with so much salt was the immediate thirst the sight of it brought on.

They forced us to sit on the floor, then Lard Butt tied our feet. Without another word of what was to happen next, they were gone. I heard them padlock the door as they left.

Typical of farm sheds, the hinges were on the outside of the door. The drafty old building had enough cracks and gaps in the wooden siding that we had enough light to see each other.

I heard the truck's engine start and the crunch of tires as it turned around and headed back the way we had come in.

Andrew had been largely silent through the whole ordeal and somehow I needed to snap him out of his despair. Beanpole had made one critical mistake. He had left my hands tied in front back at the house and neither of them realized it before they left. I quickly applied teeth and was free in a minute.

I untied Andrew and looked for a way out of the shed. The only way out was the door. The only weapons we seemed to have were the salt blocks, each weighing fifty pounds according to their tattered, dusty labels.

We had just hefted one and were preparing to hurl it against the door when I felt the beat of a helicopter rotor inside my head. A moment later, I heard it with my ears as well. It hovered for just a moment, then flew away.

"Wonder what that was all about," I muttered.

"Whoever it was, they didn't stay very long," Andrew replied. "Do you suppose they're good guys or bad guys?"

"I'm not sure there are any good guys in this scenario," I replied. "Come on. On three."

We swung the heavy salt lick back and forth three times, then let it fly. It thudded against the door, causing the edge to gap momentarily, then crashed to the floor.

"Let's try another," I suggested. We heaved another block, then a third, then a fourth, before giving up.

"Shit," I muttered. "There's got to be some way out of this shack." For the first time, I was starting to worry. We hadn't been told who was coming to kill us, but the fact that he was cautious enough to make sure there were no witnesses when he got there told me he was a professional. Probably Beanpole and Lard Butt didn't even know who was coming, but I was pretty sure I did. The only professional killer in this mix was Vinnie Delgado. Gilbert McKenzie may have tried hard to emulate him, but he was only a wannabe hit man, trying four times and missing every attempt. No, it had to be Delgado. He had the motive to want to kill Andrew, anyway.

I was pretty sure I didn't want to meet him.

I was also pretty sure there wasn't a damn thing I could do to save either of us.

Tired from heaving salt blocks, we sat on the floor again, leaning against the wall next to the door. "I'm sorry," Andrew said with a sigh. "This is all my fault."

"Doesn't matter anyway," I replied lightly. "If it hadn't been you, I'd be in some other scrape somewhere else."

"You're taking all this rather well, Angela," he said with a sideways glance, "considering we're both going to die soon. If not by being shot, from heat, thirst or hunger."

"Well, we all gotta go sometime," I answered with a shrug. "If our time is up, our time is up. Nothing we can do about it." I wondered if I really believed that.

"You going religious on me?"

"No. Just realistic. We'll either get a chance to survive or we won't. It doesn't look like we have many options."

We spent the next few minutes in silence. Then to my surprise Andrew said, "I wish we could have met under some other circumstances. Despite the fact that you're the most arrogant and stubborn woman I've ever me, I was really starting to like you. I wish I could have gotten to know you better before – all this," he ended lamely.

I turned to see if he was being facetious and found him studying me with those sexy brown eyes that had so captivated me – could it only be a week ago? His gaze held mine for a long time while I struggled to think of an appropriate response. I remembered the first time we had shared a semi-intimate moment had been at the restaurant, a moment before he had been shot. The last time had been at the Motel of the Neon Horse, when Andrew had unexpectedly kissed me goodbye before slipping away into the night. I finally tried to shrug off his comment with, "I'm sure you would have gotten over it in a few days. Sort of like having the flu. You think it's going to last forever while you're heaving your guts out but eventually you get over it."

He laughed, which amazed me under the circumstances, then I found myself laughing with him. He picked up my hand and gave it a squeeze that sent a tingle through my entire body. "Andrew, I –"

I didn't get to finish whatever it was I thought I was going to say, for in that moment, he pulled me to him and kissed me. I felt those sensuous lips caressing mine, felt his breath on the side of my cheek, felt his strong arms pulling me against his chest, and felt myself responding in a way I have never responded to any man before in my life – and I've had one or two. My arms went around his neck and held him tight while our lips and tongues explored each other with a passion no doubt heightened by the prospect of imminent death.

Dying in the arms of Andrew Field was a hell of a lot more appealing than a lot of other ways I've thought I'd go out.

Usually we don't get a choice in these matters. I wondered if I would now.

Chapter 24

I'M NOT SURE HOW IT HAPPENED, but we ended up lying on that hard wooden floor, fully clothed, but wrapped up in each other like a couple of hormonal teenagers, hands stroking each other's bodies while lips and tongues played tag with each other. I felt Andrew's right hand slide under my blouse and take some much-welcomed liberties with my left breast while his lips left mine, then nuzzled down my cheek to nibble the side of my neck.

Well, it would be a hell of a way to go, wouldn't it? I wondered what Delgado would think if he were to walk into that shed, expecting to find us tied up and subdued, trembling in fear, and instead found us making love on the floor of that shed as if we didn't have a care in the world. Well, maybe a little care for the splinters that would no doubt end up in our backsides.

As a fantasy, it was great. But reality gradually crept into my conscious mind, shoving the hormones aside, and alerting me to the fact that a car had just pulled up outside.

"Andrew, stop," I whispered. "Someone's here."

We quickly untangled ourselves from each other and I took a position next to the door. As soon as Delgado stepped into the shed, I would nail him on the back of the neck with all my strength and hope it was enough to knock him out. It was our only hope.

Andrew stepped up next to me, close enough that I could feel the heat radiating from his arm even though we weren't touching. I looked back at him, our eyes met and held for just a moment, then I heard the scrape of a crowbar against the hasp followed by the sound of splintering wood and a moment later the door was flung open. "Come out with your hands up!" I heard.

I waited tensely, not daring to breathe. Whoever was out there was no fool, rushing in where wise men would never go. So far he had made no attempt to enter, but I suspected he was moving back and forth, trying to see inside the shed without stepping across the threshold.

My heart pounded in my chest while we waited, one minute, two minutes, twelve, twenty minutes, an hour. Or so it seemed, anyway. It was probably more like forty-five seconds. What was going on? The footsteps retreated from the door.

I noticed a crack in the wall next to my left eye and tried to see outside. There was a man out there, but it wasn't Vinnie Delgado. Although I'd never seen Delgado before, I knew that with absolute certainty.

The man had retreated to his car door, and was standing there, leaning against it, talking into a hand-held microphone. He held the mike in his left hand, and in his right was a thirty-eight Special, pointed straight at the door to the shed.

Calling for backup, I mused. Just like we were taught. Good boy. I turned to Andrew. "Guess what, my dear? We're going to get out of this alive after all." I gave him a quick kiss on the side of the neck and called out, "Tim! We're coming out!"

With that I stepped over the salt blocks that were still lying in front of the door and walked confidently out into the sun and into the arms of Tim Reed, my former partner on the Myersburg police force. He gave me a heartfelt hug, which I returned. "Thank God you're all right!" he exclaimed.

He pushed me to the side and raised his gun as Andrew stepped out of the shed behind me. "You freeze where you are," he commanded.

"Tim, what are you doing? He's all right. He's my client."

"Sorry, Angel. He's under arrest." He stepped forward and effected the arrest of Andrew Field, my client, right in front of my eyes. "You have the right to remain silent," he began.

I grabbed Tim by the arm, cutting him off in mid-Miranda. "Why are you arresting him, Tim? He's done nothing wrong. He didn't take me. Someone else kidnapped both of us. For that matter, we'd better get the hell out of here before Delgado gets here or we're all dead meat."

"Angel, please stop interfering. There's a warrant out for the arrest of André Beauchamp for the murder of Cassandra Baxter, among other things." He finished reading Andrew his rights while I looked on, helpless.

"Andrew," I promised, "we'll get this straightened out at the station. I know you didn't kill her."

Andrew exercised his right to remain silent. Tim loaded him in the back of the unmarked car. Our unmarked car, I recognized with a pang of nostalgia. This was the same car I had been driving on that fateful day when I chased that drug runner into the reservoir.

"Angel," Tim said sadly, "I'm really sorry, but I have to arrest you, too." He held out a second set of handcuffs.

I stared at him in complete disbelief. "Me? For what?"

"Well, aiding and abetting Mr. Beauchamp, for one thing." He tried to take hold of my right wrist, but I slapped him aside.

"Tim, that's nuts. You know he's innocent."

"It doesn't matter what I think I know, Angel. You know that."

"Tim, there's a price on our heads right now. You lock us up and you're signing our death warrants. Our only chance is to keep moving. There's a very nasty piece of work heading this way to kill us both."

"Delgado. I know about him. Jesus, Angel, how did you get mixed up with Delgado anyway?"

"How did you know I was here at all, Tim? I think you need to do some explaining before I answer any questions without benefit of legal counsel."

"We've had Frank Martinelli under surveillance since he got out of prison. We followed the truck when it left his place. Unfortunately, we were blocked by a semi when the pickup exited the freeway and we had to double back. By the time we got to that dirt road, the truck had disappeared, but it came back within minutes and we picked them up before they reached the highway. They admitted to leaving two people in a shed, a man and a woman, but wouldn't say more than that without a lawyer. I did my best to persuade them to talk, too."

"I'll bet you did. Wish I could have been there," I grunted with just a trace of jealousy.

"Anyway, I suspected it was you, don't ask me how, so I came on alone to check."

"Didn't you just call for backup?"

"I was about to until you came out. Instead I told them I had found nobody at the shed."

"Why did you lie?"

"Because I'm pretty sure the guys back at the highway are on someone else's payroll besides the city of Myersburg, if you get my drift."

"They'll think Delgado has already come in here and taken us out."

"That's what I wanted them to think. Until you came out, I thought maybe he had. I thought you'd answer once you heard my voice but I wasn't keen to stick my head in that shed alone not knowing for sure who was there. Anyone else would have been trying to kill me, thinking I was Delgado."

"So what are you really going to do with us?"

"You're really under arrest. I'm really taking you to the station. And you really need to cooperate with me, Angel, for your own safety."

"I don't need to be cuffed, Tim. Don't do this to me."

He sighed and put the cuffs away. "Get in. The back, Angel, the back," he added when I started to reach for the front door.

Reluctantly, I climbed in next to Andrew, patting his knee to reassure him. He wouldn't look at me. Tim got in the car and drove down the dirt road, away from the highway where his crooked co-workers were no doubt waiting for him. A few miles later, the dirt road intersected a gravel road leading in the general direction of Myersburg.

He drove without speaking, while I sat in the back and fumed. How could he do this to me? I could understand why he had to arrest Andrew. Andrew actually had warrants out on him. But I didn't, and Tim knew good and well that I was no accomplice to anything Andrew was suspected of doing.

What was really degrading was being forced to sit in the back like a common criminal. How long had we shared the front seat of this car?

The road wound through some hills and washes, around one blind turn after another, punctuated by a sickening drop when the road fell off sharply into another wash. Visibility was limited to the next curve or hill.

Which is what made it very easy for someone to ambush us. We crested a hill and started to drop into the bottom when the side of the car was peppered by a hail of bullets fired from behind a black Monte Carlo parked on the left side of the road. Both tires blew and the car lurched violently to the side. I'd almost forgotten how completely level-headed Tim had always been. Rather than hit the brakes, he hit the gas, scrambling up over the top of the next rise before skidding to a halt and jumping out of the car.

"Damn it, Tim!" I shouted. "Let me out! I can help!"

He hesitated only for a fraction of a second, then pulled the door open, freeing me but leaving Andrew locked in the car. He opened the trunk and pulled out a rifle, leaving me to find my own weapons. I grabbed the shotgun and an extra handgun that I knew he always kept under the front seat.

Tim had taken a position behind a rock and was searching for the shooter down in the wash somewhere. I could see the car, an old black Monte Carlo, parked just off the pavement. I couldn't believe he had really expected to take us out in a hail of random, unaimed gunfire, but he had succeeded in stopping us. The fact that he had shot low, at the tires, made me suspect his intention was to capture us alive.

But how could he expect to do that alone?

Or was he alone?

Chapter 25

I FELT THE HAIR ON THE BACK OF MY NECK PRICKLE. This had to be a setup. Delgado needed Andrew alive so he could find out where Jason was. "Tim," I hissed. "This isn't right."

He didn't look at me, intent on finding the source of the gunfire that had crippled our car. "What isn't right?"

"He didn't kill us. And I doubt he'd be laying for us alone, Tim." I looked back at our car. Andrew was wisely keeping himself low and I knew the body of the car would stop a bullet so he was safe as long as nobody got close enough to shoot through a window. I quickly scanned the area, squinting against the sunlight, and was rewarded by a glimpse of the merest puff of dust behind a low mound. "I was right. Over there," I pointed as Tim finally looked around. "They're after Andrew."

Andrew was a sitting duck. I took aim with the pistol and fired a single round at the dust cloud while Tim rolled over into a crouch and sprinted toward the car. He opened the door to release Andrew, who crawled out of the back seat and crouched next to the car by Tim. I ran toward a tree, pinning myself against its trunk as tightly as I could. It was no Kevlar vest, but it was all I had at the moment.

A shot rang out from the mound, striking the rear door of the car with a dull *thunk*. Tim fired back with the rifle and the gunman broke cover and ran toward the wash. I picked him off with the pistol. One down. How many to go? I wished I knew what Delgado looked like.

I glanced down at the Monte Carlo, took aim, and shot its right front tire. A head popped up from behind the car and I knew where the first gunman was. But how many more might there be, hidden in the desert? I turned to watch Tim's back, scanning the desert landscape for any sign of movement, but saw nothing. I looked back down at the Monte Carlo and decided to flush the game. I fired one round from the shotgun. It peppered the Monte Carlo with four gauge buckshot but didn't do any major damage to what might become our own getaway car. It succeeded in flushing the other gunman, who bolted behind some rocks and fired in my direction.

Tim had been on the radio, which was both a relief and a source of concern. On the one hand, we were not in the best position to get out of this alive without backup. On the other hand, if Tim was right about his fellow officers being on someone else's payroll, I wasn't sure I wanted any of them to show up. He ran over to me. "You okay?" he asked.

"Sure," I replied with a wink. "Never better." I grinned and he grinned back. He knew very well that I enjoyed a good shootout as much as a good high speed chase. Maybe more. In the six years I worked at Myersburg, there had been three shootouts of any notice and I'd managed to get involved in two of them, the most recent with Tim at my side. Most cops go their whole careers without getting shot at, but I seem to draw gunfire like a magnet. I'd been lucky so far. I'd only been hit once. Well, twice counting McKenzie's poorly aimed graze at the gas station.

"Well, you got one," he said. "Where's the other one?"

I pointed across the wash. He fired the rifle where I pointed and the gunman ran further up the hill, out of the wash. "There's got to be another one, Tim. I haven't spotted him yet, but there's got to be another one. This is too bold a move for just two of them."

"I agree," Tim replied. "I'm also curious why they're not making more effort to kill us."

"You noticed that, too, huh? I think they need Andrew alive, but I can't figure why they haven't made a move on you and me, though. I doubt they have any compunctions against killing cops."

Tim glanced over. "You're not a cop, Angel. And as far as anyone is concerned, I shot that guy over there, not you. You know how much trouble I'll be in if anyone finds out I armed a civilian? Especially a civilian I just arrested about twenty minutes ago?"

I laughed. "Come on, Tim. You didn't give me the gun. I stole it, remember? When your back was turned?"

"I'll be in more trouble for that. Here," he said, handing me his gun. "Give me the one you shot him with. Try not to kill anybody else unless I'm down, okay?"

His thirty-eight was identical to Charley, and feeling it in my hand made me feel better about life in general. We would get out of this, somehow.

Tim used the shotgun to push the gunman further up the hill, then used the rifle to pick him off. Two down.

As the echo of the gunshot receded into silence, we continued to scan for other shooters. Ahead of our car was another blind wash. The road rose to a crest beyond which nothing could be seen. It would be the ideal spot for a second ambush. I touched Tim's arm and pointed past our car. "I'll bet he's over there," I said. "We've been on this side of the car all along. He's probably waiting for a clear shot. Doesn't want to drive us back down into this wash. He was probably expecting us to keep driving. When we stopped up here, it messed up his plans. What do you think?"

"I think you're probably right," he replied. "And now he doesn't know what to do since he's too far away to get to us without being seen."

"So what do we do about it?"

"I've got help on the way. I think I'd better go warn them. They'll be coming from that direction."

He started to move, but I grabbed his arm. "Wait a minute, Tim." I listened for a moment, and heard the helicopter approaching from behind the wash. "Can we trust them?"

"I don't know who they are. That's not our chopper."

I stared at him. "Not yours? Then whose? There was one at Martinelli's house, and one flew over that shed before you got there."

"I have no idea, but I don't like this."

The chopper moved in and we waited under the cover of the tree. Andrew had crawled back into the car and was again staying low. From the perspective of the helicopter, I was pretty sure none of us could be seen. I looked through the tree branches, trying to see who was in it. The 'copter was solid black, with a few numbers painted on its belly in white, but they meant nothing to me. It hovered briefly over our car, then rose and turned in place, doing a complete three-sixty before hovering once more over the car. It moved slowly forward, in the direction where I was pretty sure a third assailant was hiding.

A shot rang out, and the pilot pulled the chopper up, then moved to the right and came back, circling behind the gunman. The gunman fired again, but the bullets ricocheted harmlessly off the skids of the helicopter, amazingly missing the sides or rotor. I saw the door slide open on the helicopter, then a rifle protruded and a single well-placed shot sent the gunman's body tumbling off the hill, rolling about twenty feet before stopping against a rock.

While Tim and I watched in stunned and curious silence, the helicopter made several passes over the area, then returned and landed about fifty feet from our car.

Tim and I dropped to the ground and backed away from the tree on our hands and knees, lying on the ground with guns leveled at the helicopter. Three men got out and started to walk toward the car, two with guns at the ready, the third unarmed and looking primarily nervous.

I think we each realized at the same moment who our rescuers were. "Felix!" I called out while Tim simultaneously shouted, "Gil! Over here!"

We looked at each other for one puzzled moment, then both stood and walked back to the car. Andrew, completely bewildered, climbed out of the car.

Felix came over and gave me a hug. "You okay, Boss?"

"I'm fine, Felix, and thank God you are too. I had no idea if you were dead or alive."

"I would have been dead if it weren't for Mr. McKenzie here. The real Gilbert McKenzie, that is."

Tim was talking to the real Gilbert McKenzie, who was about fifty, tall, blond, clean shaven, had normal-sized ears and wore a nice suit.

"What's going on here?" I demanded of anybody.

McKenzie looked over at me. "Thanks for keeping Mr. Martin safe for us. We'll take over from here."

"Who's 'we'?"

He flipped out a badge holder and I saw a twin to the ID I had seen a few days before in the coffee shop of Andrew's motel in Phoenix. "FBI?" I sniffed. "Now where have I heard that before?"

"He's for real, Angela," Felix assured me. "I've been at the FBI field office most of the morning, telling them everything I knew about André Jacques Martin. McKenzie had been following my rental car ever since we left the motel yesterday. He lost us when you switched cars."

"I thought we were being tailed by some accomplice of the other Gilbert McKenzie."

"We were. This Gilbert McKenzie intercepted him, took his car, tailed us using the tracking device, then went to that place in the desert, not knowing we were tailing him at that point."

"So where's Dumbo now? Still in that tractor shed?"

"No, he's in jail in Phoenix. By the way, he's pretty mad at you. A scorpion stung him on the butt before we got back to him." He grinned.

I grinned back. If anyone deserved a pain in the ass, it was that pain in the ass. "Who was at that other place in the desert, anyway?"

"You'll never guess."

"Don't make me try."

"John Smith and a dozen kids."

The third man from the helicopter, presumably the pilot, had gone to check on the third dead body. He turned around and gave a thumbs-up sign to Gilbert McKenzie, who leaned over and said something to

Andrew, who was still in handcuffs. The look of pure relief on Andrew's face was all I needed to know that Vinnie Delgado had finally bitten the big one.

"So who's left?" I asked Felix. "For that matter, how the hell did you find me?"

"Long story, Boss, and we're probably not safe here."

"Tim," I said. He turned to face me. "How did you get involved in all this? How do you know McKenzie?"

"Angel, your friend there is correct. We need to get out of here. Then we'll tell you everything."

"Then someone better get busy changing tires."

"No, we'll leave the cars. I've got Myersburg P.D. on the way. We'll take all the guns with us and leave the cars for them to tow out of here. I've already called. But I can't be here when anyone gets here either."

McKenzie ordered Tim to remove Andrew's handcuffs, then he took Andrew by the elbow and escorted him to the waiting helicopter. The pilot had already regained his seat, put on his helmet, and started the engines. Tim took back his gun, tucking it back into its holster. The backup gun, the one I had shot someone with – I still didn't know who – he stuck into his waistband. He let me carry the shotgun to the helicopter, then placed it and the rifle on the floor in the back of the chopper.

There were two seats in the front and four in the rear compartment. McKenzie sat in front by the pilot. Andrew sat behind the pilot, facing Tim. Felix sat behind McKenzie and I sat next to Tim, facing Felix. We all pulled on helmets with intercoms in them while the engines reached a high whine and the pilot lifted us off.

"All right," I said once we were in the air, leaving behind two dead cars and three dead men, one of whom I surmised was Vinnie Delgado, although nobody had confirmed this to me. "Will someone please tell me what's going on? Tim?"

Tim looked at McKenzie, who nodded. I wondered why my former partner was looking to an FBI agent for permission to speak. "Angel, when you called me last week, my casual inquiry got picked up on the FBI's radar and the next thing I knew, McKenzie here was demanding to know why I was interested in the André Beauchamp case. It took awhile before I was convinced he was for real, but once I was, I knew you were in a lot of danger. I tried calling your office several times that morning but could never raise you. Even your answering service didn't know where you were, and your cell phone number wasn't working either."

"Sorry," I replied. "You must have called back when Felix was driving me to the airport and later that afternoon the cell phone battery died. I guess we forgot to check for messages after that. We were kinda busy."

"I know. Anyway, once McKenzie told me the whole story behind your friend here," he continued, nodding in Andrew's direction, "I realized you were in big trouble. I knew you knew that Frank Martinelli was released from prison. But I also knew, based on the fact that you didn't mention it, that you had no idea you were dealing with Martinelli's son." He reached over and put his hand on my shoulder, squeezing it firmly. "I knew Martinelli wanted you dead. I also was able to find out why he was out of prison years earlier than he should have been. But more on that later."

His hand stayed on my shoulder, and I found the gesture at the same time patronizing and yet comforting. "I was afraid Frank Martinelli was somehow using his son to get you where he could kill you. Remember, I tried to warn you to get away from André. I knew there were mob connections; I just didn't know the nature of them.

"Anyway, we were already keeping a general eye on Martinelli, but I convinced my superiors that Martinelli needed to be put under twenty-four-hour surveillance. I kept your name out of it, but told them I was in touch with an informant who had been specifically threatened by Martinelli. It was a lie, but it worked. We've had round-the-clock surveillance on Frank Martinelli's estate for almost a week. He picked someone up at the airport yesterday, then today that blue pickup truck came and left. By that time, McKenzie had notified me that you'd been taken at gunpoint and were probably on your way here in a blue truck. He didn't know they already had André. To make a long story short, as soon as I got word of the truck leaving again, I ordered it followed. We caught them coming out after they dumped you in that shed. I came on in and found you. The rest, I think you know."

I patted Tim's hand, which was still on my shoulder. "Thanks for saving my life, Tim. I don't think I said that before." I felt an answering squeeze, then turned my attention to McKenzie. "Your turn now, McKenzie. Who did you kill back there? Delgado?"

"Yes."

"How did you know he would be there?"

"We have our ways. Sorry I can't be more specific."

"Like hell you're sorry," I muttered. Still, he may have saved all our lives with that shot, so I decided to cut him some slack. "What about Frank Martinelli? Is he still free as a bird?"

"We've got nothing on him at the moment. His release from prison was highly irregular, and smacks of a political payoff of some kind, but it was legal, and he's keeping his nose clean so far."

"You call kidnapping us 'keeping his nose clean'?" I spat.

"He didn't kidnap you."

"No, Beanpole and Lard Butt did." McKenzie glanced back and looked at me strangely. Andrew smiled. I could feel Tim shake as he chuckled silently. I ignored all of them. "But they took us to him. He said we were to be killed."

"You're still alive, aren't you? He's still being watched. And as soon as we get André somewhere safe, he'll be picked up on an arrest warrant for the murder of – " he broke off when Andrew interrupted.

"Don't say it!" he nearly shouted. "She doesn't know anything about it!"

Chapter 26

I GLARED AT MY CLIENT, WITH WHOM only an hour before I had been rolling around on the floor of a shed in an amorous embrace. "Who? Who did he kill? You owe me that much of an explanation, Andrew!" I snapped.

"No," Gilbert said before Andrew could say any more. "He's right. You're better off not to know."

I sighed with pure annoyance and looked at Felix. He shook his head. "I have no idea, Boss."

"Okay," I said, "so after Martinelli is arrested, then what happens? There are still other people who want Andrew dead, and probably me as well. In fact, how did you get Felix out alive?"

"I was there when they took you," McKenzie replied. "I didn't interfere because I was pretty sure they would lead us to André, and he was the one whose testimony we needed. Unfortunately, the men we had following them lost them right after that, but we were pretty sure we knew where they were heading by then."

"Gee, thanks," I retorted sarcastically. "As long as the end justifies the means, everything is fine. Never occurred to you that they could have killed me at any time, did it?"

He went on as if I hadn't spoken but I noted a reddening of his cheeks in front of his helmet at my criticism. "After they left with you, we went into your room to see if there was any evidence left behind. We found Felix."

I looked at my secretary. He had a few cuts and abrasions on his face, and his left eye looked like mine usually did on the rare occasions when I applied eye shadow. "What happened to you after they got me?"

"They beat me up," he replied with a shrug. "That's all. Left me unconscious. I'm okay."

I raised an eyebrow but said nothing. It must have taken some doing to take out my black-belted assistant.

"Felix was able to fill in a lot of blanks for us, Ms Virago," McKenzie continued. "We were able to figure out why Mr. Beauchamp here felt he had to flee from our protection. We also found out he had returned to Phoenix, but fell into the clutches of someone impersonating me. It was crucial we get him back, get his testimony as quickly as possible, and get him somewhere safe again until the trial. Through Felix, we learned that his primary motivation for staying out of sight was gone. Jason Delgado was safe. Unfortunately, Brian was already dead. But being dead, he no longer needed André's protection."

"He was only seven," Andrew said quietly. "He deserved better. I let him down."

"You did everything you could," I said. "And you saved his brother."

He nodded, then turned his head away. I saw a single tear escape the corner of his eye and run down his cheek, finally dropping onto his shirt. My heart went out to him. What would happen to him now? To both of us? I remembered again the intensity of feeling that had overcome me in the shed, with his lips on mine, his hands on my body. How could I ever let him go?

Gilbert's voice brought me back to the present. "We've contained nearly everyone now. We've got Martinelli under surveillance. Delgado is dead. John Smith is under arrest in Phoenix. My imposter is under arrest. Felix told me about Fred Gaines. He's been cooperating with Smith because he was being blackmailed. You see, he knew all along his adoption of André wasn't legal. We picked him and his wife up for questioning and he couldn't sing fast enough once he found out the statute of limitations ran out years ago for any criminal charges relating to that adoption. Gaines feels terrible for putting André, the son he raised, through this. We haven't figured out the wife's angle yet. She claimed not to know anything. I've got a funny feeling about her. For the moment, they're both in protective custody."

"Sounds like we're about out of bad guys," I said lightly, feeling some relief after the recitation of arrest statistics. Everyone who wanted us dead was under control. There were no more loose ends, and I could finally look forward to wrapping up this case and getting back to my life in Clarkdale.

Tim's hand still rested lightly on my shoulder and I glanced over at him. There was still one more loose end, I realized. "Tim, you said there were cops on the take involved with this case. How do you know?"

He pulled his hand back and I saw his face shift into "Evasive" mode. I'd seen that expression a number of times, usually when we were conducting some kind of undercover job, and occasionally when we were explaining ourselves to our superiors after one of our more, shall we say, energetic arrests. Seeing it now, when it was I who had asked the question, was disturbing. I was about to be lied to. Was it for my benefit or the other listeners'?

"I don't know that they are. I suspected it from the way they handled the prisoners who kidnapped you. I could be wrong. Probably I am. Forget I said anything." Good. The evasion was for the benefit of the other listeners in the helicopter, not me. But who? McKenzie? The pilot? Andrew? Why wouldn't he want them to know what he suspected?

I played along. "Then it sounds like we're home free. So where are we going? Phoenix? Does anyone know where my car is at the moment?"

McKenzie replied, "Yes, we're going to Phoenix. Well, near Phoenix, anyway. We won't come in at the airport. I don't know where your car is. Probably been impounded somewhere."

Tim again rested his hand on my shoulder and I took a great deal of comfort in the knowledge that Tim would never betray me. He had managed to convey to me, without saying a word about it, that he had reservations about trusting our rescuers one hundred percent. I wondered what had caused him to be concerned. I glanced over at the pilot. I couldn't see much of his face from that angle since the helmet covered most of it, but I could see a neatly trimmed beard and mustache, and I recalled he had worn a military-style green cap pulled down over his forehead when he came out of the helicopter to check Delgado's body. The wraparound dark glasses he wore under the helmet made him look like something out of a spy thriller movie. I supposed he had a name, but nobody had bothered introducing us. He was just another anonymous government agent. I supposed the FBI was staffed with hundreds of them, performing routine tasks like flying helicopters and identifying bodies so that Special Agents like McKenzie wouldn't have to get their hands dirty.

Identifying bodies. It seemed strange that the pilot was the one to ID Delgado's body. McKenzie had taken his word for it without even looking at the body. Why? I wished I had gone to check for myself. What if this guy was wrong? What if it wasn't Delgado at all, but someone carrying Delgado's ID? I was quite sure the pilot hadn't checked fingerprints or dental records out there in the middle of nowhere. How did he know it was Delgado? And who else was dead back there? Nobody had even glanced at the other two bodies. Why?

With more questions than answers, I decided to go fishing. "So how long have you been working this case?" I asked McKenzie.

He glanced back at me. "About a year."

"How about him?" I asked, nodding at the pilot.

"Oh, he's not working this case at all. He just happened to be the chopper pilot for the day," he replied.

I glossed past this quickly with, "So you're the one in charge, I assume. Or are there other higher-ups interested as well?"

"It's my case. The higher-ups are there for the purpose of approving budget requests."

Some ego. "How long will it take to get to Phoenix in this thing? And is there any water in it?"

"Oh, sure. Sorry. There's a pack behind Tim's seat with supplies in it."

I groped behind the seat and found a backpack from which I pulled out some emergency water rations – flat foil packets containing a half-pint of water each. I took two for myself and gave two to Andrew. Tim and Felix declined. We each drank the entire contents of both packets, and I couldn't help noting how even water can be made to taste bad once the government gets involved with it. At least I had confirmation that this was a government helicopter.

"So how much longer?" I repeated, dropping the empty packets on the floor of the chopper.

The pilot spoke for the first time. "Couple hours."

"Oh," I said flatly. "Wish I'd known that before I drank all that water." In about forty-five minutes, I would no doubt need a restroom – and I didn't see any sign saying "Ladies" anywhere in the chopper.

McKenzie grinned, and I saw a smirk on the left side of the pilot's face. Tim stroked the back of my neck. "I'm sure we can persuade them to set it down if you need a pit stop," he said.

"Sure, sure, no problem," McKenzie agreed.

The pilot said nothing.

Andrew had barely spoken since getting into the helicopter. I looked at him, but he was looking out the window. I found myself wondering about the status of his bladder. After all, I had gone potty at Frank Martinelli's house, but Andrew hadn't been to a restroom since I joined him in the truck that morning. How the hell did he do it?

We flew for another hour, and I began to squirm as predicted. "I don't think I'm going to make Phoenix," I finally confessed. "Where are we?"

"Over the middle of nowhere," the pilot replied. "Near Kingman, I guess."

"Any bushes down there?"

The pilot leaned to the side to look out the window at the ground. "A few."

"Well, I need to go water one. Probably Andrew does, too."

"Set it down," McKenzie ordered.

We landed in the middle of a windswept plain. McKenzie opened his front door and stepped out to help Felix open the left rear door while Tim opened the rear door on the other side. As he turned away from me to follow Andrew out of the right-side door, I saw my chance. I reached around his side and smoothly relieved Tim of the gun in his waistband and turned it on the pilot in the same motion.

He turned to face me and froze, his face a mixture of surprise and cunning. I knew in that moment my instincts had been correct … and I was very, very lucky.

Chapter 27

"GET OUT," I ORDERED. "NOW." I held the gun to his head while I reached over his shoulder to relieve him of his sidearm before he unplugged his helmet cord from the dash, opened the door and climbed out. I kept the gun on him as I jumped out of the back door, landing next to Andrew and Tim, who comprehended immediately what I was doing and pushed Andrew back out of the way so he could back me up. The pilot glared at me but held his hands elevated as I walked him around the front of the helicopter to where Felix and McKenzie had been expecting me to jump out of the left-hand door.

"What the hell?" This came from Gilbert McKenzie, who suddenly realized his pilot was at the end of my gun. He started to reach for his own handgun, but by this point Tim had him covered too.

"Toss your gun in there, Gilbert," I commanded, gesturing toward the helicopter. "Both of you, on the ground, spread-eagled." I jabbed the pilot in the back with the barrel of my gun.

After they complied, Tim and I frisked them to be sure they weren't carrying backup weapons. They were. "Felix," I said over my shoulder to my completely astonished assistant, "come hold a gun on this bozo while I go water the bushes. I really do need to pee, you know."

"Ms Virago," Gilbert mumbled from the ground, "you don't have to hold us at gunpoint to go to the bathroom. We wouldn't have left you."

"I know you wouldn't have, you moron, but what do you know about this pilot you're so willing to trust our lives to?"

Tim was going through said pilot's pockets and tossed me a wallet. "Bernard Williams," I read. "Age twenty-three, brown hair, brown eyes."

"He's no twenty-three," Tim stated flatly. "He's forty if he's a day, probably more." He pulled off the dark glasses and looked at the man's eyes. "I wouldn't call those peepers brown. Hazel, maybe. Who do you suppose he really is?" He pulled off the helmet and tossed it aside. The man had a large area of baldness extending halfway back his scalp. The rest of his hair was black.

After seeing that we had things under control, Andrew had walked around from the other side of the helicopter. I wasn't very surprised when he blanched at the sight of the now-unmasked pilot lying on the ground.

"Delgado!" he exclaimed. He looked sharply at McKenzie, who was by now sitting up, looking as shocked as Andrew. "You told me you killed him," he said accusingly.

"I thought I had." He shook his head. "Tim, what's going on? How did you know he was an imposter?"

"I didn't know for sure until Angela took him at gunpoint. And for the record, we are not headed for Phoenix. We're almost in New Mexico." He pulled out the handcuffs he had almost put on me a few hours earlier. "Would you like to do the honors?" he asked, handing them to me.

"With pleasure." I took the cuffs and walked over to Vinnie Delgado, the Orkin man. I grabbed his right arm and twisted it behind his back while kneeling on his kidneys. "Hey, Orkin man," I said, "you have the right to remain silent." I snapped the handcuff on that wrist and shoved my knee deeper into his spine while I grabbed his other arm. "If you give up your right to remain silent, anything you say can and will be used against you in a court of law." I snapped the cuff on his other wrist, then stood up and kicked him over gently with my foot. "Hey, Tim," I said, "what exactly are we arresting him for, anyway?"

"Let's go with kidnapping for the moment, okay? Of us. He did cross state lines, too. That makes it a major federal rap."

"Okay." I looked down at Delgado. "You have a right to an attorney. If you can't afford one, oh, hell, you know the rest of it. You've been arrested a dozen times. You understand your rights?"

Delgado said nothing.

"He says he understands his rights, Tim. What do we do with him now?"

"A bigger question might be, how the hell are we going to get out of here?" McKenzie asked. "I don't see a road anywhere."

"Tim will drive," I replied. Tim had flown the helicopter for the Myersburg Police Department for two years before becoming my partner. I was pretty sure he could figure this one out.

"Whose body did you ID, Vinnie?" I asked our prisoner. He didn't reply. I shrugged. "Oh, well. I guess we'll have to read it in the papers tomorrow."

I handed my gun to Felix and disappeared behind a bush to take care of nature, aware that Andrew was discreetly watering another bush on the other side of the helicopter. When I returned, Tim and Felix had loaded Delgado into the back of the chopper and tied his feet securely. I pulled Tim aside. "I have to ask this, Tim. Are you very, very, very sure that McKenzie is who he says he is?"

"Frankly, I'm not sure of anything anymore," he replied.

"Then I say we cuff McKenzie until we get to civilization."

"I'm probably going to regret this, but that's probably our best bet right now." Tim turned to Gilbert, who was still unarmed. "Gilbert, I hope you don't mind, but at this point I'm not inclined to trust even you." He pointed his gun at the FBI agent.

"Tim, what are you doing?" Gilbert protested. "This is a federal offense, you know."

"Sorry, but self-preservation comes first." He handed the other set of handcuffs to Felix, who had witnessed everything without comment or comprehension. "Cuff Mr. McKenzie, please." Felix complied without a word.

"Tim, you're going to regret this," McKenzie warned. "You're going to blow the whole thing this way. I'm one of the good guys, remember?"

"Probably, but I can't take any chances. Get in." He gestured toward the helicopter.

Tim took the controls, this time with Andrew next to him and McKenzie behind Andrew, facing the rear of the helicopter. I sat behind Tim, in a position that enabled me to watch Andrew, McKenzie, and Delgado. Felix sat facing me, holding one of McKenzie's guns, where he had a good view of Delgado, who was trussed up like a turkey behind the empty seat.

Two hours later, we actually reached the outskirts of Phoenix. Wherever Delgado thought he had been taking us, we would never know. McKenzie directed us to the small airstrip from which they had originally come and Tim set the helicopter down on the helipad and killed the engine. He pulled off his helmet and climbed out of the helicopter. I slid my door open, pulled off my own helmet, and looked down at him.

"Now what do we do, Tim?" I asked.

"I have no idea, Angel. Delgado's a slam dunk. There's a warrant out for him. If McKenzie is for real, we're probably in a lot of trouble right now. If not, we may be heroes. I have a name of a man who can sort this out." He showed me a card with the name Jake Boswell and a local phone number, then pulled a folding cell phone out of his front pants pocket and dialed. "Everyone just stay put for now. I don't want any witnesses to see us holding guns on these guys till I know who's who."

While he waited to be connected, I looked at Andrew, who had removed his helmet but remained in the front seat. My client had been very quiet since the unmasking of Vinnie Delgado. I wondered what this all meant to him now. "What do you want to do, Andrew?" I asked.

He hesitated before answering. "I want to get this over with, I guess. None of these guys ever work alone, and I'll never be safe until I'm dead and buried again."

"There you go with that 'dead again' business, Andrew."

"My death as André Beauchamp was reported a year ago, Angela, when I entered the witness protection program. That's the only reason I've been alive all this time. But the Andrew Field identity broke down. I need another one." He turned to look over his shoulder at McKenzie. "I think he's on the level, but you must understand, I've never met him."

"Who have you met? Officially, I mean. Who set up your identity?"

"He's dead," McKenzie injected. "That's part of the problem. Look, I understand why you felt you couldn't trust me. Jake will vouch for me, then we can get this all straightened out. The important thing is we have Delgado, and we have André to testify against him. Now that the gun has been found, we can finally put this guy where he belongs."

"Sounds like Andrew has a lot of people to testify against," I mused. "What I'd like to know is why is the FBI involved in this at all. We're talking a simple, domestic, attempted murder with Delgado. Frank Martinelli is another domestic murder rap. Why the federal interest? Because of John Smith's baby selling racket? Sounds pretty lame to me."

McKenzie looked around at Andrew, who shook his head. "Please don't," he said simply.

"It was because of who Martinelli killed," McKenzie answered. "For the moment, I won't tell you who it was, since André is so adamant about it."

"This was almost thirty years ago. Who the hell did he kill? Jimmy Hoffa?"

"Not quite, but let's just say the story was on the front page all across the nation at the time."

Since I had been no older than Andrew at the time, I had no idea what high-profile murder from that long ago might still be unsolved. Why didn't Andrew want me to know? I had gotten accustomed to his lies and evasions while I tracked down his own murky past and present, but this was the final piece of the puzzle and I felt cheated by not being in on it.

Tim snapped the phone shut. "Jake described him to a tee. Just need to check one thing." He climbed in past me and pulled Gilbert's shirt out of his pants and exposed the man's belly. There was a scar on the left side, probably a bullet graze had caused it. "It's him," he confirmed. "Sorry about that, Gilbert. No hard feelings, I hope?" He released the handcuffs.

"Forget it, Tim. At least we got what we wanted, and we're all still alive." He rubbed his wrists a moment while Tim opened the left-side door and got out. McKenzie followed him, tucking his shirt back in, and Felix and I hopped out our own door and walked around to the other side where we helped Andrew open the front door and climb out with us. We left Delgado where he was behind the rear seats.

"All right, André," McKenzie said, taking the handcuffs from Tim. "I have to bring you in under arrest. Are we going to do this nicely or not?"

With a sigh, Andrew put his hands behind his back but McKenzie settled for cuffing himself to Andrew. Andrew's eyes met mine and I felt a pang of regret – regret that Tim hadn't waited another fifteen minutes before liberating us from that shed. Chances were, once McKenzie took him away, I would never see him again.

Felix must have been reading my mind, for he put his hand on my shoulder and gave it a comforting squeeze. "Come on, Boss. I think our work here is done," he said quietly.

I stepped over to Andrew and threw both arms around his neck, frustrated that he could only hug me back with one arm. "I'm sorry, Andrew," I whispered. "I'm sorry this happened this way."

"I'll be all right, Angela. I'm not in any trouble, they're just not going to let me out of their sight until after all the trials are over. I'll probably be in protective custody for at least a year."

I kissed him, unashamedly, aware that Tim and Felix were both looking on. "I don't want to lose you, Andrew," I said. McKenzie looked away, embarrassed.

"I don't want to lose you, either. But there's no other way. I have to cut all ties. I never meant this to happen, Angela." He raised his hands to touch my face, dragging McKenzie's arm with him. "I wish we'd met under some other circumstances." He kissed me again, then McKenzie pulled his arm back and nudged him in the side.

"Come on, André. The car's here."

Andrew stepped away from me, and I looked over at the dark gray sedan that had arrived. It was a twin to the car the phony Gilbert McKenzie had driven the day I followed Andrew to Phoenix. A second car pulled up behind it. Tim got Delgado out of the helicopter and led him over to the second car and turned him over to two armed agents.

Felix had appeared at my elbow and was watching me watch the car with Andrew Field inside drive away. "You going to be okay?" he asked gently.

A felt a tear trickle down my cheek. "I'll survive." Angrily, I brushed the tear away. "Fuck it. He's just another lying hunk of beefcake. Not my first. Won't be my last." I tried to smile. "At least I hope not."

Felix patted my arm. "Come on. Let's go find your car."

"Wait a minute, Felix. I have to talk to Tim first." I walked over to Tim, who was watching the car with Vinnie Delgado inside it leave the airport.

"They could have offered us a ride," he muttered.

"I guess they didn't need us any more," I replied.

Tim turned to me and held his arms open. "You look like you need a hug," he said. I stepped into his embrace, clinging tightly to him while I fought down a sob that threatened to escape. "Looks like he was more than just a client, Angel. How did that happen?" His hand gently smoothed my hair.

I sniffled once. "You know me, Tim. I'm a sucker for anything in pants. Right now, it's a damn good thing you're married and I like your wife because I have a pent-up need that badly wants relief."

He laughed. "What about your assistant, there?"

"He's gay, thank God. Lord knows, it's bad enough my having the hots for a client. I don't need to be screwing the help."

Tim gave me a kiss on the side of my neck then took my hand in his and led me over to where my resourceful assistant was using Tim's phone to arrange for ground transportation.

We collected the guns out of the helicopter and closed the doors. A taxi arrived and we took it to the nearest hotel. Two men and a woman checking in with a rifle and a shotgun and no luggage or car raised several eyebrows, but after Tim identified himself as a police officer, the desk clerk relaxed and gave us a suite of adjoining rooms. While we were checking in, Felix made arrangements for a rental car to be delivered as soon as possible.

Felix and Tim offered to share a room, but I didn't want to be alone that night. To keep my relationship with Tim safe from moral corruption, I chose Felix as my roommate. I knew I wasn't his type.

I was glad the case was over, but there were still loose ends dangling and they were driving me nuts. I knew I wouldn't rest until Frank Martinelli was again behind bars. He wanted me dead too badly. Reginald was another story. The worm was obviously a part of this, but I didn't even know what to charge him with. Conspiracy? Planting a bug was illegal, but I had no proof he had done so. It's still fairly legal to watch a crime be committed and not get involved, so I couldn't even have him picked up as an accomplice to our kidnapping. The most I could hang on him at the moment was trespassing, and that would never stick since he had left my office when requested without fuss or incident. If anything, he had a potential charge against Felix for assault.

There was another loose end, and that had to do with whether Randolph Bellamy was dead or alive. And another, I recalled. Who had actually ambushed us in the wash? We had all assumed it was Delgado, but Delgado had helped engineer our escape.

There were other unanswered questions, including the really big questions of where was my car, and would I ever see Charley again, but they would have to wait.

Tim called his wife from the motel and told her where he was. He learned his captain had called her shortly after the shootout in the wash to tell her Tim had disappeared. Tim asked her to call the department and tell them only that she had heard from him and he was all right and working undercover. He did not tell her what had happened, nor that I was involved.

Felix called Ricardo and told him he would probably be home in a day or two then he went next door, leaving me the room while I took a shower and rinsed out my underclothes, drying them with the built-in hair dryer so I wouldn't have to subject him to the sight of them hanging all over the towel racks in the bathroom. Then I called my answering service to see if there was any chance I had any business waiting for me back home. There were four messages from Tim, all left the morning I had come to Phoenix. There was one new message, left only a few minutes before I had stepped into the shower.

It was from Andrew.

Chapter 28

HE HAD LEFT A PHONE NUMBER. I called it, and he answered on the first ring. My heart pounded when I heard his voice. I wanted so much to see him again.

"Are you okay?" I asked. "You must not be in jail."

"No, I'm at McKenzie's house under guard. They're going to move me in the morning. I was hoping to talk to you again."

And I was hoping to do something besides talk, but we don't always get what we want. "What's going to happen to you?" I asked.

"They're taking me before a grand jury tomorrow. As soon as I testify against dear old dad, they'll issue the indictment and they can arrest him. There won't be any bail, so you'll be safe from him."

"Are you sure your testimony will be enough?"

"Yes, and don't ask any more questions, okay?"

I sighed. "Okay." I paused a moment, then plunged ahead. "Andrew, I think I love you."

He was silent for a long time, and I wondered if we had been cut off. Then he said, "I love you, too, Angela. But we have to forget all that if we want to stay alive."

"Can't I see you one more time?"

"I may not be in jail, but I'm under guard, Angela. There's no way I can get out of here. I'm sorry."

"Well, I'm not guarded. Where are you?"

"You can't come here. They'll never let you in."

"Try me. I can be very persuasive."

He laughed, and I felt that same tingle that I was starting to know so well. I had to see him. Hormones had been raging unchecked for a full week, and there might never be another chance. He finally gave me the address and wished me luck.

While I was in the shower, Tim and Felix had been in Tim's room swapping war stories, probably about me. I dressed quickly, then walked into Tim's room and announced that I was going out for a while.

"Out where?" Tim asked.

"To see Andrew," I replied. Of all the people in the world, these two knew me better than anyone and I knew there was no point in trying to lie to either of them.

"Are you nuts?" This from Tim.

"Way to go, Boss." This from Felix.

I smiled at both of them. "I gotta do this. I may never get to see him again. He's going to testify tomorrow and they'll probably move him to a safe house immediately after."

"Where is he now?" Tim asked.

"At McKenzie's house. He gave me the address."

"I can't let you do this, Angel," Tim said. "You know you'll only regret it."

I shook my head. "Don't even try to stop me, Tim. I've never felt this way before, and who knows if I'll ever feel this way again."

"It's just the adrenaline talking," Tim warned. "You know that. I don't want to see you get hurt, physically or emotionally. You know better than this. Let him go now. It will only be worse if you see him again."

I continued as if I hadn't heard him. "I need a gun, Tim. There may still be danger."

He sighed. "In the drawer. Take the cell phone, too."

"Thanks." I took the thirty-eight, leaving behind the one that ballistics tests would one day prove had killed a man in that wash up in Utah, and tucked it and the phone into my jeans.

"You want me to go with you, Boss?" Felix asked.

I grinned at my assistant. "Not on your life, buster. The last thing I need right now is competition. I know you want him, too."

"I saw him first, you know," he teased. "But go ahead, have your fun. But be safe." He pulled out his wallet and tossed me a square plastic packet.

"Thanks." With that, I left.

I found McKenzie's house with no difficulty and demanded he let me in to see Andrew. At this point, I didn't care who knew what was going on – or what I hoped would soon be going on – between Andrew and me. To my surprise, he let me in and pointed up the stairs. I nodded to the armed guard at the foot of the stairs.

Andrew was lying on the bed in an upstairs bedroom, watching television in the dark. He looked up in surprised amazement when I walked into the room and closed the door, locking it behind me. "You made it," he said.

"I told you I would."

He was dressed only in a terry cloth robe, and was freshly showered and shaved. Apparently McKenzie was taking good care of his star witness. Andrew got up from the bed and walked over to me. We embraced and kissed, then he led me to the bed.

I stared at him hungrily, knowing I might never see him again after that night. He stroked my hair lightly with one hand, then lay back on the bed with one arm outstretched to the side. I snuggled against his side, his arm around me, and whispered to him, "Is it really all over now? Are you going to be safe?"

"I'll be safe. I wish I could take you with me, but it's impossible. You have your life, your work. I'll probably be moved to some other part of the country, new name, new job. One of the conditions of protection is that I have to cut all ties to my past. Any phone call to anyone could blow the whole thing." He looked at me with a tenderness I'd never seen in him before. "Tonight is all we have."

I placed a finger at the base of his throat and drew it lightly down his chest, parting his robe, tracing his chest hair down to the point where the tie on the robe stopped my progress. "If tonight is all we have, then I'd like to make the most of it."

Wordlessly, he turned to me, and again I felt his lips on mine, his breath on my cheek. His free hand began working on my buttons while mine worked on the sash on his robe. In a minute, we were both unencumbered by clothing.

We spent the next hour in mutual exploration of each other's bodies, slowly caressing and teasing until we couldn't stand it any longer while the TV droned in the background. When at last I wrapped my legs around his hips and welcomed him inside me, it was as if it was always meant to be. For once in my life, the reality beat out the fantasy by a mile.

I'd been on an adrenaline roller-coaster, from being abducted and chloroformed the night before, to learning that Frank Martinelli planned to kill me, to being locked in a shed with Andrew, expecting to die at any time, to the giddy relief of being liberated by Tim, then being plunged into the ambush and shootout in the wash, the rescue by Felix and McKenzie, and the unmasking of Delgado. Now I was lying, fully satisfied, in the arms of a man I'd lusted after like I'd never lusted after anyone before. Only I was way beyond lust. I'd gotten to see the many sides of Andrew Field in the last few days, and I'd fallen in love with most of them.

We'd been lying still for about a half hour when I felt the tears start to well up. "What's the matter?" Andrew asked, stroking my cheek lightly.

"I sure can pick 'em, can't I?" I replied. "Here I am in love with someone who essentially has one day to live, so to speak, and has several prices on his head to boot."

He trailed a hand across my left breast, making gentle circles around the nipple, then moving to my abdomen. I reached across and pulled him back on top of me, again wrapping my legs tightly around him, not letting him go until once again our mutual needs had been satisfied.

The trials of the day caught up to me after that, and I fell asleep in his arms. It was about four in the morning when I heard a sound that sent me into full alert. Without a second thought, I rolled to the side and grabbed the gun from the nightstand, pointing it at the door. I quickly shook Andrew awake and hissed, "Someone's coming."

Sure enough, a key was turning stealthily in the lock. Andrew rolled away from me, silently, off the bed. I did likewise on my side of the bed, landing on the ground just as the door swung open and a hand with a gun came into view in the dim light from the still-flickering television.

If the gunman was surprised to find nobody in the bed, I'll never know. I didn't wait to ask him. As soon as he stepped far enough into view for me to determine that it wasn't McKenzie, Tim, or Felix, I fired.

Chapter 29

SORRY, TIM, I THOUGHT AS HIS SECOND GUN became a candidate for a ballistics test. The body fell to the floor, his gun discharging when he landed. The shot took out a bedside lamp.

I hit the light switch on the wall and checked the body. He was dead all right. Dazed, Andrew stared down at the crumpled figure.

I heard the sound of footsteps and McKenzie's voice from the hall. "Andrew, we're naked," I reminded him.

He quickly tossed me his robe and pulled on his jeans, which were lying on a chair. McKenzie appeared in the doorway. "What the hell happened?" he asked, seeing the body on the floor.

"Oh, just another shitty day in paradise," I quipped with disgust. "This is how you protect your star witness? Damn good thing I was here."

McKenzie turned on his heel and went downstairs, I assumed to check on the guard that had been stationed there when I arrived. I stepped into the hall and glanced down the stairs. No surprise that McKenzie was bending over another prostrate form. So much for his security.

I came back to Andrew. "Recognize him?" I asked.

"No."

"Get dressed," I said. "You're coming with me."

He finished dressing while I put on my own clothes, wistfully remembering the events of only a few hours before. I dropped the robe on the bed and tucked Tim's gun into my waistband. Then, leaving my latest kill lying where he fell, we walked downstairs and headed for the front door without a word to McKenzie. He protested briefly when he realized we were leaving, but politely demurred when I calmly leveled Tim's gun at his head and told him to fuck the hell off.

I drove the car back to the rental agency and exchanged it for another one, presumably one that didn't have the inevitable tracking device planted on it. I was getting rather tired of being ambushed every time I turned around.

Then I checked into a different hotel and called Tim, instructing him to get Felix up and meet me by the fire escape. I took Andrew with me while I swung by and picked up the other men in my life. After assuring ourselves that we weren't being followed, we returned to the second hotel and tried to go back to sleep for a few hours.

The sun was high when I woke up to find my arm draped across Andrew's chest. Tim and Felix were snoring on their respective sides of the other king sized bed in the room. Still amazed to be alive, I lay awake for a while, wondering what to do next. Obviously even the FBI couldn't keep Andrew alive, and it was really more luck than skill that had enabled me to do any better job than they did.

I glanced at Tim on the other bed. There was still an unanswered question, well, two, really if we counted the question of whom did Andrew see his father kill. The other involved my former fellow officers on the Myersburg police force, officers that Tim had said were on the take. Could they have a part in any of this?

I sat up, waking Andrew. He smiled, and I stroked his arm with my hand. "Feeling okay?" I asked.

"Never better," he lied with a straight face. Having been shot twice in a week and nearly killed a few other times in the same period hardly qualified as the best he'd ever been. But I considered maybe he was referring to the previous evening, when even my fondest fantasies had finally been fulfilled, and I had to admit to myself that I would have answered the same had he asked me the same question.

"Me, too," I said, then kissed him quickly. I turned to Tim and Felix. Having not spent (I assumed) several hours having sex as Andrew and I had, I had to believe they had gotten far more sleep than we had. If I was up, it was time they were, too. "Wake up, guys," I said, tossing a pillow at Tim.

He groaned and opened one eye to glare at me. "What time is it?" he mumbled, flinging the pillow back at me.

"Almost nine. Time to get up and figure out what in the world we're going to do next."

I had told them on the way to the new hotel part of what had happened at McKenzie's. Much to Felix's unexpressed dismay no doubt, I spared them the torrid details, focusing only on the intruder I'd killed and the fact that the man had neutralized an FBI agent to get to the room in the first place.

Felix stirred, and I got up and hit the bathroom while the men were still yawning and stretching.

An hour later, Room Service arrived with four breakfasts. If the guy wondered why a lone woman was sharing a room with two beds with three apparently healthy men, he kept his thoughts to himself. By the time we finished eating, it was ten o'clock and I was ready to make plans for all our survival.

Luckily, Felix had managed to collect our belongings, including my gun and the laptop, after McKenzie rescued him from the last room we had shared. Unfortunately, everything was in a locker at the FBI field office in Phoenix. A couple phone calls located my Firebird in a police impound yard. It had been towed from the street after Andrew was taken from it at gunpoint. Hopefully my purse was still in it. Since it was probably sporting a tracking device and possibly bugged as well, I decided to go bail it out but leave it in a parking garage until this matter was concluded and I was going home.

Finally I turned to Andrew. "Well, Andrew," I said, "you're still my client. What do you want to do? I can't turn you over to McKenzie after seeing what kind of protection he offers. Do you want to run?"

He glanced at Tim. "I didn't have the impression I had any choices here."

"Well, let's pretend you do," I replied, knowing I could get Tim to go along with me now that I'd proven his buddy McKenzie was about as competent at keeping Andrew alive as Dumbo the Elephant had been at killing him.

He thought for a minute, then sighed. "I have to go through with it, Angela. Without federal protection, I'll never be safe. And the only way to get protection is to testify against the people I'm not safe from. My father. Delgado. Smith. They may be in custody, but they won't stay that way if I don't testify. And I need to do it today."

I studied his eyes, seeking the meaning behind the words. It was a knee-jerk reaction to expect everything that came out of his mouth to be a lie, but it seemed Andrew Field was no longer lying to me. His eyes reflected sincerity, and resignation to his fate. He needed to go through with this.

And again I knew that once he did, I'd never see him again.

At least we had last night. "Okay," I said. "I'll call McKenzie."

McKenzie was furious when I reached him, and I could hear him struggling not to rage at me. Clearly he was torn between a cold fury at having me waltz out of his house with Andrew, leaving him with two bodies to deal with, and the relief of knowing that I hadn't decided to hide Andrew somewhere in Kansas. Suspecting his phone line was probably bugged, I told him to call me back from another phone. Two minutes later, the phone rang.

"He wants to testify, Gilbert," I said simply. "Where and when?"

McKenzie calmed down considerably when I said that, and he told me where to go, or maybe I should say – he gave me directions to the courthouse. I was to have Andrew there by two o'clock. He gave me the number of his cell phone. If I had any notion at all that we were being followed, I was to call him at once and he'd have us surrounded with agents within minutes.

Right. I'd already seen his idea of security measures – lying on the floor at the foot of his stairs.

I hung up the phone. "Two o'clock," I said. "Downtown." I tossed the car key to Tim. "You and Felix go pick up our stuff and get the car out of hock. Park it at the rental agency, and switch rental cars again while you're there. In fact, get a second car. We'll probably be better off in two vehicles. And pick up a prepaid cell phone while you're at it. Mine should still be in my purse, but I'm sure my batteries are dead again and there's no time to charge them."

Tim looked at me, then at Andrew. "You go with Felix. I hate to say it, Angel, but you've lost your objectivity on this case," he said. "And these aren't amateurs we're dealing with."

"No, Tim, they're pros, but so are we. So far the FBI hasn't been too reliable, but we're still alive somehow."

"I'm not leaving you here alone," he insisted. "It's far too dangerous. And," he continued bluntly, "I seriously doubt if we leave that you're going to sit here with a gun trained on the door. I know you too well for that."

Felix spoke up then, more serious than I'd ever heard him before. "He's right, Boss. And you know it, too. I'm with Tim. You want to take care of the cars and that stuff in the locker, you and I should go. Let Tim stay and guard Andrew. He's the cop, after all."

I knew I was licked when Andrew concurred. "As much as I'd love to have a couple more hours alone with you, Angela," he said sadly, "I don't want either of us to die that way. Tim and Felix are right. We need to stay on the alert. Go with Felix. I'll see you when you get back, even if it's only for a few minutes."

I sighed. "I'll call you as soon as I get a phone, Tim. Be careful." I hugged him, then kissed Andrew. Taking Tim's gun again, we left.

Since Felix knew where the FBI office was, I let him drive. He was silent for a few miles, then started, "I know it's none of my business, Boss, but –"

I cut him off. "Don't ask, Felix. I can't talk about last night right now."

"I wasn't going to ask about your sex life, Boss. I was just going to ask what you're going to do after he testifies. Will you try to go with him?"

"No," I said quietly. "He'll never be safe unless he goes anonymously. I'll never see him again." Tears ran down my face and Felix patted my thigh.

"Then you're going back to Clarkdale?"

"Yes."

"Why don't you go now?"

"What?"

"Go now. Let me take you to the airport right now. I'll bring the Firebird home. Go home now. Don't see him again. It will only make it worse."

There was something in his voice that gave me pause. I looked at his face carefully. "Been there, done that, huh?" I asked.

He didn't answer for a while, and I left him alone while he struggled with what I assumed was his own memory of what might have been. Finally he said, "I never told you much about my past, Boss."

"You don't need to tell me anything now if you don't want to."

He glanced over. "Something similar happened to me once. Fell hard for the wrong guy. At least I had a few weeks with him. You only had one night, and even that ended with a shooting."

"So what happened?" I prodded. "What was his name?"

"Bernie. He was everything I ever wanted, Angela. Sexy, smart, strong, gentle. I've never been in love like that, ever. We met at a party. Hit it off from the first moment. One afternoon he calls me up and tells me he has to leave town. Immediately. Wouldn't say why. I found out later an old lover was stalking him, but I didn't know that at the time. Bernie said he was scared for his life. He had to leave, and he didn't want me to know where he was going. He was afraid I'd be in danger if I knew."

"Sounds familiar. What happened? Did he go?"

I saw tears well up in Felix's eyes, something I'd never seen happen before, ever. "I tried to find him, Boss. I had to see him again. I thought maybe he was blowing me off, that maybe he'd found someone else." He stopped for a red light and wiped his eyes before continuing. "I went straight to his apartment. He was already gone. He must have packed before he even called me. I don't know why, but on a hunch I went to his bank. I thought he might have gone to cash out the account before he left. I got there just as he was leaving. I followed him to the airport. All I wanted to do was see him again, try to talk him into letting me go with him."

"Did you catch up with him?"

The light turned green and he continued. "I was being followed, Boss. I led the guy to him. He was shot to death in front of my eyes." The tears started to flow again, and Felix pulled to the curb while he composed himself. "I've never talked to anyone about this. The police did nothing, even when I told them what happened and gave them a description of the car and driver. I heard from a reporter that the detective in charge made a comment about not wasting the department's resources on another fag dead from a lover's quarrel."

"I'm sorry, Felix. It must have been terrible." I put my hand on his shoulder, rubbed the back of his neck.

"Thanks, Boss. But that's why I think you should just leave now." He looked at me through red-rimmed eyes. "They're not going to stop trying to get him. Chances are they'll succeed. Bad enough you'll have to read about it in the paper, but you sure don't want to be there when it happens. There's nothing in the world worse than seeing someone you love murdered in front of you. Unless it's knowing that you're the one who made it possible. How will you feel if someone picks up our trail, maybe when you bail out the car, and follows us back to the hotel? Won't be hard at all to ambush us when we come out to go to court."

Damn. He was right. He had stopped the car near a pay phone. "Stay here," I said. I called Tim.

"I can't come back, Tim," I told him. "You're right about me losing my objectivity. I'd only put you and Andrew both at risk. Can you get him out by yourself?"

"Sure, but what do I do for wheels?"

"I think you'll be safe until I get my car. I'll go one direction and have Felix go another. When he's sure he's not being followed, he'll come get you. I'll go back to the first hotel. If we're being followed, they'll probably stick with me, not Felix. I'll have him call you and hang up so you'll have his new cell phone number when he leaves the rental yard. You watch the parking lot when he pulls in. If anyone pulls in after him, call him and tell him to go to the desk and check out, then leave again. If the other car follows him out, call a cab."

"Will you meet us at the courthouse?"

"Probably not."

"Do you want to talk to Andrew now?"

I swallowed hard. "No." I hung up and returned to Felix, filling him in on the impromptu plan I had just concocted. He pulled back into traffic and we drove to the FBI office and retrieved our things.

After dropping me at the police impound lot, Felix drove back to the rental car agency to exchange cars and pick up a phone. About the time I finished the paperwork and pulled out into traffic, he called me on the car phone and hung up. I knew he would do the same for Tim. The plan was in action. There was nothing more for me to do but continue to lead any possible follower on a classic wild-goose chase. I didn't know if I had a tail, but if I did, I hoped he had a full tank of gas.

First I drove past McKenzie's house. Then I drove out to the airstrip where we had landed in the helicopter. I went inside the office and chatted with the receptionist for about fifteen minutes, asking detailed questions about chartering a flight to Oregon.

Next I drove back to the first hotel we had checked into the previous night and booked another room for that night, a room I had no intention of using other than for about half an hour. I went into the room and called my answering service, leaving word that I was going to Portland and would be home in three days. Then I called McKenzie's number and told his answering machine that I would have Andrew in Portland as planned by the next morning. I still had no idea if I was being followed or if McKenzie's phone was being monitored, but I was trying to leave a trail of crumbs that would draw attention from Andrew's true whereabouts.

Leaving the phone off the hook, on hold to a talk radio station to give the desk clerk the impression I was still there, I left the room and walked out the back entrance and around to my car. I got in and drove out, noting with satisfaction that nobody was behind me – for the moment. I drove quickly to a different rental agency and left the Firebird in the parking lot, driving out twenty minutes later in a red Mustang. Down the street at another rental agency, I abandoned the Mustang for a white Toyota Corolla. Being near the airport, I had my choice of rental companies, and before I left the area, I had visited four of them, using a different name and credit card at each.

Having done my part to boost the local economy I finally felt safe in calling Felix. Two coded sentences were exchanged, each of us communicating to the other "Mission accomplished" while revealing nothing to any listener other than that the call was a wrong number.

So I knew that Felix had picked up Tim and Andrew, did not believe he had a tail, and was proceeding to the courthouse. He knew I had left a trail of crumbs and did not believe I had a tail. It was twenty to two.

Despite Felix's tragic experience, I was tempted to try to see Andrew again. I called McKenzie's cell phone. "Are you where you said you'd be?" I asked cautiously.

"Yes," he replied. "Where are you?"

"Making arrangements to get him to Oregon, as we discussed," I said, emphasizing the last three words.

To his credit, he understood immediately. "Will he be there on time?"

"Yes. I'll only send him up if I get to see him afterward. Can you arrange that?"

He hesitated. "I'll see what I can do."

"How long will he be in there?"

"An hour. Maybe two. Probably no longer than that."

"And he'll be safe?"

"We sent ten men up to Portland to meet him," he confirmed. "He'll be safe."

"He better be. I'll call you when it's time to leave." I broke the connection. McKenzie had done pretty well picking up the real message from the midst of the red herring. I almost hoped his phone was being monitored. I'd hate to have all that cleverness go to waste.

I drove down a few side streets just to be sure I still was not being followed, then drove to the courthouse, arriving at ten after two. I saw Felix and Tim waiting at the curb, nodded to them, and drove on past without stopping. They followed me and we found a parking garage nearby, driving to the top floor before stopping.

"Well, that's over," Tim said, leaning against the side of his car. "We delivered André Martin to the grand jury right on time."

"Was McKenzie there?" I asked.

"Yes, with about ten agents. They surrounded André and took him through a back entrance."

"Well, I left a trail leading to Portland in case anyone wants to follow it. And I have rental cars scattered from here to Timbuktu and back. Well, Glendale, anyway."

Felix came over and looked me straight in the eyes. "Why did you come here?"

"I'm sorry, Felix. I understand your concern and I know you're probably right, but I have to see him again. After he testifies. Probably right here in the courthouse before they take him into hiding."

"I think you're making a huge mistake, Boss."

"You're probably right. But it's my mistake, and I'm going to have to make it."

"Angel," Tim said, "I have no idea how you keep yourself alive."

I gave him a quick grin. "Well, it's a lot harder now that I don't have you watching my back, but Felix is coming along nicely."

"He told me he was your secretary. Why are you wasting his talents by having him do filing and typing?"

"Someone's got to do it, Tim," I replied, giving Felix an affectionate glance. "And this is the first time I've had him in the field with me. I didn't know how valuable he was. I suppose now I'll have to give him a raise."

"Thanks, Boss," Felix said.

"For that matter, I probably owe him a couple thousand just in overtime this week. The expenses on this job are going to kill me, between the motels, the cars, and all the cell phones we've gone through. Good thing Andrew left me about twenty-five grand as a retainer."

"Twenty-five grand?" Tim asked. "Are you kidding? I may be in the wrong line of work."

"That's just because you refuse to take bribes, honey," I retorted. "Speaking of which, you never explained about our buds on the force. Who's on the take, and how do you know?"

"Lange, Jackson, and Medina as far as I can tell."

"How do you know?"

"Lange and Jackson were with me when we picked up those fake cops, what did you call them? Beanpole and Fat Ass?"

"Lard Butt."

"Right. Anyway, I had the strong idea that they all knew each other. Oh, they went through the motions of roughing them up and arresting them, but I noticed Lange slipping a finger under the handcuff when he locked it. Like he didn't want to hurt him."

"Probably took it off him as soon as you were out of sight."

"That's what I figured. I've been suspecting something fishy was up with those three for quite awhile. Little things. Mishandled evidence. Bad arrests. Too many guys walking on technicalities when the arresting officer was one of those three. Nothing consistent enough to violate statistics, you understand, but I picked up a pattern that all the bad arrests involved suspected mob figures."

"So who's really watching Frank Martinelli?"

"The FBI, as well as a couple of uniforms from Myersburg P.D."

"How come you're so cozy with the FBI all of a sudden?"

He turned away from my steady gaze and I saw his Evasive expression again. He didn't want to answer. Then he took a deep breath, straightened his shoulders, and turned to face me. "I'm quitting the force, Angel. I'm going to work for the FBI, undercover."

"All this came up since I called you last week?"

"They needed me, bad. I talked to Jake Boswell, McKenzie's boss, and told him I suspected a lot of cops were on the take up there. You know part of the FBI's job is investigating corruption in public offices, including police departments. I told him I'd help with the investigation, but they had to get me out of there once we broke the case. He agreed. When this is over, I'll be moving to Colorado. We're going to be neighbors again, Angel."

I grinned. "That's great, but what about your wife and kid?"

"They're on the way already. That call I made to her yesterday was her signal to move. You're not the only one who talks in code, kiddo."

"Hell, you're the one who taught me to do it." I paused, studying my former partner's face. "Tim, who did Frank Martinelli kill?"

"Well, since Andre's testifying right now and the indictment will probably come down in a few hours, I guess there's no reason not to tell you now. It's a very old case, you know. It involved another crooked public servant. The FBI was investigating a congressman from Utah, suspected of accepting bribes from the mob. They had agents working undercover, inside the mob, trying to get the evidence they needed to indict the congressman. They had almost everything they needed and were about to pull the agents out and go to the grand jury. Martinelli hit one of the agents, the one with the most information. His young son, André, saw it. Of course, André didn't know who the guy was until recently. To all appearances, it was another internal mob hit. The FBI, of course, knew who the guy was. They had to abandon him to protect two other agents who were also on the case. But the hit did the job. The other two bailed. One died in a traffic accident a week later. The other disappeared to South America. They lost the case against the congressman. They never got it back, either, because he got wind of what happened. He stayed dirty, but they were never able to prove it."

Suddenly I remembered a bit of political trivia from the last presidential election. "Who was the congressman, Tim?"

He gazed at me, then looked at Felix, then back to me. "He's moved up the ladder a bit, Angel. It's the Vice-President."

Chapter 30

AND TO THINK I'D VOTED FOR THE MAN. Now I learned that he was connected to the recent attempts on my life, and Andrew's. No wonder Andrew hadn't wanted me to know. Apparently some pretty powerful people were behind all this.

"So what's going to happen after the indictment comes down? It's still a simple domestic murder from a legal standpoint."

"Not quite. The killing of an undercover FBI agent is not considered a domestic murder, Angel. In this particular case, there are national security issues at stake. It's considered an assassination."

"There are now," I argued, "but there weren't thirty years ago. He was only one of a few hundred representatives then."

"You're too young to know this, Angel," Tim said, shaking his head. "So was I. Congressman Edie was a key member of the House Appropriations Committee. Being on the take meant that a lot of tax dollars may have been spent in some very inappropriate ways. He greased a lot of wheels for himself. Now he's the VP and he's still just as crooked. When Martinelli goes on trial, a lot of this is going to come out."

"Yeah? How's that going to happen? Who's alive to testify to it?"

"Martinelli."

"Like he'd talk."

"He'll talk to stay alive. The FBI is less interested in him getting the chair for killing the agent than they are in getting the information that will expose Edie. They'll plea bargain life in prison without parole, or even as low as twenty-five to life, if he'll come clean about Edie."

I looked from Tim to Felix, then back again. Felix looked as stunned as I had been. "So what you're saying, Tim, is that Andrew's testimony about a hit he saw at the age of five is going to be leveraged to topple the Vice President of the United States. And everybody is clinging to the fantasy that he's going to be safe, buried in the federal Witness

Protection program?" I shook my head. "And, knowing all this, you helped deliver him? Are you insane, Tim?"

"Angel, he'll be all right."

"Bullshit." I dialed McKenzie's number on my cell phone. "Where's Andrew?" I snapped as soon as he answered.

"He's testifying right now."

"You realize he's a dead man, McKenzie. I just found out where all this is leading."

"Then you must realize national security is at stake."

"Fuck national security, McKenzie. This is nothing but politics as usual. Been going on since Watergate. In fact, this was probably a part of Watergate. You've just set Andrew up to be killed. Wherever you hide him, whatever you call him, they'll get him. Because this is all an inside job, McKenzie. How can you use the federal government to protect the man who's about to bring down the Vice President? Don't you idiots realize that if he's crooked, chances are the President is, too? How the hell are you going to hide Andrew from all the President's men when all the President's men run the fucking witness program?"

There was silence on the phone. Then, "Shit."

"Shit, my ass," I spat. "You get him out of there, now. I don't care how."

"He'll be all right until the indictment comes down. These proceedings are secret. Nobody knows he's here."

"Except me, and Tim, and Felix, and you, and your superiors, and all those agents you surrounded him with when he got here, and everyone in the fucking jury room and their wives and husbands, and the judge, and the prosecutor, and probably half the Myersburg police force to say nothing of John Smith, Fred Gaines, Vinnie Delgado, Randolph Bellamy, and last but not least, Jason, Sylvia, and the goddamn dog Max. I'll be surprised if I don't see his testimony on the six o'clock news."

"Now, Ms Virago, calm down. It's going to be all right. I promise."

"Jesus Christ!" I shouted. "Aren't you listening to me at all? I —" Tim suddenly stepped forward and pulled the phone from my grasp. I whirled on him in fury. "Give it back!"

Felix stepped in and caught my arm as I was about to deck my former partner. He swiftly twisted it behind my back and restrained me while Tim walked around to the other side of the car to talk to McKenzie. "Calm down, Boss," Felix murmured, holding one arm across my chest while his other hand kept me restrained. I was shaking with fury and fear, and in a moment the anger I was feeling over the betrayal of Andrew Field gave way to tears. Felix released my arm and turned me to face him, where I buried my face in his chest and sobbed.

He held me for a long time, patting my back, murmuring words that were no doubt meant to be soothing. I finally composed myself long enough to look up and see that Tim was off the phone.

"Thanks, Felix," I whispered. "No telling what I might have done."

"I know."

Tim stepped closer, touching my arm. "You going to be all right?"

I pulled loose from Felix and hugged Tim. "I'm sorry I went for you like that, Tim. I guess I'm a little nuts about all this."

"I know. You need to get out of here, Angel. You've been a good cop and a good investigator, but if you go off half-cocked like that again, you're liable to get us all killed, and Andrew too." He hugged me tightly.

"I can't go home, Tim. I know they're going to kill him. I have to help him."

"Angel, he's here of his own choice. He knows the score. He knows the risks. And, as I'm sure you've seen, he's pretty resourceful."

"Tim, I've saved his life three times in a week, and there were several other attempts that were only unsuccessful due to the poor marksmanship of the shooter. I don't think he's that resourceful."

"And I've saved your life," Tim reminded me. "Let me take care of this. Please. Let Felix take you home. Go get your car, drive home, or fly home, or take a bus. Whatever you want. But go home." He put his hands on my shoulders and held me away at arm's length, so I was forced to look at his face. "If Andrew's going to get killed, he's not going to be any less dead if you also get killed trying to save him. Go. Now. I don't want any more arguments. You're not a cop anymore. You're a woman in love." He took his hands away from me. "Now get the hell out of here and let me do my job." With that, he pulled his gun out of my waistband, tossed my cell phone on the seat of my rental car, climbed in the other car, and drove away, leaving me and Felix alone.

I watched him drive away. I knew he was right. I was no good to him in the condition I was in. Felix took me by the hand and led me around to the passenger side of the car, opened the door, helped me in. He got behind the wheel and we drove away, away from the courthouse, away from Andrew Field.

It took a couple hours to retrace my steps, returning the rental cars I'd left in each other's lots. We drove the Firebird to a service station and had it put up on a rack while we searched the underside for tracking devices. The only one we found, we tossed into a dumpster by the service station. Then we drove home.

Chapter 31

IT WAS A WEEK BEFORE I HEARD from Tim. He had left Myersburg P.D. and was now working for the FBI, and I discovered the day after I came home that his department-issued cell phone had been deactivated already. I had no other way to contact him. I had stewed all week, hoping to get word, and knowing nothing more than what was in the newspapers.

Felix and I had returned home while Andrew was still in front of the grand jury, speaking little on the trip, stopping overnight in Flagstaff before continuing to Clarkdale in the morning.

We picked up Felix's car where he had left it at the airport, and I had Andrew's Suburban towed back to his own house. Since the rent had been paid for a year, I figured the Suburban could legally be parked in his driveway for another six months. Maybe someone in the Witness Protection Program would come to dispose of his belongings once he was in his new life, assuming he managed to survive testifying against all those who had recently tried to kill us. He would need new underwear and socks again, I supposed.

The cash under the spare tire was already in my safe. I used some of it to pay myself my agreed fees plus expenses. The rest I left alone. It wasn't mine.

I was largely in a daze, depressed and worried. The shock of all the people who had died since that fateful day when the incredibly sexy Andrew Field had first darkened my door had finally set in. When on the police force, it was routine for a cop involved in a shooting to undergo counseling to help put things into perspective and ensure he didn't go off the deep end. I knew I should have sprung for a little counseling for myself but I really didn't want to talk about it. Felix tried hard to play psychologist for me, but I couldn't even talk to him about how I felt. The truth was, I wasn't sure how I felt, or how I should feel, or how I wanted to feel. I had wallowed in my depression and self-pity for seven days. I had nothing else to do, anyway. There had been no new business, not even a simple employment check.

The Phoenix police had finally shipped Charley back to me, and I was sitting at my desk cleaning and reloading him when the call from Tim came in.

"How you doing?" he asked.

"Business is slow. I haven't killed anybody in a few days," I answered lightly. "Not even myself."

"Well, I'm glad to hear that."

"Is Andrew still alive?"

"Yes. He's fine. I've been guarding him myself, Angel. I thought you'd like to know that. Nobody but me even knows where he is. Not McKenzie. Not Jake Boswell. Nobody. Not even my wife, by the way, so don't ask her."

"Thanks, Tim. You still in Arizona?"

"We're still in this country. I won't say more than that."

The caller ID on my phone indicated the call was a Washington, D.C. area code, but I figured that was because he was calling through the government switchboard.

"Is he done testifying?"

"Only at the grand jury level. You probably read about the Frank Martinelli indictment. He's locked up. They picked him up the afternoon you went home."

"How goes the case against the VP?"

"Martinelli's not willing to talk yet. His attorney thinks Andrew's testimony is too weak. He thinks he'll get him off at a jury trial. It will take time to develop enough corroborating evidence to convince him otherwise. One advantage we have is that we have DNA technology now that we didn't have thirty years ago. Once Andrew went on record, it gave us what we needed to get a warrant to collect DNA from Martinelli. It will take a few weeks to develop it and compare with the DNA evidence collected thirty years ago. We think his lawyer will see our point of view once that comes in." He paused. "You see, Andrew didn't just see the hit. He saw his father dispose of evidence. Martinelli doesn't even know yet that we have the tire iron he used to subdue the agent, complete with fingerprints and tissue evidence, and we have the gun he used to finish the job."

"Where was all that?"

"Andrew, at the age of five, actually hid the tire iron in their attic. The house has been sold four times since then, but it was still there."

"What about the gun?"

"I thought you knew."

"Knew what?"

"That was the gun you found at Andrew's house. The one registered to Vinnie Delgado. Frank Martinelli gave it to Delgado after the hit and was smart enough to get the registration out of his own name. Of course, Delgado didn't know he'd done that. It's the same gun that was used to hit Randy Bellamy a few years back. It also killed Cassandra Baxter."

I felt like my head was spinning. "Did Andrew know all that?"

"He does now." He paused. "This thing turned out to be bigger than any of us realized, Angel."

"It started out as a simple stalking case on my end, Tim. Who would have figured?"

"There's just one thing Andrew's worried about. A loose end. He asked me to tell you."

"What's that?"

"We still don't know where Randolph Bellamy is. Or if he's dead or alive. Or if he's any danger to you."

I turned to face my window, staring out at the blue sky above. "Tim, do we really know he exists?"

"He exists. But he's disappeared."

"Do you know what he looks like?"

"I'll fax you a photo. He may still be in Clarkdale. That's the last place anyone saw him. If you run onto him, be very careful. Andrew called him a loose cannon, and I think he's right." I found it ironic that he would use the same words to describe Randolph Bellamy as had been attributed to me by the police shrink before I was hired as a cop.

"But what is his connection to anything?" I asked. "He had some connection to the kids, but they're gone now and Cassy is dead. Is he wanted for anything? Is he dangerous?"

"He worked for Andrew's father. He had entered the Witness Protection Program for the same reason as Andrew. To testify against Martinelli, and secondarily, to protect him from Delgado. Somehow Martinelli bought him off. He and your ex, Reginald, may still be working together, somehow. And they might still be after you. If you see either of them, call me right away." He gave me the number of his new, government-issued cell phone.

I hung up and stared at the receiver for a moment, thinking about what he had said. That's just great. I was back on the outside looking in and now I find out there were two people running around loose, still on the payroll of the man who wanted me dead. I buzzed Felix.

He came into the office. "Yes, Boss?"

"I just heard from Tim." I filled him in on the new information regarding the gun, then added, "And Randolph Bellamy may be running around loose somewhere, looking to kill me on behalf of Martinelli. There should be a fax coming in with his photo sometime soon."

I had omitted any mention of Andrew, but Felix didn't let it pass. "How is Andrew, Boss? Did Tim say?"

"He's okay. Tim's guarding him. Nobody knows where he is but Tim. He's probably as safe as he can be for the moment, but it obviously can't last forever." I fought back the tears that came unbidden to my eyes.

"No, I suppose not." He paused when I suddenly turned away from him, my eyes brimming. "How are you holding up now?"

I wiped my eyes quickly and turned back, trying to smile. "I'll survive, I suppose. Felix, I killed several people last week. And others died, not by my hand, but dead all the same. I can't help wondering what the justification was. All those people wanting Andrew dead because of something he saw when he was five."

"Maybe that's why Brian was killed. Maybe he knew something, too."

"We'll never know." Despite my concerns, I had to admit that hearing from Tim that Andrew was still alive had managed to lift my spirits somewhat. "You want to go to lunch with me? I think it's time I got out of this hole I've dug for myself."

"Sure, Boss. Let me forward the phones to the service and we can go."

We locked the office and drove to what had become Felix's favorite restaurant, the one where Ricardo worked. Ricardo grinned when he saw us, and I smiled back. At least Felix's relationship had some hope of working out.

Knowing I was Felix's boss, Ricardo was attentive to my every need, and quickly charmed me out of my blue mood. I could see why Felix liked him so much. He was witty and cheerful and sensitive. No doubt he knew much of what had happened while we were gone, and he did everything he could to cheer me. It was a pleasant contrast to the tension and stress of the previous week to see him and Felix banter as if they had been together for years.

Since Felix himself had been in mortal danger a time or two, I supposed their reunion upon his return had been about as emotional as the one night I had with Andrew. Something about surviving death tends to make one appreciate life more fully. I just wished I had someone to appreciate it with. I found myself feeling somewhat jealous of Felix, but happy for him at the same time, especially now that I knew a little of his own painful past.

We were gone about two hours before returning to the office. I was in a much better mood, and joked with Felix about ways to drum up a little business. He suggested that we call a few married women at random, hanging up when they answered the phone. After a week of that, we should mail them a flyer geared toward domestic surveillance.

We had a laugh about that as we rode the elevator to our floor. I was almost tempted to try it, but was still hopeful some business would come in through more legitimate avenues.

A fax was waiting when we arrived, and I found myself looking at the face of Randolph Bellamy. So that's what he looked like. Notes at the bottom said he was forty years old, five foot ten, about 190 pounds, brown hair, brown eyes, no distinguishing marks. The face in the picture was clean-shaven, reasonably nice-looking with a suggestion of wrinkles, read that, "character lines," around the eyes. He looked like anyone's boy next door now heading into middle age. I showed it to Felix, then dropped it on the corner of my desk. I also noted the fax number stamped on the edge of the page. If the number was correct, it had been faxed locally. I wondered if that meant Tim and Andrew were nearby.

Since there still was nothing to do at the office, I decided to go on home.

I pulled into the garage and entered the house through the side door that leads from the garage into an entryway near the living room.

Since returning from Phoenix, I've made it a habit to search every room of my house when arriving home, before taking off my holster. I had even taken apart all the phones a few times to check for bugs. Today I was even more paranoid than usual for some reason, and checked each room in the house twice before I was satisfied. Finally, I was able to relax enough to set about doing some mundane chores that had been neglected. I was still edgy enough to leave Charley right where he was for the time being, and kept my cell phone in my hip pocket. I had started the dishwasher and was just putting a load of clothes into the washer when I felt more than heard a door open. I froze, listening. I heard a floorboard creak and knew whoever it was had come in through the side door, the door to the garage.

The garage I had not searched. Shit. They could have been anywhere in there, including up in the rafters, or hiding behind that pile of boxes in the corner. I hadn't even thought about someone being in the garage. I must be slipping.

I pulled Charley out and grabbed the cell phone with my other hand, quickly hitting the speed dial code for my office. Felix answered and I quickly whispered, "Someone's here. Call the cops. Then call Tim. Now." I hung up.

There was only one way out of the utility room, through the kitchen. From the kitchen, I could go to the living room or to the hallway leading to the two bedrooms and the bath. The side door to the garage opened into an alcove off the living room, near the hallway. A six-foot-high divider separated the kitchen from the living room.

The creaking floorboard told me the intruder was actually in the living room. I darted from the utility room into the kitchen area. Peeking around the corner, I saw that the intruder's back was to me at that moment. I glanced through the still-open door to the garage and debated for a moment about simply making a run for it, but I knew I'd feel better if the situation were contained right now, rather than leave this unknown assailant loose to try again. I pointed Charley straight at the back of the intruder's head and cocked the hammer.

It had the desired effect. The intruder froze, straightened, dropped a pistol to the floor, then raised both hands in the air and turned around.

It was a teenaged girl.

Chapter 32

"WHO THE HELL ARE YOU?" I ASKED. "Why are you here? And kick the gun over here. Now."

She kicked the gun to me and I picked it up, half expecting it to be a toy replica, but this was the real thing – a fully loaded forty-five semi-automatic. Hardly a toy for a child to be playing with. I unloaded it quickly and set it up on top of the room divider.

"I don't have to answer your questions," she spat. "Not without a lawyer."

"Fine, then I'll just shoot you now," I said, closing one eye and taking careful aim at the center of her chest. "Only cops have to give you a lawyer. I have the right to defend my home from armed intruders."

"Wait!" she shouted. "Don't shoot. Please."

"You have three seconds to tell me who you are and why you're here."

"I'm Michelle Bellamy," she replied hurriedly. "You killed my stepmother. Well, she was like a stepmother. They weren't actually married. I came to kill you."

Michelle. The third child mentioned by John Smith a.k.a. Howard Bellamy, and whom I had wondered if even existed. It may have been the only truthful statement he made to me that day. I lowered Charley and uncocked the hammer. "Turn around. Hands on the wall."

I frisked her and found no other weapons. "Sit down," I commanded, pointing to a chair.

"What are you going to do? Kill me too?" she asked.

"Who put you up to this? Randolph?"

Her face fell. "He told me where you lived. He showed me how to get in here and where to hide."

"What makes you think I killed Cassandra?"

"He said you did. And I checked with the police. They said you found the body."

"Well, I did find the body, but I didn't kill her. I had no reason to kill her. And he's using you to get rid of me, one way or another. If you'd killed me, I'm out of Randolph's way and probably you would have gotten a few years in therapy. I kill you and I'm the one in prison, which means I'm still out of Randolph's way. If Randolph killed me, he's a prime suspect and once caught, he'd get the death penalty. See? He's using you to get what he wants while keeping his own hands clean. No matter which of us killed the other, he would have gotten rid of me."

"Then who killed Cassandra?"

"Frankly, Michelle, I suspect Randolph did. Then he staged his own apparent death to make certain people stop trying to find him."

"That's a lie. Why would he kill her? He loved her. She loved him."

"She was in love with another man. A man who happened to be her long-lost brother, but she didn't know that. And Randolph works for a mob boss who happened to be her father. He's a very twisted man who put a contract out on his own son because he knew too much, and who shed no tears over knowing his daughter, Cassandra, was dead. He's a man who wants me dead because I once sent him to prison."

"Who was she in love with?"

"Someone she worked with."

"Who? Mr. Field? She said he got her fired from work."

"She got herself fired from work, Michelle." I paused a moment while she absorbed that. I was not going to elaborate. "Michelle, where have you been the past two weeks?"

"I've been with my dad ever since Cassandra left him, right after she got fired. I had to take care of the other kids, Jason and Brian. We stayed in her house until she was killed, then we moved to an apartment. Uncle John took the boys away."

"What did Randolph tell you about Jason and Brian?"

"The day Cassandra died, Dad told me Jason and Brian had to go back to the adoption agency. Uncle John was coming to get them. I know Brian was killed that same day. I don't know what happened to Jason."

"He's safe. He's back with his real mother."

"I'm glad. I was so worried about him. It was awful about Brian."

"So you've been hiding out since then?"

"He told me we had to stay out of sight until they caught her killer. You. When the police didn't arrest you, he told me we had to get revenge ourselves."

"So he convinced you to hide in my garage and ambush me. Have you ever fired that gun before?"

"Oh, yes, he takes me to the shooting range all the time."

"You do realize I'm going to have to have you arrested, don't you? And that we're going to have to find Randolph before he hurts anyone else?"

Her face fell. She was only fifteen. "I know. I'm sorry. But he told me —" She looked up at me, past me, really, and turned pale. I heard a sound over my shoulder and turned around. There was a gun pointed at my head, another forty-five. I was sure this one was also loaded.

I had finally met Randolph Bellamy.

"Drop the gun," he said calmly. Reluctantly, I let Charley slip to the floor and raised my hands. I had called for backup, but so far there was no sign of rescue. I had to stall for time.

"So you do exist," I replied. "I was beginning to think you were another of Andrew's aliases."

"Where is he?"

"Who?"

"Andrew Field. I know you're protecting him somehow. He's the one I want."

I debated for about a half second whether it would be better or worse for me to reveal that Andrew was in FBI protective custody. Somehow I felt that my life was worth more to Randolph if he thought there was a chance he could get Andrew than if he knew for certain he couldn't. "I don't know where he is right now," I replied. It was the truth, anyway.

"I don't believe you. I saw you together at the restaurant. You were holding hands, looking into each other's eyes. You know very well where he is."

"You saw us at the restaurant?" I quickly put two and two together and came up with three. Never let a killer know you know he's a killer, I could hear Tim lecturing me over and over again. "Then you must have seen Cassandra shoot him. Did you tell the police what you saw?"

"Yeah, that's right. Cassy shot him. Then you killed her. But it was his fault, all of it."

I knew he was lying to try to keep Michelle in his corner. I had no idea how much of my explanation had sunk in with her. Hopefully, since I hadn't killed her when I had the chance and a legal excuse for doing so she would realize I was not the blood-crazed monster Randolph had tried to make me out to be.

"You know I didn't kill her, Randolph."

"Then Andrew did," he said quickly. "Either way, you helped him do it, then you helped him escape. Now you're hiding him. Tell me where he is now, or I'll kill you."

"If you kill me, you'll never find him now, will you?"

He lowered the gun fractionally. "You'll tell me where he is. Come on. We're getting out of here now. For all I know you've called the police."

I started to walk to the front door, but he stopped me. "Don't be an idiot. The car's out back."

I walked through the kitchen to the back door, still wondering how he had gotten into the house. If he and Michelle had both been there all along, why had he allowed me to disarm her and spend several minutes telling her what a slimeball he was? More likely, he had been outside in a getaway car, and had come in only when he didn't hear gunshots. If he hadn't been inside all along, how had he gotten inside? I had searched everywhere but the garage.

The answer to that question would have to wait. At the back door, he stepped back while I unbolted the door, then he pulled it open and shoved me through it with the barrel of his gun. I stumbled down the steps, just catching sight of a movement to my right. I hit the dirt and rolled. A shot rang out and Randolph's gun, which a moment ago had pushed me through the door, flew out of his grasp and landed a few feet from me.

Tim had come to the rescue.

Epilogue

EIGHT MONTHS LATER, FELIX BROUGHT me the newspaper with my morning coffee. "No thanks, Felix, I don't drink it," I said as usual.

"Guess I'll drink it then," he replied.

I browsed the front page, but the headline was anti-climatic. I had been on the phone with Tim half the night before and I already knew that Vice President Edie had committed suicide yesterday morning, the day before a formal investigation was to begin – an investigation that would have led directly to his mob ties and the murder of an FBI agent thirty years before.

Frank Martinelli's plea bargain went straight into the toilet at that point. He would never see the light of day again, and the prosecutor was optimistic that a death penalty would result.

John Smith had been convicted three months before for baby selling.

Delgado had already plea bargained for life without parole for his many sins.

Dumbo the Elephant, whose real name was Cecil Cromwell, turned state's evidence. Once he finished testifying against everybody else, he, too, was placed in the federal Witness Protection Program. At Tim's urging, they promised to locate him on the eastern seaboard somewhere. He would not be allowed to travel west of the Mississippi, ever. I wasn't too worried about him. He had proven to be a completely incompetent hit man.

Randolph Bellamy had been convicted the previous week of the murder of Cassandra Baxter. He was expected to draw twenty-five to life. He'd be up for parole in about three weeks, I figured with disgust. I had been called to testify in that case, since I had found the body. The defense made a feeble attempt to pin the crime on me, but the jury nailed him anyway after only two hours' deliberation. His DNA had been found under Cassandra's fingernails. Ironically, the whole thing had been nothing more than a lover's triangle. He had become jealous of Cassy's continued obsession with Andrew and tried to kill Andrew in the restaurant. Then he had lured Cassy to Andrew's home, making her think Andrew had a change of heart and wanted to see her, then killed her with the gun he found in Andrew's desk – not knowing it was the same gun he himself had been shot with by Vinnie Delgado. He hadn't known Martinelli was Cassy and Andrew's father until after his arrest at my house that afternoon.

And apparently, Cassandra had discovered nothing about Andrew's past, despite Andrew's initial concerns and evidence to the contrary. Reginald's bug, planted in my office that day, had been the key to Andrew's betrayal.

Michelle was placed in a youth home until she was eighteen.

Hours after Martinelli was arrested at his home in Myersburg, Reginald had found a stash of money under the salt blocks in the shed where Andrew and I had been held captive. He was last seen buying a one-way ticket to Rio.

Andrew was still in Tim's care, and although I suspected he was in the area, I still did not know where he was. I supposed it was for the best, but I still ached with desire whenever I thought about him.

After perusing the article about the Vice President, I looked at Felix, who grimaced as he sipped his coffee. "I guess it's finally all over," I said.

"Guess so, Boss."

"Stop calling me *Boss*. We're partners now, remember?" We had collected some reward money for our role in capturing Delgado and had decided to combine forces as equal partners until the money ran out or we started turning a profit, whichever came first.

"Doesn't matter. You're still the boss. I like it that way."

"So, we got any business lined up this week?"

"Maybe. A man called a while ago. Wants to see you about a missing person case. He'll be here at ten."

"Good." There had been a slow trickle of business since our return from Phoenix, one or two domestic surveillances, seventeen pre-employment checks. I even accepted one lost dog case in which the dog was found in the custody of an ex-lover. But my name was now being mentioned in the papers in connection with the Edie affair, and I was optimistic that the attention might bring in some business. I hadn't fired a gun nor had the Firebird over sixty-five miles an hour for months.

I was jealous of Tim in his new position with the FBI, and not just because he had access to Andrew and I didn't. He was seeing action, stopping criminals, arresting people, while I mostly sat in an office and searched for information on a computer.

All the while, I wondered where Andrew was, reliving our only night together, seeing his face in my mind's eye, trailing my finger across his mustache, down his cheek, tracing the scar on his neck, stroking the hair on his chest. Tim had told me several months ago that Andrew had requested plastic surgery to alter his appearance immediately after his last testimony was given. I wondered what he looked like now.

Felix finished his coffee and leaned back in his chair. "Want me to go hang up on some married women for a while?"

I smiled. "No, Felix. With any luck, this new client will keep us busy for a few days, anyway."

"Hope so." He hesitated. "You know, Boss, you really need to get out of this funk you're in. Why don't you go to a bar, pick up some good-looking piece of meat, and get yourself laid? That's what I'd do."

I smiled. "Just what the doctor ordered, huh? I don't think so, Felix. I know I only knew him a couple weeks, but I think it's going to take me a long time to get over Andrew Field. A woman spends all her life waiting for Mr. Right to come along, and it's hard to lose him, especially the way I did."

"Well, that only shows it wasn't meant to be, and the real Mr. Right is still out there waiting for you to find him. How are you going to find him by moping around over something you know you can't have?"

"Maybe that's true, Felix, but I'm still not ready yet." I glanced at my watch. "It's almost ten o'clock. I guess I'd better set the stage for my new client."

Felix left the office and I spread a few files on my desk and turned my desk calendar to a dummy page on which several fake appointments had been written. It wouldn't do to have a client think I was in so little demand I literally had nothing else to do with my time. I always try to project an image of briskness and professionalism – and that I was much, much busier than I could ever hope to be.

It was two minutes past ten when Felix buzzed me and reported, "Ms Virago, James T. Wright is here to see you."

"Send him in," I replied.

James T. Wright was about six feet tall, clean-shaven, had short blond hair and wore black horn-rimmed glasses. He was dressed in a white button-down shirt with a pocket protector, a green striped tie, and a loud red plaid sport coat. His wrists stuck out from his sleeves and his pants were high-waisted and baggy. I took one look at him and decided, "Loser."

"So what can I do for you, Mr. Wright?" I asked, glancing down at the clutter on my desk. Boy, was that name a joke.

"I'm looking for Mrs. Wright," he replied in a nasal voice. It was worse than I thought. Nerd all the way.

"Is she missing?"

"You could say that," he replied.

I glanced at the pocket protector. She was probably hiding. Who can blame her? Then I caught a whiff of his cologne. He wasn't a complete loser; he was wearing my favorite cologne, the one that worked as an aphrodisiac on me. It had been months since I'd smelled that fragrance. Andrew had been wearing it the night he was shot in front of my eyes at the restaurant.

I found it disturbing that an obvious loser like this would be wearing such sexy cologne. I glanced at him again. Despite being a total nerd, he was kind of cute. He was staring at me as if he'd never seen a woman before. His brown eyes bored into mine and I looked away, self-consciously, disturbed by the unjustified hormonal reaction I was starting to experience. Probably just the cologne. "When was the last time you saw her?"

"Eight months ago."

"Why did you wait so long to start looking for her?"

"You might say I've been locked up for a while."

Oh, great. A jailbird. Major loser here. "What were you in for?"

"Being in the wrong place at the wrong time."

"So you got out of jail and she was gone? Have you checked with her friends, family?"

"Oh, I know where she is." He slid a finger into his collar and pulled out a chain with a medallion on it. "She's not far away at all." He idly fingered the chain, watching me, and my eyes were drawn to the dangling medallion like a moth to a flame.

It was a gold figure of a horse, with flowing mane and sapphire eyes. It appeared to be real gold and real sapphires.

I looked up and saw the smile, the smile I remembered so well, the smile that could make me melt. I bolted around the desk and Andrew stood up and took me in his arms.

"I didn't even recognize you," I said. "What did you do to yourself?"

"A little plastic surgery. A little hair bleach. The rest is costuming. Tim helped me."

"What does this mean, Andrew? Is it safe now? Are you coming out of hiding?"

"Andrew is dead, Angela. You must never call me that again. I'm James Wright now. You can call me Jim." He pulled off the glasses and with them went all appearance of geekdom. He kissed me, a long, penetrating kiss, while I clung to him, desperate that he might walk out of my life again.

"Did Felix know about this?" I gasped when he finally released me.

"No. The fact that neither of you recognized me is very important, Angela. Tim said if I didn't pass this test, I'd spend the rest of my life in Seattle."

"How will he know you passed?"

The door to the outer office swung open and Tim stepped into the room. "Because I was listening, Angel." He smiled at me. "He's all yours, now. Take good care of him. I'm being transferred to Denver, so I'll be checking up once in awhile." He turned to leave.

"Wait, Tim," I said. He looked back at me. "Thanks for everything, buddy. And do me a favor, will you?"

"What's that?"

"Tell Felix to take the rest of the day off. And make sure he locks the door when you both leave." I turned back to Andrew. Oh, that's right – Jim. "I think my new client and I have some things to discuss. Alone."

Tim gave me a wink and shut the door behind him. I reached over and unbuttoned that hideous sport coat, threw the pocket protector on the desk, and pulled the necktie loose. "First, Mr. Wright," I said, "I would advise you that if you want to find Mrs. Wright, you need to lose the wardrobe. All of it."

"That's your advice, is it?"

"That's my advice."

And in a flashback to my fantasies of my very first meeting with him, he proceeded to remove both our clothes, then throw me across the desk and make passionate love to me on the spot. Or maybe I threw him across the desk first.

It didn't really matter. As Felix had predicted, I had finally gotten my man.

THE END

Acknowledgments

I would like to acknowledge the assistance of a couple of people who helped with some technical details of this book:

First, I would like to thank Brenda Sanford, one of the first real-life policewomen in this country, who gave me some insight into the realities of police work and training from a woman's point of view.

Second, I would like to thank Tessa Nicolet, who told me all about helicopters since I'm afraid of heights and couldn't ride in one myself and she frequently rides in them in her work with the US Forest Service.

My apologies to policewomen everywhere if it appears I have made light of their contributions to law enforcement. Thankfully, real-world policewomen are much more professional than my fictional "woman with a gun" and I applaud their valuable contributions to law enforcement.

K D Ryder

November, 2014

www.ingramcontent.com/pod-product-compliance
Lightning Source LLC
Chambersburg PA
CBHW060324260626
47160CB00007B/2670